To Steve + Ma

I hope you fellows enjoy
this glimpse of old San
Francisco. The research
took me five years in all.

Best Wishes,

John

RING *of* FIRE

JOHN CLAY WINCH

Ring of Fire. Copyright © 2020 by John Clay Winch. All rights reserved.
Print ISBN: 978-1-09831-481-1
eBook ISBN: 978-1-09831-482-8

Front cover concept by George E. Winch.

Front cover art by Leigh McLellan.

Front cover photo: View of San Francisco. Ca. 1860. Goat Island. Courtesy of the Bancroft Library, University of California, Berkeley.

Back cover photo by James P. Wollak.

To Esther and George, for all their love and care.

ACKNOWLEDGEMENTS

I wish to thank my primary readers, Mr. Michael O'Laughlin and Mr. James P. Wollak, for their careful reading of the manuscript. I also wish to thank the Orinda Mystery Writing Group: Chris L'Orange, Karen Clayton, Mary Ann Bernard, Pat Craig and Phyllis Nagle. Finally a special thanks for Susanne Lakin, the CMOS martinet who whipped the final draft into shape, and various mentors and friends in the past including Donna Levin, David Corbett, Brad Newsham, and Waimea Williams.

RING of FIRE

CHAPTER *1*

June 1866

Major Hampton Ellis stood in the warm, smoky interior of the El Dorado Saloon, enjoying a second whiskey-and-lemon cocktail, chatting with a barmaid as the young woman waited for her order. Glancing at the far end of the crowded bar, Ellis saw a man he knew to be dead lifting a shot glass.

Their eyes locked through the hazy air, with its din of loud talk and barking laughter. Ellis put his drink down as he stared at the lean handsome face, now wearing a trim mustache, the cool and purposeful eyes.

"Daniels," Ellis said aloud in disbelief. "Thaddeus Daniels."

The man was an infamous Confederate spy, but word had gone around Washington that Daniels had been executed when Richmond fell, or had committed suicide after Jefferson Davis's capture a month later. Ellis was certain he had heard of the man's death from one of the intelligence officers on Grant's staff.

In a dark suit and matching top hat, the ghost nodded to Ellis, put his glass down on the bar, and turned into the crowd. Ellis pushed his way through the mass, some drinkers voicing annoyance, but lost sight of the specter. By the time he reached the end of the bar, Daniels was gone.

Outside the El Dorado, Washington Street was lost in a flood of mist -- the cool, wet air refreshing as Ellis lifted his kepi to wipe a palm across his balding head. Looking up and down the lane, he could only see seven or eight yards in either direction. A pair of gas lamps marked the edge of the boardwalk, their reddish light haloed by moisture. Distant fog bells clanged a monotonous knell from the wharves.

"Daniels?" Ellis peered at the shadowy building facades visible along the street. The man could be anywhere, less than a dozen paces away. Out of the gray oblivion, Ellis heard the distinct clicks of a pistol hammer being cocked. Ducking behind a lamppost, he glanced back and forth at the misty darkness while his hand searched his coat pocket for his derringer. A sharp report startled Ellis as he glimpsed the muzzle flash. The lamp rang with the bullet's ricochet, metal bits stinging his cheek. Whirling, he ran in the opposite direction, damp darkness enveloping him as his boot heels clattered on the boardwalk.

Ellis stopped after several blocks, to lean gasping against another lamp, studying the swirling gray vapor as his aching lungs drew air. Surely, he had lost Daniels—but he was lost as well. He had been in the city less than a month and was still getting familiar with the streets.

Sweat ran from beneath his cap brim, his heart sledging in his chest. Indistinct at first, then clearly through the mist came the steady click of boots on wood. A top-hatted silhouette emerged from the fog. Ellis pulled the derringer from his pocket but started backing up. Losing his nerve, he ran across the street and ducked around a corner. Quickening footsteps followed him. Turning another corner, he spotted glowing windows and sprinted toward them. Yellow light spilled through an open door, shone through grimy windows. It was a grog shop—vile liquor for pennies a glass—he had been warned about such places. Stepping inside, Ellis stuck his head out the door, not quite able to believe he had outrun his assassin. He waited for Daniels to show, gripping the single-shot pistol with damp fingers, but saw only roiling vapor in the wavering glow of the lamps. Years ago, Ellis had met Daniels at a reception in Georgetown, where the Southerner in the course of their conversation had asked leading questions about the ordnance shipments Ellis supervised on the military railroads. Knowing the capitol was full of Confederate operatives, Ellis had reported the incident. Why Daniels would try to kill him now the war was over made no sense whatever.

"Welcome, Major. First drink is on the house." The barman grinned—a skinny man with predatory eyes. He wore an old graying shirt and stained vest.

From beneath the kepi's brim, Ellis glared at him and the down-and-out customers sitting at the dingy tables. He waited for a full minute as his breathing slowed. Checking the street once more, he walked out into the night, derringer in hand, thumb on the hammer.

The whiskey from the El Dorado lurched in his stomach, yet he forced himself to march. Crossing an intersection, he passed in front of the Customs House, realizing he was on Battery Street and nearing the Barbary Coast. His luck was improving—he was only a block from Madame Cecile's cathouse. If he could reach it, he would be safe.

Drawing near the corner, he saw a figure detach itself from the shadows and stride toward him. Ellis jerked up his pistol and fired, the shot screaming off into the night. Daniels smiled, planting his feet as he pointed his own weapon. Ellis saw the octagonal muzzle aimed squarely at him. Dropping his pistol, he raised his hands, fear locking his knees. "Please, God. No!" The muzzle roared, spitting fire and sparks.

Ellis smashed against the ground. In the ringing silence, the hard vibration in his skull grew to an overpowering tremor; black and gray blurs skewed in his vision. He felt himself falling into an abyss.

CHAPTER *2*

Lieutenant Blake sat at his desk in the inspector general's office, sifting through the reports he was summarizing. The three other desks in the room were empty, the officers who occupied them gone for the day. The door to the inner office of the assistant inspector general was closed. Colonel Wagner, the AIG, had left for the day as well. Through the bay windows across from him, the fog-clotted sky was visible but its gray-hued light was fading. Along the whitewashed walls, wooden shelves were filled with thick leather-bound folios containing reams of reports, inventory lists, and copies of requisitions orders necessary to their work.

Boot heels clumped along the hall beyond the open office door. Peterson, a sergeant major in the provost marshal's department, walked in and glanced around the room. He wore a cape-shouldered regulation blue overcoat and cap. Coming to attention, he saluted. Blake remained seated, returning the salute with a distracted motion.

"Is the colonel here?'

"Gone for the evening. To a dinner party, I believe. At the Selby's on Rincon Hill," Blake answered.

"Major Ellis, one of the staffers with the quartermaster, is in the morgue. Someone shot him in the head. General Halleck received word this afternoon from Isaiah Lees, who's a detective with the local police."

Blake returned to his work. "I'll let the colonel know in the morning."

"General Halleck asked that the provost marshal follow the matter, but Major Colton has his hands full, what with running the stockade and rebuilding the batteries at Fort Alcatraz with convict labor. The major was wondering if one of you fellows might be able to consult with the police on this."

Blake looked at the sergeant major. "You can't spare a single man?"

"Most are working at the stockade. The rest are out chasing down deserters. Major Colton would consider it a personal favor if your commanding officer would take this over."

Blake smiled to himself. That was the Army way—delegate troublesome work to the next fellow whenever possible. "I'll take the news to him personally. That will be all, Sergeant."

At the coat rack beside the open office door, Blake shrugged into his skirted uniform jacket and buttoned it. Removing a red silk sash from a wall hook, he wrapped it around his waist, and buckled on his pistol belt. In San Francisco, only Quaker gentlemen did not carry a handgun or a knife beneath their coats at night. As a soldier, he had the advantage of wearing a revolver openly. It had the proper effect—on the dark city streets, the shabby denizens stepped out of his way and beggars never asked him for spare pennies. Blake checked the small mirror hanging on the wall to make sure his dark-brown hair was neat, glancing into his skeptical gray eyes. He seated his kepi on his head, canting it to the left to give it the jaunty angle he favored. He pulled the office door shut and locked it.

* * *

"This is the Selby's house," replied the Negro butler, immaculate in a white shirt, silver brocade waistcoat, and dark swallow-tailed jacket.

Blake stood at the door of a grand two-story house mounted on a hillock overlooking Harrison Street, a boulevard lined with prominent mansions. He was slightly out of breath having climbed several flights of stairs up from the plank sidewalks.

"Who may I ask is calling?"

"Lieutenant G. W. Blake. I'm here to see Colonel Wagner on Army business. It won't take but a moment. However, I must speak with him."

"Come in, sir."

The tall African stood aside, opening the door. Blake stepped into a richly paneled entryway, taking off his kepi. From an adjacent room came the noise of many voices talking at once. The party was still in the opening stages of cocktails and gossip. Supper had not yet been served. A plump middle-aged woman strolled in from the crowded room. She wore an elegant green silk dress with a yellow lace collar. Her hair was done up in the latest style.

"And who is this handsome young man, Nathan?" she asked, glancing at the butler as she placed her gloved hand in Blake's palm.

Clicking his boot heels together, Blake bowed slightly from the waist. "Good evening, ma'am."

"This is Mr. Blake," Nathan said. "Here to see the colonel."

She looked reprovingly at him. "What could possibly be important this late in the day?"

"Mrs. Selby, it pains me to disturb your party, but I am here on urgent military business."

She smiled. "Oh, you're a delightful liar! Isn't he cute, Nathan? Do fetch the colonel, will you?"

With a sober nod, Nathan walked into the crowded, brightly lit room, disappearing among the people. Mrs. Selby slipped her arm through Blake's.

"Have we met before, Lieutenant?"

He looked over at her, feeling uncomfortable. "Uh, no, ma'am."

"Where has Colonel Wagner been keeping you?"

"Busy at the inspector general's office. I arrived here in April, just a few months—"

"And where are you from?" she asked.

"New London, Connecticut. But I came out from Washington, DC, where I was working—"

"Are you married?"

"No ma'am."

"Engaged?"

Blake smiled. "No ma'am."

"Would you like a drink?'

"Thank you, no. I wouldn't want to disrupt your party."

"Nonsense."

Withdrawing her arm, she stood back and looked at him with gauging eyes, fingering one of her garnet pendant earrings.

Nathan reappeared with the colonel in tow. Wagner was a tall man with graying temples and a cavalryman's mustache. The brass buttons on his uniform shimmered like gold, having been doubtlessly polished that afternoon by an orderly. Blake stiffened to attention and saluted with a crisp motion. The colonel regarded him with a disapproving frown, returning the salute.

"Dallying with the ladies, Lieutenant?" asked the senior officer.

"Mrs. Selby," said Blake, looking at her. "If you will excuse us?"

"Don't be grumpy, Colonel. He's a very nice young man and from a good family, I'll warrant," she said before returning to her room full of guests.

Blake waited until Nathan likewise removed himself from the entryway, then relayed the conversation he had with the sergeant major from the provost marshal's office. Wagner listened, a grave expression on his face.

"I played poker with Major Ellis at my club just last Friday evening. This is troubling news. I want you to follow up—make sure the police are doing a thorough job. Have you got anything pressing on your desk at the moment?"

"Not really, sir. I'm summarizing the inspection at Ft. Crook and doing preparation for the inspection at Ft. Humboldt."

The colonel nodded. "Give this priority for the moment. And keep me informed."

"Understood, sir."

Nathan emerged from the crowded parlor. The two soldiers looked over at him as he approached.

"Mrs. Selby would like you to join her supper party, sir. What shall I tell her?"

"The lieutenant is honored to accept." Wagner smiled, his voice ironic. "Give Nathan your kepi and sidearm, Mr. Blake. We wouldn't want to disappoint the hostess. Lord knows she seems to enjoy our young officers."

The parlor of the Selby house was extensive, brightly lit by two chandeliers as well as wall-mounted gas lamps. Ornately carved chairs and couches were arranged about the long room, their polished wood gleaming in the light. Most of the guests were standing. A table stood to the right of the doorway, where a servant poured punch from a large silver bowl or sherry for the ladies and whiskey for the gentlemen. Amid the competing conversations, Wagner raised his voice to Blake.

"Whiskey, soldier?"

Blake shook his head. "Not on an empty stomach, sir. I'll have punch instead."

"A wise decision. Better to keep your wits about you, or Mrs. Selby will have you married off to one of her daughters before you leave the house."

Blake smiled. "I received a thorough interrogation prior to your arrival."

Drinks in hand, they mingled with the other guests, the colonel introducing Blake to several whiskered men in evening dress. A tall gentleman with a bald pate and an expansive gray beard gestured with his hand as he expounded on local politics.

"I don't care if this fellow Middleton is the president of the Central Railroad! He's a fraud. His proposal for the Second Street cut will ruin this neighborhood if it goes through. What do you think will happen to our property values then?"

One listener whose hair was dark and slicked with pomade shook his head. "You can't hold back progress. The days of pioneers and miners are over. The vitality of civilization cannot be halted …"

Blake let his gaze wander, taking in the young ladies in the crowded room. He saw a pretty blonde in a red taffeta dress whom he recognized from the last party he attended. Her name was Angeline, but he couldn't recall her family name. Looking to the corner of the room, he saw another young woman standing alone next to a tall potted plant. She dressed in the style of the Californios—a long dark skirt and a white silk open-necked blouse that revealed her flawless brown skin and fine collarbones. An elegant shawl draped her slender shoulders. Her dark hair was pulled up and held in place by a silver comb. She had a slender face with a strong tapered jaw. Her eyes were large, her nose high-bridged and elegant. She caught him staring and gave him a brief smile before she looked away. When her gaze came back to him, he was still had his eyes on her.

"Tell us about the war, Lt. Blake. Did you see much campaigning?" the tall bald bearded gent asked.

"Excuse me, gentlemen," Blake said, walking away.

She watched as he threaded his way through the crowd. The expression on her lovely face grew surprised as he moved past the last knot of guests and stopped before her.

"Good evening, señorita," he said. "May I present myself?"

Suppressing a smile, she nodded.

"I am Lieutenant Gordon Williamson Blake. However, my friends call me Liam."

"Good evening, Lieutenant," she answered, offering her hand.

Pressing her fingers against his lips, he bowed while his eyes looked into hers.

"I am Elena Caltera. My cousin is Don Miguel Noe."

"I have heard of him. His family owns one of the local ranchos."

She smiled. "You are well informed, señor."

"Are you from the city?"

Elena shook her head. "Monterey. And which part of the United States are you from?"

"New England. This is my first posting to California. I'm with the inspector general's office."

They continued to chat, Blake losing himself as he watched her. Realizing he was staring, he looked down at her shoes, then focused on her brown eyes. She made the other women in the room seem very plain by comparison.

"Were you in the recent fighting in the East?" she asked.

He nodded, frowning with unpleasant memories. "My battalion was at the Battle of the Wilderness Tavern two years ago. I was wounded in the hand-to-hand fighting. I spent a month recovering in a hospital in Washington, DC."

Her eyes were sober, her curved lips forming a straight line. "It must have been very trying."

"The angels were with me that day. I survived where many did not."

"Forgive me for bringing up such an unpleasant subject."

"Do you live in San Francisco, Miss Caltera?"

"No, I am just visiting my cousins."

"Will you be in town long?" he asked, hoping to that he might call on her.

"A few weeks."

"And were you raised in Monterey?" he asked.

"I was born there and left when I was thirteen to go to a convent school in Mexico City. I left the convent last month after six years, which included a year of teaching."

Blake nodded, impressed. "Teaching is a noble if impecunious profession."

It was then he saw the ring inset with small diamonds on her left hand—all of the quickened hope of the last few minutes fading. She noticed his gaze and stood straight, her chin lifted.

"You're married?" he asked, disappointment in his voice.

"Engaged," she answered, but there was a look in her eyes. Blake wasn't sure what it indicated—uncertainty, perhaps.

"How long have you been engaged?"

"The marriage was arranged when I was seven years old. I have not yet met the man I am to marry. His name is Don Carlos Bejarano. He lives on a rancho outside of Los Angeles."

"An arranged marriage?"

She nodded, holding her punch cup in the palm her hand.

"Wouldn't you rather decide for yourself who your husband should be?" he asked.

She looked away, then back at him. "I must do as my parents wish. It was decided a long time ago. One must obey the family traditions."

"I see."

They stood facing each other, the silence between them awkward. She attempted a smile but then glanced away.

"When … are you to be married?" he asked, keeping his voice even.

"In a month."

"Well, then," he said, raising his glass. "Here's to your every happiness."

Her eyes searched his, looking perhaps for sarcasm. "Thank you."

Sipping his punch, he struggled for something to say. She gazed across the crowded room as the competing voices clamored around them. She returned her attention to him.

"What sort of name is Liam?"

"Short for Williamson. Our family butler, Mr. O'Connor, gave it to me when I was a boy. The whole family calls me that now, with the exception of my father, who still calls me Gordon."

Elena smiled, showing fine white teeth, her eyes amused. "That's very sweet."

"Do you like San Francisco?" He wanted to keep the conversation going, despite his disappointment.

She shook her head. "It's very big and crowded."

The guests standing close by parted and a lean Californio man appeared, dressed in the Spanish style. He led a woman who looked to be his wife, elegantly attired in a blue taffeta gown, by the hand.

"Don Miguel," Elena said. "May I present Lieutenant Liam Blake?"

The Californio gentleman shook his hand. Blake bowed to the señora, who offered him a bland smile. The don spoke to Elena in Spanish.

She looked at Blake. "We are leaving. It was a pleasure to meet you, Lieutenant."

The don and his wife had already turned away and were parting the crowd. He touched Elena's arm, not wanting her to go.

"May I see you again?" he asked.

"I will be at the noon Mass tomorrow at St. Mary's." Her dark eyes held his for a moment, then she walked away.

He watched her leave, enticed by the prospect of seeing her again and yet troubled that she was destined for another.

* * *

After a seven-course meal, the guests separated into two groups: ladies in the sitting room for tea and cordials, gentleman in the billiard room for cigars and brandy. Blake stood on the veranda, outside the billiard room, feeling uncomfortably full. Cigar fumes nauseated him. Preferring the cold night air and the darkness of the veranda, he thought of Elena, wondering why she had affected him so deeply. It wasn't just her beauty—she had an innate grace that was impressive. Further, she was straightforward rather than coquettish, which he much preferred, and she was educated, an important trait in a woman.

"There you are," a female voice said.

Surprised, Blake turned to his right, where the veranda led past the sitting room. The young blond woman he had seen earlier was looking at him with her bare arms crossed.

"Angeline?" he said, uncertainly.

"Yes, Angeline Whitfield, in case you'd forgotten. I saw you earlier talking to the Noes. How have you been?"

"Busy but well. And you?" Blake recalled chatting with Angeline some weeks earlier. She was pleasant, but he was not drawn to her, in spite of her amiable blue eyes and winsome manner.

"I am fine."

She walked over to stand next to him, smiling as if amused by a private thought as she gazed out at the other houses glimmering with lights. She looked at him.

"I didn't see you at the ball the Wexworths gave last month."

"I don't think I was invited."

"You were. I helped Elisa Wexworth write the invitations."

Blake shrugged. "I guess I was busy that night."

"Surely the Army doesn't require you to put in such long hours," she spoke teasingly. "You must be seeing someone."

He glanced over at her, unsure if he should be annoyed. "What if I am?"

"Then I should die from jealousy," Angeline replied, raising her fine eyebrows.

"Never fear. I wouldn't let that happen," he answered, wondering what she was driving at.

"How very gallant of you. Who says there are no gentlemen left?"

He was not in the mood to be teased, wishing to be left alone with his musings on Elena but he let it go. "How's your cousin?"

"Jim Sanders? Speculating with his money like every other fool in the city. But, otherwise, he is fine. Have you been to see Woodward's Gardens since it opened to the public?"

"No," he answered. "I would love to stay and chat, but I'm afraid it's been a rather long day. It was very nice to see you."

He shook her gloved hand, smiled briefly, and turned away.

* * *

She watched Blake slip through the glass doors to the billiard room. Angeline had been hoping he would ask her out. She frowned and walked back toward the sitting room, hugging her arms to her chest. The night was very cold.

CHAPTER *3*

Daniels stood at the window of his hotel room, chewing on the end of a slim black cheroot. He was reluctant to light it because smoking before breakfast made him too lightheaded. He looked out at the various colored buildings of San Francisco—most were squat structures of wood, etched in the clarity of the morning sunlight. It was a pretentious hick town, putting on airs of respectability amid its dirty unpaved streets and bumpkin residents. The morning papers were spread out on the rumpled coverings of his bed. There was no mention of the murder. He knew from experience the best place to hide after a killing was in a city.

"Too many faces," he said aloud, watching the pedestrians going about their errands on the street below like a nest of ants.

Turning away from the window, he retied the sash of his silk dressing robe. He sat on the bed and closed the thin sheets of paper, then took the cheroot from his lips and stared across the room. He missed Jeannette and the days not so long ago when they shared an apartment in Paris. He closed his eyes so that he could picture her face. Heart-shaped it was, with high cheekbones and full lips. Her dark brows and green eyes always seemed to hold a look of amusement, as though the world were hers. Back then, it had been—for both of them. To be young and wealthy in Paris had made him feel invincible. He had seen the envy in men's eyes when he introduced Jeannette to them, and he had carried his possession of her as the natural tribute due to any young lord—though, admittedly, it was the family fortune that separated him from sweaty workingmen, not noble birth. Still, by American standards he was an aristocrat, as much as any effete French baron or drunken English duke. Jeannette had been a fitting lady—beautiful, sly, and intelligent.

He rolled the little cigar between his fingers, recalling her slow smile whenever he reached for her in their rooms and the way her buttocks tightened in his hand and her back arched as their love-making climaxed, her breathy cries in his ear.

He threw away the cigar, rose from the mattress, and returned to the window, looking out again over the placid buildings. Often he wondered how she had died--anguished, her face tear-streaked, praying hopelessly in the final seconds? When he read the news in Richmond, he had felt a sharp, deep pain in his guts. Yankee ships outside of Wilmington, North Carolina, had sunk the *Aberdeen*, a blockade runner of Scottish registry and the ship he knew Jeannette Fayant to be a passenger on. It was a back-page article in a month-old copy of the Washington *Sentinel*, dated August 3, 1864. The article noted that all lives aboard the *Aberdeen* had been lost.

He untied the silk belt of his robe. It was time to dress and eat. There was much to do. The Yankees still owed him for Jeannette's death and the fall of Richmond.

* * *

The early morning sun shining on Portsmouth Square was a benediction after days of relentless fog. Blake slowed to a stroll along the boardwalk, enjoying the warm light. He lingered for a moment, then passed through the shadowed entrance doors of City Hall and made his way over to the police department, asking a desk sergeant where to find the city's detectives. The sergeant sent him down a wood-paneled hallway to a room at the back of the building. The door was open, and half a dozen men in store-bought suits sat at desks. Several were talking, the others writing.

"Can I help you?" asked a sturdily built man with deep-set eyes and bushy hair that was parted on the side. He had a mustache and small pointed chin beard.

Blake took off his kepi. "I'm looking for Captain Lees."

"That's me," the gent said.

"I'm here representing the provost marshal, among others, to inquire about the investigation of the murder of Major Ellis."

Lees nodded. "Better talk to Detective O'Gara. He's handling it."

He turned to two men who sat at their desks drinking coffee from porcelain mugs and looking through papers. "Tom, this fellow is here to see you."

Lees went back to his desk while one of the two men walked over. He was barrel-chested and had red hair closely trimmed to his large head. A flaming mustache almost covered his mouth. His brown cravat was knotted in a loose bow at the collar of his shirt.

"Tom O'Gara," he said, offering his hand. His knuckles were scarred, and he had a powerful grip.

Blake introduced himself. "Have you arrested any suspects in the murder of Major Ellis?"

O'Gara folded his thick shirt-sleeved arms across his vest. "Matter of fact, we brought in a skellum just yesterday morning. He's down in the holding cells."

Blake nodded. "Have you gotten a confession?"

O'Gara smiled wryly. "Not yet. But we will."

Blake looked in O'Gara's steady eyes. "Would it be possible to see this man and talk with him?"

"What for? We've got him by the balls. He was carrying a pawn ticket for Major Ellis's watch, and the dumb bastard still had the major's empty wallet. Best of all, he had a recently fired derringer in his pocket. He'll confess. Don't you worry."

"I'm not questioning your abilities, Detective. It's just that my colonel will want a full report. If you have the culprit, the colonel will want to know as much about him as possible."

O'Gara pursed his lips, then nodded. "All right. I'll take you down to the cells. But you'll need to leave your sidearm here."

Blake unbuckled his belt and handed it to the policeman. O'Gara laid it on the blotter, then walked toward the doorway, gesturing for Blake to follow him.

It was cold in the basement hallway where the cells were. The corridor was lit with gas lamps, which gave off little light in the shadows. The jailer opened a wooden door with a barred window, and Blake entered with O'Gara at his back. A ragged man sat on an iron bunk suspended from chains anchored to the wall. The room was rank with the smell of unwashed flesh and the faint stench of sewage from the covered slops bucket in the corner. As gaunt as an Andersonville survivor, the prisoner wore a tattered coat, the sleeves hanging about his skinny wrists. His hair was cropped close to his scalp.

"Has he been arraigned in police court?" Blake asked.

"Not yet. He still hasn't admitted to the crime."

"Might I have a word alone with him?"

O'Gara gestured with his thumb. "I'll be out in the hallway. Should I lock the door?"

"That won't be necessary."

The jailer and the policeman left, pushing the door shut. Blake looked at the suspect. The only light came from a small grilled air vent set in the ceiling at the back wall no wider than two hands placed side by side.

"What is your name?" Blake asked.

"Finnegan," he answered in a rasping voice.

It was hard to see in the dimness, but Finnegan's cheek and eye looked bruised.

"Have you been fighting, or did something else happen?"

"The coppers done this." Finnegan pointed to his eye. "I wasn't doin' nothin', just gettin' drunk, and they arrested me."

"Detective O'Gara told me you had a pawn ticket for the dead man's watch and his wallet when you were arrested outside a grog shop."

"Well … yeah, I took the man's wallet and watch. But … but he were already dead. I didn't kill him."

"What about the derringer in your pocket?"

"It was in the soldier's hand when I found him. I took it along with the wallet, figgerin' to keep it for protection. Street punks rob me all the time."

Blake studied him. "There's no point in lying. You will hang for this. Tell the truth now and you can save your soul, if not your life."

Finnegan rose slowly from his perch. "Honest Injun with God as my witness, I didn't kill nobody. How could I shoot anybody with these hands?" He held up fingers that shook with tremor.

"I need a drink bad." He closed his trembling hands into fists.

During the war, Blake had seen hardened dipsomaniacs among the federal soldiers. Many ended up wearing a barrel shirt, corporal punishment for being drunk on duty. Others were discharged by the regimental doctors as unfit for service. Most folks saw drunkenness as a moral weakness, but Blake viewed it as a ravaging disease.

"I just took the money so's I could drink. That's all. They can't hang me for that, can they?"

"You had better come clean. Murder can't be hidden."

"But I didn't do it," the wretch insisted. "Can't you tell them that?"

"I'm not sure my word would carry much weight."

"But you're a gen'leman and a soldier. They'll listen to you. You gotta help me."

Blake shook his head. "You have to help yourself. I don't think there is much I can do."

Finnegan sat on his bunk, staring at the dirty floor.

"How did you find the major?" Blake asked.

"I was working on a bottle," he said in his gravelly voice. "But it were just a small one. I's in a doorway across from the Customs House and hears gunshots. So I went to take a look. The fog were pretty thick, but I found the major laying on the sidewalk. Blood was leaking from his head something fierce, and his eyes was closed. Plain to see he were a goner. So I took his wallet and watch—the pistol too—figgerin' he wouldn't need 'em no more."

"Did you see anyone else?" Blake demanded.

"There was a feller down by the Custom House lookin' toward me, then he turned away and the fog swallered him. I sold the watch and went up to The Brown Dog, along the street. Bought some bus-thead and pickled eggs. Woke up outside on the curb later with a patrolman kickin' me in the ribs. But I didn't kill that man," Finnegan said hopelessly.

Blake nodded, turned, and went out through the door. While the jailer locked it, Blake and O'Gara started along the corridor to the stairway.

"Schmitt and I will work on him some more. We figure to have a confession by nightfall."

Blake stopped at the wooden staircase leading to the first floor, laying his hand on the banister. "I don't think that man is responsible for the major's death."

"He had the gun, the pawn ticket, and the wallet."

"But you have no witnesses."

"The district attorney has convicted murderers on circumstantial evidence before. Look, Lieutenant, the evidence points to him." O'Gara gestured with his palms as though the conclusion was obvious.

Blake started up the stairs with the detective alongside him. "I don't dispute the fact he robbed the major. I just don't believe that old soak killed him. Finnegan's delirium tremens is so bad, I don't think he could manage to shoot a man in the head. And if he didn't kill Major Ellis, then who did?"

Upon reaching the top of the stairs, they walked toward the front entrance. O'Gara told him to wait while he retrieved Blake's sidearm. A minute later he returned and handed the gun belt to Blake, who buckled it on. Blake held out his hand.

"What are you going to tell your commanding officer?" O'Gara asked, shaking the offered hand.

"That you don't have the right man." Blake was not surprised by the police taking the path of least resistance but felt they were making a serious error.

"Damn it, he's guilty."

"Of robbery, sir. Nothing else."

"Well, I don't see it that way, Lieutenant."

"Nonetheless, thank you," Blake said, having no reason to antagonize the detective. "Do you mind if I return later to see how things are progressing?"

"Suit yourself."

Knowing the matter was far from resolved, Blake gave the Irishman a casual salute and walked out the front doors.

* * *

Daniels stood on California Street, finishing his post-breakfast cigar. He wore a black suit, its frock coat generously cut to hide the holstered revolver at the small of his back. He flicked the cigar stub into the refuse along the curb stones and mounted a short staircase to a building with a granite façade whose windows were painted with letters advertising "Marine Insurance." He entered the office just inside the main doors and stood at a small gateway that separated the desks of the salesmen and underwriters from the reception area. Outfitted in a suit, starched collar, and tie, a clerk sat behind a small wooden counter adjacent to the door.

"Help you, sir?" the clerk asked, putting down his pen.

"I'm interested in talking with a sales agent."

"Right away, sir."

The clerk walked over to a middle-aged man with reddish-brown hair and a graying beard. The fellow stood and motioned Daniels over to the desk, which had two leather chairs facing it. Daniels opened the thigh-high gate and advanced. Shaking the agent's offered hand, he said "Thomas Jackson. I'm here representing a new and somewhat small mining operation in the Comstock."

"Please sit down, Mr. Jackson."

Daniels sat erectly in the chair, not allowing his back to rest against it. "As I said, I'm part of a business concern from Nevada. We are mining and smelting silver ore. We are too small to have a government contract with the Treasury Department in Washington, but we do have one with the government of Mexico. Consequently, we will be transporting bullion to Acapulco by clipper ship."

"I see," the agent said, settling back into his chair, his hands folding together at the fingers.

"What concerns me is that … well, in any seaport there are thieves who hang around the docks, waiting for opportunities to pillage cargoes that sit on the piers—or even after they have been loaded onto the vessels."

"Hence the need for insurance, sir!" said the agent, sitting up.

"Precisely. However, since I am new to town, I'm looking for even more specific information. Who are these wharf rats? What sort of grip on the situation do the police have? Is it safe at all, or are we better off shipping the bullion to Los Angeles?"

"Of course not!" the man insisted. "We do have a criminal element along the wharf led by a blackguard whose name is Liverpool Wilcox. However, San Francisco has harbor police in three stations along the wharf to keep these brigands in hand. Fearless men, I assure you, these harbor police."

"No doubt, however—"

"We have several policies indemnifying loss due to theft. Whatever your needs, great or small," the agent said, with a smile of his yellowed teeth.

Taking a handful of printed brochures, Daniels left after reassuring the salesman he would be back once he had made up his mind. Outside on the street, he walked to the corner of Battery, where an ex-soldier stood with a Yankee forage cap pulled low over his eyes, the sleeve of his faded blue shell jacket pinned up on one side.

"Spare some pennies, mister?" the veteran asked.

"These are precisely what you need." He handed the pamphlets to the cripple and walked on.

* * *

Blake entered the inspector general's office to find Lt. Schaeffer sitting alone at his desk in the white-walled room. The scratching of his pen was the only noise. Blake took off his kepi.

"Is the colonel in?" he asked, walking to his desk.

Schaeffer lifted his graying head, looking at his young cohort. He pulled the gold watch from his vest and glanced at it. "At 8:53, I'd say the old man was finishing the coffee he had with breakfast at his club. He'll be here in, say, twenty minutes. Where have you been?"

"Over at City Hall. Wagner asked me to look into this murder."

"You mean Ellis? What happened to him? Killed by a Sydney ticket-of-leave convict in some Barbary Coast gambling hole?"

"He was shot over on Battery Street. The police have a man in custody, but I'm fairly convinced he didn't kill the major."

"So you're a detective now as well as a young adjutant. You university fellows are quite remarkable."

Blake looked at him. He did not always appreciate the older man's teasing humor. Schaeffer stood up slowly and limped over to the bookshelf to pull down one of the volumes. At forty years of age, he was something of a relic for a junior officer. Under orders at Missionary Ridge in the battle for Chattanooga, Schaeffer had led a charge into the Confederate lines. The rebels were loaded with buck and ball that day, and Schaeffer had fallen along with half his men. Hit in five places, he had somehow survived and astonishingly lost none of his limbs to the surgeons' saws—neither of the two musket balls nor the three buck pellets striking bone or artery. He spent half a year recovering in the hospital. When he was able to walk, he had been told that the Army was going to retire him due to his wounds. Rumor had it he went to General Halleck and begged in tears not to be cashiered because he had a wife and a child, and he was now unfit for working as a carpenter in the civilian world. Halleck had assigned him to the inspector general's office in California.

"Well, when you see the colonel, please tell him I'll make my report when I get back," Blake said, averting his eyes as he often did when Schaeffer moved about the office.

Schaeffer put the volume down on his desk and eased back into his chair. He regarded Blake with his steady, perceptive gaze. "Do I frighten you, Liam?"

Surprised, Blake looked at Schaeffer as he considered the question, then shook his head. "You were unlucky."

"Unlucky to get hit or unlucky to survive?"

Blake raised his eyebrows. "That's a question worth pondering, old man."

Schaeffer smiled enigmatically, returning to his work. Blake put his cap back on and headed for the door.

"Where are you off to now?"

Blake paused. "I'm going over to the quartermaster's department to get more information on Ellis."

* * *

"That's Ellis's over there." The staff sergeant pointed to a desk in the corner of the room next to a window overlooking Portsmouth Square. Like Blake's office, this one had a battery of desks and men working at them. The wall facing the square had half a dozen windows, which filled the room with sunlight.

"I'd like to take a look at it," Blake said.

"Have at it," the sergeant replied, returning to his work.

Blake went over to the desk and sat in the chair. He paused, not certain of what he was doing, what he should be looking for, and he was thinking of Elena. He had been recalling their conversation and her beautiful face all morning. It was distracting him from his work, but he could not help it. He hoped to finish before the noon Mass ended at St. Mary's Cathedral so that he might see her again.

Reprimanding himself silently, he focused on the desk and began searching through the drawers. Each was neatly organized and held the usual writing implements, ink pot, blotter, paper, and printed forms. In the main drawer was a small wooden box shaped like a matchbox. Blake slid it open and found a meager collection of business cards. He thumbed through them—most were from dry goods suppliers, butchers, and iron foundries. He stopped when he saw one that was rose-colored with a floral display imprinted on the card stock. It advertised Madame Cecile's House of Pleasure. The address was on Battery, near Washington Street.

Blake unbuttoned his uniform coat and slipped the card into his vest pocket. He continued searching through the remaining drawers but found nothing out of the ordinary. Closing the final drawer, he scanned the blotter and desktop which were clean. Blake walked over to the staff sergeant's desk.

"Do you know where Major Ellis lived?"

"I believe he put up at the Cosmopolitan Hotel. Had money of his own, I hear."

"What sort of fellow was the major? Was he well liked?" Blake asked.

The staff sergeant shrugged. "He was good at his job. He was sent out from Army headquarters to audit us. I'd say he was meticulous but fair."

"He didn't rankle anyone here? Have words with anyone or make accusations?"

"No sir."

"Thank you, Sergeant."

The two men saluted each other, and Blake walked out the door. The Cosmopolitan was over on Montgomery Street, near Pine. Donning his kepi, he left the building.

Shops with awnings and office buildings lined the block of Montgomery between California and Pine Streets. In several windows facing the sidewalk, Blake saw saucers piled with gold nuggets. These were the stock broking establishments, enticing speculators. Most brokers were considered to be little more than well-tailored thieves. He strode on, passing men in hats and women in bonnets. Approaching the hotel, he slowed as he saw Angeline Whitfield walking toward him, arm and arm with a man dressed in a handsome dove-colored morning suit, his matching hat slanted at a rakish angle. Blake recognized the man as Angeline's cousin.

"Good morning, Miss Whitfield." Blake stopped, raising his cap.

She nodded coolly. Her cousin noticed her reaction, raising his eyebrows, then looked at Blake and offered his hand.

"Lieutenant Blake, if I recall. James Sanders. Good to see you again."

"Likewise. Are you here to invest in the silver mines?"

James laughed. "Not today. I'm escorting Angeline home. She volunteers mornings with the Contraband Relief Society."

Blake shrugged. "I'm afraid I haven't heard of it."

"For the relief of the slaves freed from the war. Their secessionist masters kept them in appalling conditions. Remind me again what is it you do for the society, dear cousin?"

"I write letters on behalf of the society, asking for donations," she answered, her tone annoyed.

Leaning forward conspiratorially, Sanders put his hand to the side of his mouth as though to keep Angeline from hearing him. "The society is going to set them up as gentlemen."

She cut her eyes toward him, an exasperated look on her pretty face. "The Negroes deserve a helping hand to keep them from poverty."

"No doubt," Blake said. "But education is the best way to help people."

"Well put, my friend," Sanders said.

"We mustn't dally, James. Mother is expecting us for luncheon."

Blake tipped his kepi once again to Angeline, who regarded him impassively, and the two strolled on. He watched them go, swallowed by the groups of pedestrians moving along the street, wondering what he had done to make her so unfriendly. Shrugging, he continued up the block to the tall arched doorway of the Cosmopolitan Hotel.

* * *

The porter led Blake down the carpeted corridor of the Cosmopolitan Hotel's third floor. He stopped in front of Room 320 with a pass key in his gloved hand, but the door was already ajar. The porter looked at Blake with puzzled eyes and pushed open the door. Blake followed him, unsnapping the flap of his holster with his right hand. In the middle of the richly decorated room stood Sgt. Major Peterson folding clothes into a trunk on top of the bed.

"Peterson," said Blake, closing his holster, "What are you doing?"

The sergeant dropped the trousers onto the bed and came to attention.

"My CO sent me over to pack up Major Ellis's possessions to be shipped back east to his family. I asked over at the quartermaster's office, but they were shorthanded this morning."

Turning, Blake nodded to the porter, who left the room.

"Carry on, Sergeant." Blake sat in a stuffed chair against the wall, looking at the heavy curtains and cream-colored floral print wallpaper. An Oriental rug matching the color scheme of the wallpaper covered most of the floor.

Peterson went back to folding clothes heaped on the bed.

"Col. Wagner has me looking into Ellis's murder," Blake said.

"Making any headway?"

"A little. Have you ever heard of Madame Cecile's House of Pleasure? Ellis had one of the madame's cards in his desk."

Peterson grinned, his mustache widening. "It's a cathouse over on Battery. In fact, now that you mention it, I saw Ellis there a few weeks back. There was a row over one of the ladies—a mulatto. Some soldier from the Second Artillery was having words with Ellis about who was going to have her."

"What happened?"

Peterson shrugged. "The madame stepped in between them. Ellis was insistent he have her first. Pulling rank in a whorehouse—that's one for the newspapers."

"I'm sure it wouldn't be the first time. Who was the soldier he was arguing with?"

The sergeant major rubbed his forehead in an effort to recall. "His name is John … John Hallinan. He's a private. During the war he made it up to sergeant but was busted down for some offence."

"Anything else you recall about that night?"

"Hallinan made some threats, but it was Dutch courage. He'd been to a few saloons before he showed up at the madame's. She sent him packing. He never came back that night, to my knowledge."

"Have you checked the drawers of this desk?" Blake gestured to the simple fold-down desk in the corner of the room.

"Found a letter to his wife that the major never mailed and a diary. I glanced through it—pretty dull stuff. Although he writes in glowing terms about the mulatto whore he kept company with."

"At Madame Cecile's? What's the girl's name?"

"Janey."

"Do you know her?"

Peterson smiled. "Not in the Old Testament sense. But I've seen her in the parlor. I prefer the Celestial sporting ladies."

Blake stood. "Where's the diary?"

Peterson pulled a leather-bound book from the trunk tray on the bed. Blake put it under his arm.

"Carry on, Sergeant."

* * *

Azariah Dekker sat at the table in the dining room of his modest two-story house on Taylor Street, at the foot of Fern Hill. He sipped coffee from a china cup and looked moodily at the papers, lingering over his breakfast. As he read, he ran a hand over his thick head of graying hair, which he kept scrupulously barbered and combed. He tugged at his full mustache, scanning another article, when the maid, an Irish girl named Mary, appeared in the entranceway.

"Mr. Dekker, there's a gentleman at the door who wishes to speak with you."

The older man mused for a moment. "Is he alone?"

"Yes sir."

"Show him in."

While she was occupied, Dekker went to the china cabinet against the wall and, using a key from his vest pocket, opened a locked drawer. From it he took a small Colt .31-caliber revolver and slipped it into his waistband, then pulled his vest over it. He returned to his chair. Mary ushered in a man wearing a black suit with a burgundy cravat holding a gray top hat. He looked to be thirty or so and had dark hair and a slender mustache.

"Mr. Dekker, I presume, former editor of the *Democratic Press* newspaper?"

"I am he," Dekker said, holding his hands at his waist, the left covering the right, which gripped the butt of his hideaway. "Who are you, sir?"

"Thaddeus Daniels."

"I believe I have heard of you," Dekker said, relaxing a bit. "You worked with Captain Bulloch in London, procuring vessels for the Confederate Navy."

"You are particularly well informed, sir."

Dekker got up from his chair and shook hands. "I grew up in the Florida Keys with Stephen Mallory, secretary of the Confederate Navy. We stayed in touch throughout the war. Please sit down."

Daniels took a seat at the table while Dekker shut the doors to the dining room and glanced at the one leading to the kitchen to see that it was closed, then returned to his chair.

"When the news of Lincoln's assassination reached San Francisco, a mob ransacked the offices of the *Democratic Press*, smashing the press and destroying the furniture. I was home with a bout of influenza, luckily for me. No doubt I would have been shot or lynched," Dekker said. "How have you faired since the cause was lost?"

Daniels stared at him with an unflinching blue-eyed gaze. "I am here to resurrect the Cause. I mean to revive the Knights of the Golden Circle."

"But we are scattered. Many were arrested or disappeared. One or two deported. There are others, of course, but with the war lost and Jefferson Davis captured…"

"There are others, yes," Daniels replied. "There are thousands of Southern men waiting for a signal to take up arms again. I mean to supply that signal. Will you help me?"

Dekker dropped his gaze to the rug on the floor. It was worn, its colors faded, its edges beginning to tatter.

"My funds are nearly exhausted. I haven't worked in over a year. I'm fifty-two years old -- the Yankee papers in this town won't hire me. And if they did, I'd be a pressman, not an editor. I don't know what help I can be."

Daniels leaned forward to whisper. "I'll handle the financial end. I need your contacts. I need soldiers, willing to fight and die for the Cause. Are you with me?"

Dekker looked into the man's earnest face. "Yes."

"Good." Daniels sat back and placed his hand on the table. Cupped in it was a derringer.

"If you had said no," he told Dekker, "I would have had to shoot you."

CHAPTER 4

Blake stood at the inner doors of St. Mary's Cathedral. Down the nave, a robed priest intoned a Latin prayer to the sparse assembly of parishioners seated in the pews. The cool air of the church smelled of stone and lit candles. Clerestory light came through the windows, illuminating rectangular sections of the pews. There was a calming peacefulness to the place, yet Blake kept peering at the backs of the parishioners trying to see if Elena was among them.

Realizing he would have to wait, he gazed at the floor, cap in his hand, wondering who had killed Ellis and why. The intention was not robbery, or else Finnegan would have turned up nothing with which to binge. *If not robbery, then revenge perhaps? Who were his enemies?* Blake would have to wire for Ellis's service record and interview Private Hallinan.

The priest had stopped speaking, and the people were leaving. He saw her walking down the aisle, her head bowed. She wore a cream-colored dress with a white collar. A light-brown mantilla covered her hair, and one side was thrown over her shoulder. She looked up as she left the nave and smiled when she saw him waiting.

"Hello, Lieutenant."

He took her hand and kissed it, his morning-long anticipation fulfilled by her presence. She gestured with a finger toward the pews. "My *duena* fell asleep."

Blake saw a lone figure sitting on the benches, unmoving.

"I pinned a note to her shawl that says I've gone shopping and she is to wait for me here."

"How long have you got?" he asked, thinking how lovely she looked.

"She usually sleeps for about an hour."

"Would you like something to eat?"

They sat in the tea room of the Lick House on Montgomery Street. The room was large and airy, with Corinthian pilasters dividing the walls into sections decorated with mirrors and murals of gardens. The small tables were draped with linen and set with silver cutlery. Ladies in their hats and finery sat talking and sipping from cups. Here and there among the females lounged men in suits, talking with their lady friends. Blake sat with Elena at a corner table near the windows. He ate a finger sandwich and followed it with a swallow of tea. Elena sipped from her cup but had yet to touch any food.

"Do you like Army life?"

He considered the question. "It has its frustrations and boredom, but it can be very exciting. Even terrifying."

She nodded, her lips pursed. "Were you terrified in the battles?"

"The only major action I was in happened at the Wilderness. The rest were minor skirmishes. There were moments of terror—taking artillery fire, the Confederates charging our lines with their bayonets."

He looked into her wide brown eyes, which seemed to invite his frankness. "As … much as I was scared of dying … I was even more afraid of not acquitting myself honorably under fire. When the rebels rushed us, it was a wave of men and bristling steel. I thought my time was at hand, but I kept shouting for my men to hold. Rifles were going off around me, the air dense with smoke. Then they were upon us. I had my sword and revolver in hand. I parried one man's bayonet, but another's took me through the shoulder. I shot him in the face and he fell, dragging me down with him. But the line held. My men were true. After the rebels fell back, two of them carried me to the ambulances in the rear and from there I was evacuated to a field hospital. I received a commendation, but it was the soldiers who earned it."

Tears blurred his vision, and he wiped them away. Her hand, soft and warm, touched the back of his as it lay on the table. Her gaze was intent on his face, her expression concerned. He laced his fingers through hers, grateful for her touch and her understanding. He had never spoken of that day to anyone but knew he could trust her.

They walked arm and arm down Kearny Street, heads leaning toward each other, past other pedestrians crowding the sidewalks in front of the shops and restaurants. Wagons and carriages rolled by in the dirt street, horse harnesses jingling rhythmically. Blake looked over at her, and Elena smiled back. As they approached California Street, she withdrew her arm.

"I should go on alone from here," she said.

"Nonsense, I'll walk you back to the church."

She shook her lovely head. "The duena must not see you."

"Oh," he said, hooking his thumbs on his gun belt. "I understand."

She placed her hand on top of his. "Thank you, Liam. This has been very special."

He nodded. "You walk ahead. I'll follow at a short distance. Just to make sure you are not disturbed."

"Not too close. The old woman must not know."

With a final look, she turned and walked smartly along the boulevard. Blake followed keeping a good fifty feet between them. The sunlight was making him overly warm in his wool uniform. He loosened the buttons to let the upper portion hang open. Elena crossed California Street and went up the hill to the steps of the church, where an old Californio woman waited, clutching a black purse. Blake stopped at the corner to watch the two women walk up toward Dupont Street. He saw Elena glance over her shoulder at him. He stared for a moment, then turned away, not wanted to give away the ruse. Lifting his kepi, he ran a frustrated hand through his hair, knowing he would spend the rest of the day thinking about her. Trying to ignore a surge of despair, he started back for the office.

* * *

"Who is that young man looking at you?"

"I don't know what you mean," Elena answered as she and the duena reached the level of Dupont Street.

"The one in the uniform down on the corner. Is he the one you talked about meeting at the party last night?"

Elena laughed. "What you are talking about?"

"I may be old, but I am not blind," Teresita said. "You must not disgrace the Noes. They are responsible for you while you are away from your family. You must not act wantonly."

Elena's face tightened. "I have done nothing wrong."

"Walking off alone when I am asleep is not right, and I will not have it. Do you hear?"

"I have done nothing wrong."

"Do not consort with gringos. They will only bring you misery. As they have only brought misery to the Spanish families of California."

"Do not lecture me, old woman," said Elena, her voice angry. She signaled for a cabriolet driver to stop. The taxi man halted his carriage at the curb. Elena gave him the Noes' address, then climbed in after Teresita. The driver's whip flicked at the single horse in the harness, and they started along Dupont, heading for Market Street.

"I wondered why you didn't just go to Mass at Mission Dolores. You wanted to see that young man."

Elena glared at the old woman. "Do not forget your place, Teresita. You are a servant."

"I am an old *friend* of the Noes."

Elena did not reply. She had done nothing wrong. The old woman was a tiresome gossip. She watched the wooden buildings pass as the cab threaded its way down the street, shading her eyes with her gloved hand whenever the sun found her face. Liam was a nice man, she told herself, not only very handsome in his blue uniform but also sincere, unlike so many men whom she found to be arrogant and duplicitous. And why shouldn't she like him? She knew she was destined to marry another, but that did not mean she could not feel affection toward the soldier, nor refrain from spending time in his company. As the carriage rolled toward Market Street, she saw occasional couples on the sidewalks, walking arm in arm or hand in hand. She looked away, frowning.

* * *

"I don't believe the police have the real culprits in this case," Blake said, summing up his progress report to the colonel. Wagner sat at his oak desk in his vest and shirtsleeves, the blotter covered with neat rows of reports that he reviewed before signing.

"Have you interviewed this Private Hallinan or the mulatto jezebel?"

"That's my next step, sir. However, I need to convince the police they don't have the killer in hand yet." Blake said, wondering if what he had uncovered would be enough to get O'Gara to listen.

"Good work, Lieutenant. Carry on."

Blake executed a proper about-face and left the small office. Back at his desk, he looked at the work waiting for him but decided he could finish it later. He wanted to follow up with O'Gara and walked toward the open door.

"Where are you off to now?" Schaeffer asked, looking up from his work.

"Off to find a murderer. Want to come?"

"The old man wouldn't let me. Somebody's got to work around here."

"Don't stay too late," Blake grinned.

"Worthless youngster," Schaeffer replied, returning to his writing.

Fifteen minutes later he was walking the back hallway to the detectives' office at police headquarters. He entered the room and saw only O'Gara and another cohort at their desks. The other detective was Schmitt, whom O'Gara had mentioned helped with the interrogation of Finnegan. Schmitt had a rectangular face that was clean shaven and pitted with smallpox scars along the jaw and temples. His dark wavy hair was threaded with gray.

"Well," O'Gara said, standing up and dropping his pen. "Finnegan still hasn't signed his confession yet."

Blake stopped in front of O'Gara's desk with his cap in hand. "You've got the wrong man. Finnegan didn't kill him."

Schmitt looked up. "How do you know?"

"He told me as much. Undoubtedly, Finnegan robbed Ellis once he was dead or dying, but he didn't shoot him. His hands are so tremulous he couldn't hit anything smaller than a building with a pistol. Haven't you noticed how he shakes?"

"Who the hell cares what you think?" Schmitt stood from his chair. "Get out of here before I throw you out."

"Easy, Karl," O'Gara said. "The lieutenant is entitled to his opinions, but the police court judge will make the decisions."

"He shouldn't be prosecuted for murder," Blake insisted.

"All right, soldier boy …"

Schmitt reached for Blake's shoulder, but he knocked aside the policeman's hand.

"Meddling son of a bitch!" The policeman tried to grab again.

Tossing his hat on the desk, Blake backed up, fists raised, knees bent in a boxer's stance. O'Gara stepped abruptly between them.

"Karl, let me talk to him. Go get some air. I'll straighten this out."

Schmitt hesitated, then walked around them as he kept his eyes on Blake. "I'm going for a drink, but I'll be back." He grabbed his hat and coat off the wall rack and left without a backward glance.

"What the hell are you trying to do? Get your teeth knocked out?" O'Gara asked, sitting down. "Look, the case has been solved. This rummy is a career criminal. He's served sentences on the chain gangs and in jail numerous times. He's a thief and a drunkard. Captain Lees is satisfied with the outcome. There's no reason to halt the machinery of justice."

"I believe in justice for honest men," Blake said. "And, frankly I'm not overly concerned about the fate of a larcenous wastrel. But if Finnegan didn't kill Major Ellis, it means the assassin is still loose. What then?"

"You're making this more complicated than it is."

"I know of a private, garrisoned at the Presidio with the Second Artillery, who had an argument with Major Ellis over a Negro prostitute. I spoke to a sergeant who witnessed the event. I think we should talk to this private."

O'Gara stared at Blake, weighing his words. "Schmitt's going to be mad. Hell, he's already mad. Maybe Captain Lees, too."

Blake picked up his kepi from O'Gara's desk. "Do you want to do the job right or just do the job?"

O'Gara shook his head. "You're a persistent cuss. All right, I'll meet you at the Bank Exchange Saloon at seven this evening. We may as well talk to the hooker first since she's closer, then question the private."

Blake put on his hat. "Thank you, Detective. Seven o'clock then."

* * *

Jim Sanders walked along Montgomery Street, threading his way through the pedestrians. The late afternoon breeze blew grit from the street, causing him to squint and raise his hand to shield his face. He brushed the dust from the front of his morning suit, pausing to check his reflection in the plate window of a men's clothier store. He straightened his black silk cravat and tugged his waistcoat flat. He enjoyed spending time with Angeline, who was witty and sweet, and his Aunt Martha, who had been something of a mother to him ever since his own had passed away. The only problem was that Martha was a temperance advocate who didn't serve liquor in her home. For a bon vivant, he considered drinking lemonade with luncheon far too tame. Craving the smooth bite of good whiskey, he decided to stop in at the bar of the Occidental Hotel where he lodged.

Minutes later, he entered the wide lavishly decorated lobby of the Occidental and walked to the establishment's saloon. It was long and narrow with white marble floors and fifteen-foot-high windows facing the streets. Potted plants were situated at intervals around the room, and gleaming brass spittoons placed strategically along the foot rail of the bar. Just past four o'clock, there were only a few patrons—the crowds of businessmen who came for libations after work had not yet been released from their labors.

Sanders stood at the bar and greeted Floyd, the bartender. A somber ex-prizefighter, Floyd shaved his craggy head, reputedly so that no unruly patron could grab his hair when it came time for him to eject any belligerents who had had too much to drink.

"Bushmills with soda, my good man," Sanders ordered.

While Floyd was mixing the cocktail, Sanders noticed the other man standing at the bar. He had one elbow resting on the dark mahogany, and he clutched his forehead as he stared down at his drink. When Floyd put the bubbling glass on the bar, he asked, "What's troubling him?"

The bartender shrugged his wide shoulders.

Sanders sipped his drink and sighed with satisfaction. "Well, give him another of whatever he's having, with my compliments."

Floyd nodded and went to work. Sanders had another sip, then took off his top hat and inverted it, laying it on the polished wood. He was feeling expansive, watching as Floyd placed a new drink in front of the troubled man and said a few soft words while pointing to Sanders, who raised his glass. The man, who wore a pair of wire-rimmed spectacles, nodded and waved hesitantly to his benefactor.

Having done his Christian duty, Sanders addressed his libation with another long sip. He admired the painting of Salome that hung behind the bar. She was a voluptuous naked female with a mane of dark tresses and full breasts reclining on a divan in a "come hither" pose, with only a long wisp of cloth lying across her hips to guard her virtue. Sanders thought of Sally Newhall, the divorced woman who ran a boardinghouse on Second Street. They had been keeping company the last few months—enjoying the shows at playhouses and the Academy of Music, fine dinners at Delmonico's and the Poodle Dog. Afterward, they would go to his rooms in the hotel and make passionate love. Smiling to himself, Sanders noticed someone standing next to him. It was the mournful chap with the glasses.

"I wish to thank you for your kindness, sir," he said, offering his slender hand. "My name is Francis Pettingill."

Sanders shook hands and introduced himself.

Pettingill continued. "A pleasure to meet you, Mr. Sanders. You indeed have the bearings of a gentleman. Have you been in San Francisco long?"

Sanders grinned. "My family moved here during the gold rush from Oregon, having made the trek across the plains back in '46."

"Pioneer stock," Pettingill said. "Very impressive. Did your family strike it rich during the rush?"

"My father scraped enough out of the streams to get a stake. Then he began working for a carriage maker in town. He bought the business in 1858, and we've been doing well ever since."

"Very good, sir." Pettingill signaled the bartender. "Allow me to buy you a drink, Mr. Sanders."

They ordered another round. Pettingill seemed less dejected, though he still frowned at moments. He ran his hands down the dark silk frock coat he wore and adjusted his gray cravat.

Floyd placed the fresh round in front of them, then went back to polishing glasses.

"And you, Mr. Pettingill, are you an Argonaut?"

He shook his head. "I came down from Virginia City some months ago. I have numerous interests in the mines but was tired of living in the hinterlands. The dust and the heat are very onerous."

"Life on the frontier," Sanders said. "I can't imagine wanting to stay there. I enjoy the comforts of civilization—excellent restaurants, cold champagne … and beautiful women."

"Of course," Pettingill said distractedly, staring down at his drink.

"What's bothering you, old man?" Sanders asked, feeling the lift of the whiskey.

"Nothing, but thank you for asking." The fellow scratched his head. "It's a financial concern, but just the sort of thing a gentleman has to deal with from time to time."

Sanders nodded, sipping his new drink. "Is your family from Nevada?"

"No, I was raised in Springfield, Illinois, and came west for my health. I have weak lungs. The doctors advised me to move to the desert for the benefits of the clean, dry air."

"Makes sense," Sanders said, lifting his glass.

"I arrived in 1856 just before the strike. Fortunately, I was able to get in on some excellent investment opportunities shortly after I arrived. I've been doing quite well until just recently."

"Ah, the vagaries of Fortune," Sanders said, glancing at his glass, which was less than half full, and feeling a tinge of disappointment. "What adventurers in the stock markets have not had their reversals! Diversify, I am told. That's the key to staying afloat."

"I have been told the same and have done so but …" Pettingill shook his head.

"But what?"

He looked Sanders squarely in the face. "I'm too diversified. I invested most of my ready cash in a shipping venture. So much so I took out a loan from the Bank of California to have something to live on, but now the bank's going to call in the note. I was hoping to reverse my fortunes in a poker game last Sunday night, but luck was not with me. I lost nearly a thousand."

Sanders frowned, his head singing from the Irish whiskey. "Woes indeed, sir."

Pettingill bit his lower lip, running his finger along the rim of his glass. "I have some shares in the Ophir Mine. But I am reluctant to sell them. You see, the stock is worth five thousand dollars. I spoke to James Lick about it, as we've done a bit of business in the past. Do you know Lick?"

Sanders nodded. "I know him by sight, but we haven't been introduced."

"I'm sure you know his miserly reputation then. He offered me only fifty cents on the dollar, the old brigand. If I could just get seventy-five cents on the dollar, I could pay off the bank note and still have a little left over to keep me until the shipping venture pays off. We're bringing in rubber from Nicaragua for the manufacturing of rain slickers and such."

Sanders studied his empty glass, then put it down on the bar and looked over at Pettingill. His brain was humming like a tuning fork.

"Rubber? There's money to be made in that?"

"Absolutely. Would you like another, my friend?"

* * *

Azariah Dekker and his guest climbed the last few steps of the wooden staircase leading from Taylor Street to the sandy promontory of Fern Hill. They walked along the level expanse in the stiff afternoon breeze. Dekker held a silver-knobbed cane with one hand and gripped the brim of his low topper hat with the other. Daniels buttoned his frock coat and held his hat's brim as well. Sunlight lit the tawny ground as they strolled to the edge of the hill and looked down on the steep incline of California Street toward the blue sweep of the bay and the tiny masts of the ships docked at the Market Street wharf and the others wharves along the Embarcadero.

The breeze lessened, and Dekker let go of his hat. He stabbed at the sandy ground with the tip of his cane, then looked over at the former Confederate agent.

"What precisely does your plan entail, sir?"

"It is similar to the *Chapman* operation. To outfit a vessel with cannon and small arms and use it to capture a larger ship, such as a Pacific Mail Steamship or one from the California, Oregon, and Mexican line. Then transfer some of the heavier guns to the steamer and use both vessels to plunder Yankee shipping in the Pacific."

"You have no letters of marque," Dekker said. "And even if you did, no nation would honor them now with Richmond fallen."

"Desperate times call for desperate measures, my friend. Furthermore, I mean to use the ship to fire upon the town before we slip out the Golden Gate."

"Are you mad?" Dekker stared at the younger man. "Fire upon San Francisco? You would waken the guns in forts around the bay! You would have to sail through the Ring of Fire, a triangulation of Yankee batteries—Fort Point to the south, Lime Point to the north, and Fort Alcatraz to the east. It would be sheer suicide."

Daniels remained unruffled. "It can be done."

"No, sir, it cannot!" Dekker insisted, stamping the ground with his cane. "Don't you know? There are fifteen-inch Rodman cannons mounted on the Ft. Alcatraz batteries. Not even an ironclad can survive a direct hit from a Rodman!"

"The gunners cannot hit what they cannot see. If an attack upon the city were to occur on a night of heavy fog, I believe it would be possible to lob a few volleys at the town, cut the running lights, and sail out the Gate. General Lee may have surrendered, but thousands of loyal Southerners are waiting for the right moment to take up the fight again. It is my intention to give them that signal. Shelling a Yankee building will be a call to arms like Fort Sumter."

"Even so, in dense fog you would need a pilot to get the ship out of the Gate, one skilled at steering by the binnacle alone."

"San Francisco is full of sailors, captains, and pilots. Such a man can be procured."

"But what of his silence? You may recall it was the treachery of the hired captain that scuttled the whole *Chapman* affair by revealing the conspirators' intentions to the harbor police and thus to the US Navy."

"We'll need to use our connections with the Knights to find a loyal bay pilot."

Dekker, who had spent years supporting the states' rights and Southern independence, shook his head. He had met Southern zealots before but no one like Daniels. "This is uncommonly risky."

The younger man smiled. "Indeed, but in risk there is opportunity."

Pointing to a large square gray stone building down by the wharves, Daniels asked, "What is that building, sir?"

"The U.S. Custom House."

He looked at Dekker. "That will be our first target."

CHAPTER *5*

The hills above the town were backlit with the light of the setting sun, which had sunk below the horizon. The smells of cooking food scented the air, drifting from the restaurants along Montgomery Street. Lieutenant Blake strolled along the sidewalks. He had worked most of the afternoon clearing up the reports on his desk and stopped at five thirty to head over to the Olympic Club, where he had spent an hour doing floor exercises and punching the sawdust-filled heavy bag. After a cooling shower, he had dressed and left to meet O'Gara. The day was ending, but progress had been made. The Ellis investigation was moving forward, and the hour he had spent with Elena had been simultaneously soothing and exciting. He wanted to see her again, though when that might be possible, he had no idea. He would write her a note once he returned to his hotel room this evening.

Crossing Clay Street, he walked to the Montgomery Block building, which housed the Adams Express Company. Just past the express offices, he found the Bank Exchange Saloon. The bar was jammed with men in suits, many still wearing their hats. Blue cigar smoke hovered over the crowd, the air noisy with competing voices. Blake spotted O'Gara sitting at a table in his vest and shirtsleeves, eating a sandwich, a schooner of beer at his elbow. Blake went over to the free lunch counter laid out with platters of ham and beef, baskets of sliced bread, and pots of mustard arrayed for the customers' enjoyment. He took a plate from a stack and made himself a thick sandwich of ham and cheese. Ordering a schooner of steam beer from a white-aproned waiter, he sat down at the detective's table.

O'Gara nodded hello as he chewed the last bite of his sandwich. He washed it down with a draught from his mug, then paused to ask, "Have you got the address of this sporting house?"

"Yes." Blake started in on his food.

"Ever been there before?"

Blake shook his head as he chewed. Swallowing, he spoke. "Finnegan mentioned seeing a man walking away from where Ellis was lying. But he was uncertain as to his description. I was thinking we might ask around. Perhaps someone else got a look at him."

O'Gara thought about it, shrugged in agreement, and lifted his beer for another drink. "Maybe at the grog shop where our friend drank up his unjust rewards."

In a few minutes, they were finished. Blake noticed that O'Gara's vest had two slim revolvers placed butt forward in the lower pockets, with the barrels poking down through the bottom seam.

"Did your tailor make that vest alteration for you?" Blake asked, amused.

O'Gara grinned. "My wife did it for me. It's the easiest way to carry a pocket revolver I found. What's in your holster?"

"An Adam's Patent Navy .36," Blake replied, getting up from his chair. "My father gave it to me when I received my commission."

O'Gara stood to pull on his suit coat. Even without buttoning the front, one could not see the guns he carried. He took his hat from the table, and they left the raucous saloon. It was nearly dark outside, though the gas lamps had yet to be lit.

"So where's this cathouse?" O'Gara asked.

"A couple of blocks over on Battery between Washington and Jackson. Madame Cecile's."

"I know the place," the detective said.

They walked the streets, passing only a few people as the sidewalks were nearly empty. They saw a lamplighter from the gas works company carrying a long stick with a hook and a taper at the end, lighting the tall glass-paned lamps patiently one by one. A bold-eyed wench in a low-cut blouse and long skirt, a ratty silk shawl draped around her shoulders, strolled by and smiled at them. They crossed over to the east side of Battery and walked halfway up the block to a wood-frame house with a small stairway and porch, which was illuminated by a single red light. On the landing, O'Gara knocked on the solid door, and the peephole opened.

"Detective O'Gara to see the madame."

The door opened for the two men to step inside. The doorman was taller than O'Gara and Blake and wore a suit that his muscular frame filled. He had long dark hair, slicked with oil and tucked behind his ears. His face was pocked with scars, a wide mustache draping his mouth. His eyes were calm and menacing.

"If you are here to partake of the ladies," he said in a slow, rough voice, "you'll need to leave any weapons with me."

"Just want a word with Madame Cecile," Blake answered, looking around.

The entranceway led to a long corridor with adjacent rooms, the first being the parlor with a fireplace, a rug, and four couches. An upright piano stood in the corner, where a colored gentleman in a brown suit sat playing one of Chopin's nocturnes. Several ladies in undergarments and robes sat on the couches, talking with two male patrons while another without a client sat rolling a cigarette. A tall, dark-haired woman approached, a Japanese folding fan clutched in her long fingers. She wore a black silk dress with a high collar.

"Gentlemen, welcome." She smiled. "Mr. O'Gara from the police, isn't it?"

O'Gara nodded. "Yes ma'am. We're here to speak with one of your girls. What was her name, Lieutenant?"

"Janey," Blake said, holding his kepi, which he had removed upon the madame's arrival.

"And what is this concerning?" Madame Cecile asked, her smile gone, her eyes challenging.

"A routine police inquiry … about a man she kept company with," the detective answered, glancing over at the bouncer, who stood silently in the corner by the door with his hands clasped in front of him.

"I see," the madame said. "Has Janey done anything wrong?"

"Not in the least. We just have a few questions about one of her patrons. Can we see her?"

"I suppose."

"We'll also need a quiet place to talk with her. Perhaps you have an office?"

"You can use the kitchen. It's the last room at the back of this hall. Solomon, show them where it is. I'll get Janey."

O'Gara and Blake sat in a large alcove that had a table and benches lining it. Madame Cecile appeared in the kitchen doorway and pointed at them. A young brown-skinned woman stepped past her and crossed the room, clad in a low-cut red camisole, a pink corset, and lacy red knickers that ended at mid-thigh. A purple robe covered her shoulders. Her thick, wavy hair was plaited into a single tress. She was pretty, and the uncertainty that made her bite her full lips made her even more winsome. She moved her large dark eyes from Blake to O'Gara and back. The detective smiled slowly as he looked at her long brown legs.

"Good evening, Janey," Blake said. "We're here about Major Ellis. You kept company with him in the past. Do you recall the major?"

"Yes, I know him."

"Do you remember when he last came by?" O'Gara asked.

"Must have been about a week ago, sir. He was sort of a regular."

"I heard that Major Ellis had a row with another soldier, a private by the name of Hallinan. Do you recall the night?" Blake said.

She nodded, closing her robe. "That private made a fuss. I was sitting in the parlor, waiting for Mr. Hampton, the major. The private come in and was looking over the girls. He walked up to me and said for me to go upstairs with him. I told him I didn't have time because the major was due at nine o'clock. He came by every Saturday night at that time for the last month. The missus don't like us to say no to a man, but I am fond of the major. He's good to me. That Hallinan fellow cussed me, and just when the madame come in to see what the matter was, the major come in too."

"So what happened?" O'Gara asked, his notebook opened in his palm and a pencil in his other hand.

"I went over to the major and said we should go upstairs. Then Hallinan cussed some more and said he had dibs—he seen me first. He smelled of whiskey and threatened to hit the major. That's when the missus called for Solomon to escort him out."

"Did he make any other threats?" Blake asked. "About later on?"

She shook her head. "Solomon got him by the scruff and marched him to the front door. He was hollering about getting his three dollars back. Solomon told him to come back later and get his trick then."

O'Gara looked at Blake, closing the notebook.

"Why you asking me this? Where's Major Ellis?"

"He's in the morgue," O'Gara said, rising. "Someone shot him."

"Oh, my God!" She raised her hand to her mouth.

"Have you seen Hallinan since that night?" Blake also stood.

"Yes, he come by." She looked at the floor. "I went upstairs with him. He's rough and likes to hurt a girl. I told him to never come back. He laughed at me, and I ain't seen him since."

"Thank you, Janey," Blake said, thinking she had not given them much that was useful. Perhaps interviewing Hallinan would be more revealing.

Walking past her, the two men headed for the door to the hallway.

"Lieutenant?" Janey spoke.

Blake paused at the door. "Yes?"

"I like officers. You get lonely here in San Francisco, you come see me." Her brown eyes were sincere as she gazed at him.

"Thanks again." Blake nodded.

O'Gara laughed and punched him on the shoulder as they made their way out.

* * *

Azariah Dekker stood on the corner of Sansome and California Streets, next to a tobacconist's store, which was closed and dark. With him was Henry Lee Baugh, a tall sandy-haired man from Austin with deep-set eyes of pale blue. His ears stuck out slightly from his head, and the edge of the left ear had a small semicircular notch where a Comanche musket ball had clipped it when Baugh was a trooper in Texas, serving under John Bell Hood in the U.S. Second Cavalry, patrolling the *Comancheria*. He had worked with Dekker for years on the *Democratic Press* and was a fellow Knight of the Golden Circle. Both Dekker and his companion were dressed in workingmen's clothes—dark canvas pants and old wool coats. In the wan light of the gas lamps, Dekker checked his pocket watch.

"It's ten minutes after nine," said the older man. "Where is he?"

The streets were mostly empty. People were either at home, dining at restaurants, or drinking in saloons. Footsteps sounded along the sidewalk, and the two men looked in their direction. Baugh put his hand inside his coat to grip the weapon he had beneath it. Dekker touched his shoulder to signal that it was all right. He recognized the approaching man. It was Daniels. Like his companions, he wore rough clothes.

"Gentlemen, forgive my tardiness."

Dekker gestured to Baugh. "This is Henry Lee Baugh. He is one of us—a Knight. He served with Hood, fighting Comanches in Texas before the war. Came out west after his enlistment ended and became a news reporter."

Daniels shook hands with Baugh. "I'm from Savannah myself. Always a pleasure to meet a fellow Knight."

Baugh nodded. "The same."

"I'm late because I was trying to locate the whereabouts of one Liverpool Wilcox."

"The harbor thief?" Dekker asked. "Whatever for? He's a cut-throat, and so are all of his henchmen. Smash your head in for a dollar, if they think you have one."

"But Wilcox and his gang may prove useful. I intend to engage them to procure a ship for us. However, we must find him first."

"That's easy," Baugh said. "He and his gang drink at The Kraken, over on Pacific and Drumm, the heart of the Barbary Coast. No place for gentlemen."

"I anticipated it would be a dive. Are you armed, Mr. Baugh?"

"I have an Army .44." He opened his wool coat to display the holstered weapon.

"And you, Mr. Dekker?"

The older man took his hand out of his pocket, holding his small five-shot .31 Colt.

"Commendable but perhaps something more persuasive is needed," Daniels said.

He opened his coat to reveal a sawed-off shotgun. He handed it to Dekker.

"Hold it muzzle down. That way the percussion caps are less likely to fall off. I suggest cutting a hole through your coat pocket to maintain an easier grip on the gun."

"I'm not sure I brought my pocketknife," Dekker said, holding the shotgun with one hand and patting about his person with the other.

Daniels reached to his belt and produced a short bowie knife. He traded it for the shotgun while Dekker opened the pocket and lining of the coat.

"Azariah told me of your insistence on this rough garb. We'll blend in very well," Baugh said.

"One of the lessons I learned in England in the service of Captain Bulloch. Dressing like a gentleman while operating in the shipyards in Liverpool only made you conspicuous," Daniels responded.

"There," Dekker said, handing back the knife. He folded the lapels of his coat over the eighteen-inch barrels, while his hand inside gripped the shotgun. He buttoned only one of the four buttons and looked up at his companions.

Daniels gazed at the other two. "Just a few simple directions before we brace Wilcox and his gang. Once we enter their lair, we must stay together—at each other's elbows. We'll cluster at whichever end of the bar is open, preferably near a wall. Don't let anyone stand behind you. I'll do all the talking. If I nod to you, Azariah, raise the shotgun and level it at Wilcox. They must know we are in earnest, whether our intention is to hire them or annihilate them. Understood?"

Dekker nodded solemnly, and Baugh smiled.

* * *

As they walked away from Madame Cecile's, O'Gara looked over at Blake. The streets were gloomy and the night air chilled by a strong breeze. The faint strains of a waltz came from a concert saloon across the street, its windows glowing with light, its signs advertising music and dancing.

"Think you'll go back and visit Janey?" O'Gara asked, putting an unlit cheroot into his mouth.

"No," Blake answered, annoyed the detective thought he would patronize a prostitute.

"Why not? You're not married, are you?"

Blake glanced over at his companion. "For one thing, I'm … seeing a lady. For another, before I joined the Army I spent an hour at my father's insistence with a doctor who is a friend of the family back in New London. He showed me photographs of people inflicted with venereal disease, pictures of their genitalia. He made me promise I would never bed a whore. After seeing those daguerreotypes, it was an easy promise to make."

"You can always use a condom. Of course, there are better sporting houses along Dupont Avenue over by Geary and Post."

"You speak like a man of experience," Blake said, wondering if the policeman was needling him.

O'Gara smiled and took the small un-lit cigar from his mouth. "I gave it up once I got married. Been three years now, and we have a little boy."

Blake nodded. "Shall we walk over to the Brown Dog?"

"May as well."

In a few minutes, they reached the tavern. It was small with dirty sawdust on the floor. Several men were seated at tables, talking loudly and drinking. The wood of the bar was nicked and scuffed. Behind it stood the saloonkeeper—a wiry balding man with a rough face and watchful eyes. Blake and O'Gara entered and walked to the bar. One of the patrons at the tables stood and left quickly, keeping his head down. Blake saw O'Gara turn at the rapid exit but the detective stayed by the bar.

"Gentlemen," the bartender said with a predatory smile. "What'll you have?"

"Information," O'Gara replied, holding open his coat to show his badge. "The other night an Army major got shot out on the street. You remember that night? Maybe you saw something?"

"I have a business to run. I can't be concerned with what goes on out there. I have to keep my customers happy."

"I think you mean drunk, stupid, and penniless," O'Gara said. He pointed a finger at the man. "I can close you down right now."

"What for?!"

"None of those bottles behind the bar have tax stamps on them," O'Gara said, nodding to the sparse collection of liquor bottles on the back bar.

Blake slid a silver dollar across the wooden counter. "Did you happen to see the major walk by?"

The bartender looked from the cop to the soldier. Blake repeated the question. The bartender put his hand on top of the silver coin.

"He stopped in the doorway to catch his breath. It seemed as though he might have been running. I invited him in, but he just looked at me and kept going. Not long after that I heard a shot, but I didn't go to the door. Wasn't none of my business."

"Anybody else in here who might have seen anything?" O'Gara asked.

"One of my regulars left just after the major did."

"This regular have a name?"

The bartender looked away.

"He got a name?" O'Gara demanded, slamming his hand down on the bar.

"There a problem, Fergus?" asked one of the men at the tables.

O'Gara turned, drawing and cocking one of the revolvers from his vest. He pointed the Colt at the fellow. "This is police business. Leave now if you don't want to spend a month on the chain gangs."

Without a word, all three men at the table stood, hesitated a moment, then walked out the door, their faces sullen. The cop turned back to the bartender.

"You're next," he said, extending the Colt. "And keep your hands on the counter where I can see them. Now, you want thirty days on the gangs, fixing the streets?"

The bartender shook his head.

"Give us the name then," Blake said, after glancing at the other customers, who sat quietly watching.

"It was Paddy Doolin."

O'Gara started. "Aw, Jesus Christ, not him!"

"What is it?" Blake asked.

The cop waved him off, glaring at the bartender. O'Gara said nothing as he carefully reset the hammer of his revolver onto a cylinder pin between the loaded chambers.

"How often does Doolin come around?" the detective asked.

The bartender shrugged. "Once a week or so."

"Come on," O'Gara said to Blake.

Slipping the handgun back into his vest pocket, O'Gara turned and walked out. Blake threw a final glance at the saloonkeeper, then followed. Outside, he had to step quickly to catch up to the policeman.

"What's wrong?"

O'Gara stopped to put the cheroot back in his mouth, lighting it with a match he scratched against a gas lamp. He took a puff, which seemed to calm him, and looked at Blake.

"Paddy Doolin is what we call a Barbary Coast Ranger. He's a ticket-of-leave Sydney convict who arrived back in 1852. A career criminal—robbery, arson, murder, you name it. The Vigilance Committee ran him out of town in '56. Only, he resurfaced a few years later. Getting information out of him … we might as well interrogate a cigar store Indian. And he's going to be hard to find."

"How so?"

"We'll have to go into the Barbary Coast to roust him."

"I'm game if you are," Blake said.

O'Gara shook his head. "It's too late. He could be anywhere by now, in any of a hundred places—opium den, grog shop, gambling hell, whorehouse. Who knows? We'll do better to seek him out at midday. He'll be sleeping off whatever he did the night before. I know a kid who works as a beer boy at the Billy Goat saloon. If anyone knows where Paddy Doolin is holed up, the kid will. I'll seek the boy out in the late morning and meet up with you at City Hall at noon."

"All right," Blake said. "I'll ride out to the Presidio tomorrow morning and talk to Hallinan. I'll bring him to police headquarters if I think there's anything important to be had from him."

"Good enough." O'Gara offered his hand, which Blake shook.

"I'm off to catch the omnibus for Happy Valley. I have a house over by the foot of the hill on Second Street. See you tomorrow."

O'Gara crossed the cobbled street and disappeared around a corner building. Blake strode along Battery and turned at Sacramento for the What Cheer House, thinking of the note he wanted to send Elena.

* * *

The murky streets were plagued with half-hidden obstacles—discarded bottles that rolled underfoot, hogs sleeping in the shadows that squealed when accidentally kicked, curs that growled from beneath the boardwalk. The air was rank with the stench of garbage, alcohol, and urine. Grimacing, Azariah kept pace with his companions, the shotgun beneath his coat occasionally bumping his legs. Lights and tinny music blared from the row of saloons along the lower end of Pacific Street.

The grog shops were interspersed with sailors' boardinghouses—shabby, grim-looking establishments—and closed shops that displayed cheap boots, jackknives, and oil skins in their fly-specked windows. A grey-haired, toothless woman sat on the edge of the boardwalk, dressed in ragged clothes. She smiled querulously at them.

"Just two bits, you lads. I'll do you all for just two bits."

The trio walked past her, saying nothing.

"Fucking bastards!" the hag shouted.

Azariah had never been through the Barbary Coast at night and feared he might have to use the shotgun before they even got to The Kraken. Worse than the haggard women who stood outside the bars in low-cut blouses, smoking cigarettes were the feral-eyed men, standing or sitting along the street, some in the light, others in the shadows. Most were gaunt wrecks, debilitated from a life of dissipation. But a number were young and dangerous as wild animals.

They crossed Battery Street and continued down Pacific, passing a doorway marked with Chinese ideographs. The faint aroma of burning poppy seeds emanated from the closed doorway.

"Opium," Baugh said. "The Kraken is just up ahead."

"Remember," Daniels added, "we must stay together."

They reached the saloon, whose faded street sign showed a giant squid attacking a ship. Inside, the taproom was rectangular and roughly thirty feet across. The air was hazy with cheap, bitter tobacco smoke. The walls were dark and bare. Conversation ceased as the trio entered, the denizens glaring as they walked to the bar, which was made from old hatch covers nailed together. An upright piano stood off to the right of the bar, marked by several bullet holes. Oil lamps hanging from the ceiling by chains gave the room a soft, venomous glow. The barkeep was a stoop-shouldered man with a ravaged face and scarred eyebrows. He smiled, several of his teeth missing. A meager collection of bottles lined the counter behind the bar, alongside a trio of squat kegs with wood spigots.

"And what will you brave lads be having?" he asked.

"A word with a friend," Daniels answered, who stopped at the counter, with Baugh and Azariah at his flanks.

"A friend? Who might that be, stranger?"

"I seek counsel with Liverpool Wilcox."

"Never heard of him."

A man seated at a table close by looked over. "Wha' do you want with Wilcox?" he asked in Cockney accent.

Daniels turned, smiling. "A business arrangement."

The man stood, the others at his table rising along with him. The fellow who had spoken was short and slender. He wore a blue wool jacket that looked like it might be part of a nautical uniform. His square face had deep lines; his eyes were intense. A thatch of graying hair covered the top of his head. The folds of his jacket were unbuttoned, and a Colt Navy revolver was slung through the heavy belt supporting his trousers.

"Who're you?" the short Englishman asked.

"A businessman. From Georgia, if you must know. I'm here looking for a boat. Am I correct in assuming you are Mr. Wilcox?"

"Not *mister*. Captain Wilcox," he corrected.

"Captain, then. We are here to hire you and your cohorts to obtain a ship for us. A schooner would do nicely. You see, we haven't the means to buy one outright and so must resort to … subtler methods."

Wilcox walked toward Daniels, stopping a yard away. Alongside him moved a tall light-haired man with a full beard who looked unmistakably Scandinavian. The Englishman stared at Daniels for half a minute, hand resting on the grip of his Colt.

"What do you say, Sven?"

Breathing audibly through his slightly open mouth, the Swede looked from Daniels to Azariah to Baugh. "I say we cut their throats, by God, and throw them into the bay."

Azariah cocked the hammers of the shotgun inside his coat, the metallic clicking audible in the tense silence. He unbuttoned the garment with his free hand as sweat ran down his back.

"One hundred dollars in gold eagles," Daniels said, breaking the impasse, producing a cloth sack from his coat pocket. "Another four hundred when we take possession of the ship."

He tossed the bag to Wilcox. The Englishman caught it and worked open its mouth, then poured newly minted coins into his broad palm. He looked from the specie to Sven.

"What do you say now, you big square 'ead?"

"I say we cut their throats and throw them into the bay."

Daniels stepped close to the Swede, his elbow jerking. The Swede gasped in pain. Stepping back, Daniels pulled the revolver from beneath his coat. It was cocked and leveled at Wilcox before the harbor thief could react. Azariah hauled the shotgun clear of his jacket, holding it on Wilcox's men, who protested loudly but stayed where they were. The Swede stared down at the knife hilt sticking out of his belly. Crimson and gleaming in the soft lamplight, blood ran down his pant leg, dripping onto the sawdust at his feet. He collapsed to his knees, his weight shaking the floorboards, hands clasping the hilt. He looked up in shock at Daniels, who ignored him and kept the massive Le Mat revolver pointed at Wilcox. Azariah's jaw clamped with fear, wondering how they would ever make it out alive.

"Now, sir," Daniels said. "We can continue killing each other, or we can conduct business. I leave the choice to you."

Baugh cocked the revolver in his fist, pointing it at the barkeep. The saloonkeeper raised his hands, backing away toward the far end of the counter.

"What will it be, Captain Wilcox? Mutual cooperation or mutual destruction?"

Ever so slowly, Wilcox nodded his head. Sven fell over on his side, again shaking the floor. His head fell to the grimy sawdust, eyes closing as blood pooled beside him. Wilcox glanced at the dying man as he let loose an agonized whine like a gut-shot dog.

"I'll want an extra fifty dollars for killing my lieutenant."

"I think we can accommodate you. Do you know the German Saloon?"

"On Montgomery?"

"Meet me there at noon where we can discuss this further. Come alone," Daniels said.

Wilcox nodded.

"Azariah, walk to the front door and cover the rest of the room."

Relieved to be leaving, Azariah moved swiftly to the front door, turning as he went, shotgun muzzles sweeping the crowd. The smoky air was making his eyes water, but he dared not wipe them. When he got to the doorway, he put his back to the frame and held his gun on Wilcox and his gang. Daniels and Baugh backed their way across the room.

"You all best stay put. Anyone who comes out that door in the next few minutes is going to get a mouthful of buckshot," Daniels said loudly.

One by one the trio went through the door. Striding quickly, they turned at Front and headed east to Market Street. Azariah glanced over his shoulder several times to make sure no one followed them.

* * *

Mrs. Sally Newhall heard knocking at the front door of her boardinghouse. She locked the door after dusk, insisting her boarders use their keys at night. She had only an elderly Irish maid to help her run the house, and the only protection beyond the locks on the doors and windows was a pair of derringers she kept in her desk drawer. Sitting in the parlor with a cup of mint tea and a book, she glanced at the grandmother clock in the corner and saw that it was nine forty-eight—too late for any civilized callers. She waited, hoping the knocking would cease. Mrs. Feeney had long since finished the supper dishes and retired to her room. For a moment, silence pervaded the air, though she could hear one of her boarders walking around in his room above. The rapping at the door continued, becoming louder.

Muttering, she put aside her novel and walked out of the room into the front hall. She paused at the mirror to check her brown hair -- glancing at her face, which was pretty but often had a stern expression. Her skin was dark, the legacy of her Modoc grandmother, and her eyes a clear green. She went to the broad decorated wooden door.

"Who's there?" she called in an even voice.

"Sally! It's me, Jim. Open up."

Turning the key in the lock, she pulled the door open enough to peer out, feeling annoyed and curious at the same time. She saw Jim Sanders standing in the yellow porch light. His hat sat crookedly on his head, and he was grinning. He put his hand on the door, pushing his way in.

"Good evening, my dear."

She winced at the whiskey on his breath. "Go home. You're drunk."

"I've been celebrating. Met this fellow who's desperate for cash. Gonna sell me shares of the Ophir Mine for pennies on the dollar. I'm going to see some real money out of this!"

She placed her hand on his chest and moved him back against the door. "You have to go back to your hotel. I have a reputation to maintain. If I'm seen entertaining drunken men, this boardinghouse will be ruined. You go home."

He brushed her hand aside and pulled her close. "I want to celebrate. Let's make love."

"Not here, not now," she hissed.

He tried to kiss her but she turned her face away, stepping back out of his embrace. She reached for the door and opened it. "Go home, Mr. Sanders."

"But Sally … I want to celebrate."

"You've done enough of that."

"I'm staying," he said, taking off his hat and tossing it onto the narrow table across from the door. He squinted at her to mark his resolve.

Sally regarded him as she would a petulant child. She had dealt with drunks before. Nodding, she closed the door.

"Have you had your supper?"

He shook his head. "I'm famished. Have any pork chops?"

She took him by the arm and led him to the parlor sofa. "Sit down, and I'll make up a plate for you in the kitchen."

He smiled, patting her rump through the back of her dress. "That's my girl."

"Sit." She pushed gently but firmly down on his shoulder until he was resting on the sofa. "I'll be back in a minute."

She went to the parlor doors and pulled them closed. Then she strode to the kitchen, walked through it, and made for the room off the back pantry. She knocked at the closed door.

"Wha' tis it?" answered Mrs. Feeney sleepily as she opened the door. She was in her nightgown, a pleated cap on her head.

"I need your help," Sally said. "Mr. Sanders is here, and he's drunk. I need you to help me get him into a hack."

"I'll get me robe."

"He's in the parlor."

Without waiting for her, Sally headed back to the front of the house. She quietly opened the parlor door to peer inside. Sanders sat slumped on the couch, his chin resting on his chest. She had an impulse to just let him sleep right there, but if one of her boarders found him there, it would mean all sorts of gossip and whispers—at first, around the house, then around the neighborhood. She closed the door and went to get her coat. She would have to go out onto the street to find a cabbie.

* * *

Blake sat on his bed in his shirtsleeves and stockinged feet, perusing Major Hampton Ellis's diary, hoping to find something that would help explain the man's murder.

He read an entry dated June 8, 1861:

Today I was informed by my commanding officer that I am to be the liaison officer to the U.S. Military Railroad, and it will be my responsibility to oversee shipments of supplies and ordnance to federal armies in the field. I am very pleased to have this assignment …

Blake plodded through more entries, then skipped ahead to one dated September 15, 1862:

I had a terrible row with Emmelda last evening, who insisted on voicing her support of Lee's invasion of Maryland at a supper party.

My wife has no conception of the trouble she can make for me or herself. There are numerous rebellion advocates languishing in the jails of Washington. This was after she introduced me to a "businessman" from Savannah, who indicated he knew people who would be very grateful for select information regarding the shipments I coordinate, and that for such information I would be amply rewarded in gold dollars. I reported the scoundrel to the provost marshal's office this morning but was informed that the soldiers sent to arrest him found his hotel room deserted.

He carefully read the next several entries, hoping to find the name of the man who had approached Ellis for information but found no further mention of the incident, just dull descriptions of the major's difficulties with tardy suppliers and deliveries of spoiled goods. Blake moved to the final entry, dated April 25, 1866.

I took this assignment (auditing the quartermaster's section of the Department of California) because Emmelda has remained sequestered in her rooms at home since the fall of Richmond. And while San Francisco has not the amenities available to a gentleman that Washington or Baltimore have to offer, I have however made a rare discovery. She is a mulatto courtesan, tall and statuesque, with warm brown eyes and full soft breasts. Her name is Janey, and she is as willing and loving as Emmelda is cold and forbidding. I visit her regularly and find great solace in her smooth brown arms.

Closing the book, Blake sat on his bed musing over Ellis's words. He slid the journal onto his nightstand and stood to stretch. Walking to his table he sat and took a sheet of paper from a small leather case next to the steel pen and inkwell. For a moment, he imagined Elena in his arms, bringing a rush of tenderness and desire. He smiled, his eyes closing. Shaking his head to fight off his fatigue, he picked up the pen. But he hesitated, unsure of what to write. *How could he tell her she had captured his heart in so brief a time? And with her engaged to another man what would be the point?* Putting down the pen, he rubbed his forehead, biting his lip in exasperation.

CHAPTER 6

A high-ceiling grayish-white fog blanketed the sky as Blake jogged his rented horse along the Presidio Road. Along the wide lane, a stiff breeze blew grit from the road so that he pulled his blue kepi low over his eyes, wishing he had brought along a neckerchief to tie over his nose and mouth. Extending beyond the edge of town, the road passed a small inland lake surrounded by houses called Washerwoman's Lagoon. Blake glanced at its long gray oval surface riffled by the cold wind.

A Bowman & Gardner omnibus rolled past him, pulled by four massive horses, heading for town with two passengers in the coach. Blake could have taken the omnibus to the Presidio Reservation but had decided to ride instead to keep up his horsemanship skills. The road ran west, past occasional solitary houses surrounded by animal pens or small cultivated fields. They seemed lonely, isolated places. The few people he saw standing in their yards watched him pass without greeting him or waving their hands. Further on, he passed a cluster of buildings just outside the white fence marking the edge of the military installation. The buildings were a collection of saloons, card rooms, and brothels that catered to—or preyed upon, depending on one's point of view—the garrisoned soldiers. Contemptuously known as "hog ranches," these establishments sold whiskey, female flesh, and other amusements to the hard-working, ill-paid servicemen. One place had a sign declaring it "The Presidio House." Blake saw a few uniformed men lounging on its veranda. It was hardly half past eight in the morning, and soldiers were already drinking.

Roughly a mile beyond the hog ranches, Blake rode up to a broad arch, whose apex was marked with a crossed cannons insignia. The gated doors of the garrison, built of wooden beams and studded with iron points, were open. A sentry with a long Springfield rifle slung on his shoulder stood by a small post shack just outside the gates. Blake halted his mount as the sentry saluted him.

"Good morning, Lieutenant."

"Morning," Blake said, returning the salute. "I'm here to interview one of your soldiers. Who is the officer of the day?"

"That would be Lieutenant Ayers. The duty office is in that barracks." The guard pointed to a building several yards beyond the flagstaff, just inside the gate.

Twenty minutes later, Blake and a first sergeant walked into one of the kitchens on the west side of the enlisted men's barracks. When the first sergeant asked a mess man where Hallinan was, the cook gestured with his thumb to a pantry toward the back. There they found a single man in a long-sleeved undershirt and smeared white apron straddling a small keg, peeling potatoes with a thin-bladed knife. He muttered under his breath as he worked. A small pile of brown potato skins lay between his booted feet. At his back were shelves of canned goods.

"Hallinan," the first sergeant said. "On your feet. This officer has some questions for you."

The man looked up. He had thick brown hair, insolent blue eyes, and a short pugnacious nose. He stood slowly as if it were a great effort.

"Sir?" He spoke without a brogue, and one of his front teeth was missing.

"I'm looking into the shooting death of Major Ellis," Blake said to him.

"Yes sir."

"Do you recall Major Ellis?" Blake asked, tucking his riding gloves through his pistol belt.

"No sir."

"Really? You had words with him over a harlot named Janey, at Madame Cecile's establishment on Battery Street a while back."

"Not ringing any bells for me, Lieutenant."

"You deny this occurrence?"

Hallinan looked at Blake and waited before answering. "I don't recall it ... sir."

"I've spoken to eyewitnesses who say you were there. That you threatened the major. This is a serious matter, Private. The major was shot to death. Failure to cooperate will lead to disciplinary measures, perhaps even a court-martial. Do we understand each other?"

"Wait a minute, Lieutenant. I never laid a hand on that fat bas ... the major. God as my witness. Sure, we had words over a no-account darky whore, but it was just words. I got shown the door."

"Where were you three nights ago?" Blake asked, disliking the man's arrogance and wondering if the private was hiding something.

"Three nights ago? I was here, mopping out the kitchen, like I have for the past two weeks."

Blake looked at the first sergeant for confirmation. The man narrowed his eyes as he regarded the private.

"Drunk and disorderly, wasn't it, Hallinan?"

"Drunk on duty, sir. I received a week in the stockade and KP for three months. Ask the mess sergeant if you don't believe me. He was here taking inventory."

Blake pulled his riding gloves from his belt.

"I may have more questions later, Private."

The first sergeant gestured to the bucket of potatoes next to Hallinan's leg. "Carry on, soldier."

Moving down the steps of the barracks, Blake thanked the first sergeant and dismissed him. Heading back to the post gate, he mused in frustration over Hallinan's alibi. The investigation was faltering. He could only hope Detective O'Gara would have something.

* * *

Angeline Whitfield waited for her cousin who was to walk her home outside the building where the Contraband Relief Society had a single office, paid for by the society's corresponding secretary. She rubbed her gloved right hand, which was stiff from the six letters she had penned that morning. It was tedious work, copying solicitations to be sent to the prominent families and businesses in town, but it got Angeline out of the house and gave her something worthwhile to do with her mornings. The sun was just beginning to break through the summer clouds. The light made her squint, and she wished she had brought a parasol. Pedestrians passed by on the plank sidewalks, the men often smiling at her. She looked away. *Where was Cousin Jim? Had he forgotten her?*

A taxi carriage pulled up in front of the building, its door opening. Jim Sanders stepped out to offer her his hand.

"Top of the morning, Angie. Your carriage awaits."

She smiled. "A taxi?"

"I'm celebrating. I have a colleague I want you to meet. He's inside, and his name is Mr. Pettingill. He and I have struck a bargain, and we are taking you to luncheon at the Lick House."

"How delightful!" She always welcomed a break from her routine.

Taking her cousin's hand, Angeline stepped up into the carriage and sat across from a sober-faced gentleman with spectacles. He tipped his hat to her as Jim climbed in, swaying the carriage on its springs. Jim made the introductions. Pettingill smiled, bringing her hand to his lips as he bowed forward. Jim rapped his knuckles on the roof of the coach, and the conveyance started forward.

"A pleasure to meet you, Miss Whitfield," Pettingill said, offering a shy smile.

Angeline smiled back and looked at Jim. His face was pale, his eyes a little bloodshot.

"Were you drinking last night?" she asked admonishingly.

"Who, me? Never," Jim said. "Never again. At least, not like that. I was positively boiled. Last thing I remember was walking down to Second Street, and yet I woke up this morning in my rooms at the Occidental. The work of a guardian angel, no doubt."

"Mother hopes to convert you some day, Cousin. I tell her she is wasting her time."

"I'm afraid the fault is mine," Pettingill said. "We had rather a party at the Occidental's saloon. But good things have come of it. Your cousin and I have come to a harmonious accord—one that will bring us both satisfaction."

"Pettingill has various interests in the Comstock," Jim explained. "But he now lives in town. A much better place to manage one's affairs than dusty old Virginia City."

"True, but I cannot malign a place that brings me income. Without the silver mines, I'd be working as a clerk in a counting house."

"And bored to death, I imagine," Jim added, settling back on the bench seat.

"Counting every penny I earned." The newcomer laughed.

Jim laughed as well, and Angeline smiled.

"Shall we have oysters and champagne?" Pettingill suggested.

Angeline looked at Jim to see how he would answer. He took off his hat and combed his fingers through his hair.

"I don't think I can ..."

"Hair of the dog, old man. It's the best cure."

"Not abstinence?" Angeline asked.

Pettingill shook his head. "Not when you are celebrating."

Jim smiled weakly. "Maybe I'll just have a steak and watch you two eat the oysters."

* * *

The interior of the German Saloon was dark and soothing to the eye after the bright sun of Montgomery Street. The saloon was a long rectangular room with handsomely paneled walls of dark redwood. Here and there hunting trophies were mounted—a mountain lion's head with gleaming fangs, a buck with magnificent twelve-point antlers, a shaggy somber-looking bison with leathery nose and lips. The bar occupied one side of the room and small square tables took up the rest of the space, nearly all filled with customers. The air smelled of cooking food, cigar smoke, and steam beer.

Daniels leaned against the bar, rolling a black unlit cheroot between his fingers. He glanced at the carved wooden grandfather clock in the far corner of the room and wondered if Wilcox was going to show. It was eleven minutes after the hour. He slipped his free hand beneath his black frock coat and touched the butt of the Le Mat holstered at the small of his back for the third time. *If that limey son of a bitch doesn't show, I'll hunt him down and put a bullet through both his eyes.* Daniels gestured to the bartender to freshen his glass of lager. The barkeep lifted a pitcher from the basin of ice below the counter and refilled the mug.

Daniels nodded his thanks, sipping from his glass. He had considered waiting outside and across the street, just in case the police showed up instead of Wilcox. However, professional thieves spent their lives hating and avoiding the authorities, not enlisting them for revenge, and Wilcox stood to gain the extra fifty dollars for the knifing of his cohort. *Where was he?* Daniels mused petulantly.

A man in a nautical-styled jacket stepped up to the bar on Daniel's left and signaled the bartender.

"I'll have a beer, mate, on my friend 'ere."

Daniels looked down at the smaller man. "How did you get in?"

Wilcox took a long drink of beer, nearly finishing the mug. He put it down and wiped his mouth with a sleeve before answering. "I had to make sure there weren't no coppers around, just in case you was playin' me for a fool. Often best just to slip in the back door, isn't it?"

"I suppose that explains your tardiness."

"My what?"

"Never mind. Can you get me a boat? A schooner or something larger?"

"What do you want it for?" Wilcox said.

"Suffice it to say that I have a sudden urge to sail the Pacific. Can you procure a vessel?"

"Procure a vessel?" Wilcox rubbed his stubbled jaw, glancing at Daniels. "I believe I can. There's a fat banker what keeps a right nice pungy anchored not far off Meiggs Wharf. Rendezvouses with his mistress on the boat, with his missus none the wiser, I suspect."

"Pungy? What's that?"

"Pungy schooner. Don't you know anything about boats?"

"How big is it?"

"Little over one 'undred feet long. Maybe twenty-two foot abeam."

Daniels nodded slowly, lifting his beer with his left hand, his right tucked behind him.

"When can you get it?"

"Soon as you like, but it will cost a thousand."

"For that much, I could buy one outright. Five hundred is all you will get."

They stared at each other for a long moment.

"Seven 'undred for the boat. Fifty for butchering Sven."

Daniels took a drink of beer, his eyes never leaving Wilcox's over the rim of the mug. He put the glass down, shaking his head.

"If you want the rest of the five hundred, get the boat." Daniels backed up two steps and turned to leave.

"Bloody 'ell but you're stubborn. All right, damn you, five it is."

Daniels returned to the bar, leaning toward the smaller man. "When will I have it?"

Amid the noise of the bar, Wilcox lifted his glass to the barkeep, who frowned and refilled it. He took another long sip, pondering the question. "Three days. We'll need to set up a safe rendezvous point. But first things first, eh? The fifty for Sven?"

Taking coins from his vest pocket, Daniels thumbed gold eagles onto the bar. He counted out five, then returned the remainder to his vest.

"I'll meet you back here in two days. At noon. So long, Captain."

Daniels picked up the cheroot from beside his glass and clamped it in his mouth. He retreated a few paces as Wilcox watched him, then turned and stepping in with a noisy group of businessmen in top hats as they moved toward the door. Out in the sunlight, Daniels waited in an entranceway to see if Wilcox was following him. But the slight Englishman must have lingered over his beer. Daniels stepped into a cab waiting at the curb and told the man to drive.

* * *

Entering the office, Blake paused at the coat rack to hang his kepi and pistol belt, then walked toward his chair. Schaeffer, at his desk, lifted up a small envelope.

"A young Californio boy brought this for you."

Holding the paper to his nose, he smiled. "From a young lady, I suspect."

"You're a prying old coot," Blake said as he took the envelope.

His name was written in beautiful script on the outside, which exuded a lovely floral scent. He was eager to open it but decided to wait for a more private moment. He slipped it into his trouser pocket while Schaeffer watched. Last night sitting at his table, overcome by the day's fatigue he had fallen asleep while trying to find the right words to express his feelings for Elena.

Blake went to the doorway of Colonel Wagner's chamber and waited until the senior officer, puffing on his pipe, looked up from his work. He took the pipe from his mouth.

"Yes, Mr. Blake?"

"Sir, the investigation is beginning to stall. I questioned Private Hallinan this morning. He was on KP duty the night Ellis was killed. I'd like to request Ellis's service record from Washington to see if it might hold any possible answers."

"Perhaps Hallinan had an accomplice do it. Have you considered that?"

"No sir, but it might be worth considering," Blake said.

"Go ahead with Ellis's record, but it will take weeks to get a copy. Wire the records office in Washington for a summary. See if that will give you anything to work with."

"Yes sir."

"By the way, do you have the Ft. Crook inspection ready yet?"

"I finished it yesterday. I'll bring it to you," Blake said.

"Right away, if you please."

Back at his desk, Blake glanced at Schaeffer, who was engrossed in his work. He took the scented envelope from his pocket and opened it.

Dear Liam,

Such a pleasant hour we spent together. I have thought of you often since then. There is a ball tomorrow night at the residence of Mr. & Mrs. Peter Donahue. Their house is at 461 Second Street. An invitation will be arriving shortly. I hope to see you there.

Affectionately,

Elena

He smiled, refolding the letter. He knew he was mad to get involved with her. But he felt such an extraordinary attraction—to deny it would be to turn his back on his hopes. Perhaps there was a way she could extract herself from this marriage contract. Perhaps they could be together despite circumstances.

He put the note back in his pocket and unlocked his desk drawer to retrieve the report for the colonel.

* * *

Angeline walked along upper Stockton Street between her cousin and Mr. Pettingill, gazing at the small blue strip of the bay and the brown hills beyond, minute in the distance. On the bare crest of Telegraph Hill, the staircase-encircled tower of the inner telegraph station was visible, the flag atop its pole fluttering in the breeze. Angeline slipped her arm through her cousin's.

"Well, that was a lovely meal," she said. "We must do this more often."

Jim glanced over at her, his eyes still slightly red.

"Indeed, we should," Pettingill said.

Angeline gave him a smile, which he returned. The dry goods, groceries, and feed stores they passed gave way to broad mansions, mostly on the west side of the street with views of the water. They stopped before the Whitfield home, a wide house painted a cream pastel with white trim along its windows and door frame.

"What a splendid afternoon," Angeline said as she kissed Jim's unshaven cheek. "Mother will wonder what you've done with me."

"Tell her I send her my love."

"Shall I walk you to the door?" Mr. Pettingill offered.

Taking his arm, she climbed the brick stairs to the wide carved wooden door with him. At the doorstep, she offered her gloved hand. "A pleasure to meet you, sir."

"Indeed, it was truly mine, Miss Whitfield. May I … may I call on you?" he asked.

She nodded, finding his awkwardness rather touching. "Yes, of course."

"Tomorrow then. Perhaps a carriage ride to the Cliff House?"

"What time shall I expect you?"

"Eleven o'clock, if that won't interfere with your volunteering."

"Not at all," she answered. Mr. Pettingill was not handsome or dashing, but he was pleasant and courteous, and it had been weeks since she had any gentlemen calling for her at the house.

＊ ＊ ＊

Back down on the street, Sanders looked for a taxi carriage while Pettingill stood smiling. The man from Virginia City held out his hand. Sanders gazed questioningly at him.

"I believe I'll walk, old fellow. A pleasure doing business with you, and it has been an exemplary afternoon."

Sanders shook his hand then watched him stride briskly away. Reaching to the inside pocket of his coat, he touched the folded stock certificates whose face value numbered five thousand dollars. He had given Pettingill $3,750 for them. He intended to sell them at face value and net an easy $1,250 profit. Sanders raised his hand against the glare of the afternoon sun. His headache was returning. Seeing a cabriolet, he waved his hand for the fellow to pull over.

* * *

In the daylight, the Barbary Coast was dreary and subdued. The dirt streets had refuse along the curbs, left to the various hogs wandering about, rooting through it. The saloons and dance halls were quiet, their doors open to the early afternoon drinkers. A few tattered beggars stood on the boardwalks, croaking for pennies. O'Gara and Blake walked past the Clinton Temperance House, which offered redemption and sobriety to the Coast's forsaken denizens. Next to it was a windowless hovel that had a "Steam Beer" sign tacked beside its door. Further on, O'Gara stopped at a two-storey boardinghouse whose wooden siding was weathered and gray. He looked at the faded numbers painted above the doorway.

"This is it."

He took one pocket revolver out, thumbing back the hammer and turning the cylinder to check that each chamber was properly capped, then repeated the process with the second. Blake unholstered his Adams Navy .36 to do the same. O'Gara put his hands in the pockets of his coat and pulled a long folding knife from one and a short truncheon from the other. Satisfied, he returned the implements to his pockets.

"We're bracing the lion in his lair, so let me do the talking and watch my back," O'Gara said. Blake nodded.

The policeman opened the boardinghouse door, and they entered. Stopping, O'Gara waited in the shadowed foyer that led into a dark unlit hallway. Blake looked at him questioningly.

"Better to let our eyes adjust before we go further," O'Gara said. "Doolin's room is number six."

They moved into the dim corridor.

"Who's there?" a suspicious voice demanded.

An obese woman in a faded, stained dress appeared out of a doorway as they approached. She held a meat cleaver in her right hand.

"Police, ma'am." O'Gara held his lapel back to display his badge. "Here to talk with Paddy Doolin."

"He's not here. Now get out."

"Go back inside your room," the detective warned.

She snarled, swinging the cleaver. O'Gara caught her forearm before it dropped, grabbing her face with his other hand. He slammed her into the wall, her head denting the plaster. She slid down to a sitting position, unconscious. Still grasping her arm, O'Gara plucked the cleaver from her fat fingers. He looked at it, then handed it to Blake.

"We may need that. You can see the sort of respect a policeman gets around here. Come on."

They walked the shadowed hall, which reeked of tobacco smoke and stale urine. Numbered pieces of paper were tacked to each door. O'Gara halted at number six, knocking softly on the door.

"Paddy?" O'Gara said in a thick Irish brogue. "It's me, Flinn. Open up, boyo. Open up."

"Wha'?" a rough voice answered. "Who is it? Who's disturbin' me sleep?"

The door opened a crack. O'Gara bulled his way in, shouting as he shoved Doolin back. The Irishman lost his footing and fell beside the flimsy cot he slept on, dropping the derringer in his hand. O'Gara kicked the pistol into the far corner. Blake shut the door to stand in front of it. A single set of bare dirty windows filled the narrow room with light.

"Wha's this? Who the hell are you?"

The detective pulled the club from his pocket. "I want a word with you, Doolin."

Clad in graying long underwear, the Irishman struggled to his bare feet. He was thick set and not more than five feet four. His dark-reddish hair was tousled. He had wide sideburns and several days' worth of gray stubble on his jaw. Beneath wiry brows, his blue eyes were bloodshot. His room reeked of old cigar smoke and male sweat.

"Jaysus!" Doolin said, recognizing O'Gara. "Goddamn coppers, in me own room! Get the fuck out and let an honest man sleep!"

"Sit down, Paddy. Or I'll bust your head open." O'Gara raised the short club.

"I ain't done nothin'." He sat, glancing warily from the policeman to Blake.

Even though he gripped the meat cleaver, Blake took out his Adams revolver, wanting a weapon in each hand, just in case.

"Fergus, the barman at the Brown Dog, says you saw a murder three nights ago, just up Battery, past the Customs House. Tell me about it."

Doolin looked at the detective, saying nothing. He lunged from the cot toward Blake and the door. Blake sidestepped, swatting him behind the ear with the Adams. Doolin crashed against the door and fell, rolling onto his back. O'Gara grabbed one of his hands and dragged the ruffian back across the floor to the foot of his cot. He hauled Doolin into a sitting position. Blood trickled down the Irishman's neck from behind his ear.

"If he tries that again, shoot him," O'Gara ordered.

The policeman knelt over Doolin, clutched his throat, and held the club before the Irishman's slowly blinking eyes. "What did you see the other night? What did the killer look like? Answer me, or you'll spend a year in the Broadway Jail House."

"Fuck … youse."

"You want another bust on the head?" O'Gara grabbed a handful of Doolin's hair, raising the club. He smashed it down on the man's collarbone. Bellowing, Doolin writhed. He grabbed the wrist of the hand that held his hair.

"Want another?" O'Gara shouted.

"Jaysus!" He moaned. "No more. I'll tell ye. Let … let go of me hair."

"Tell me first, you mick bastard."

"Didn't see any shootin'. It was over … when I got there. A gent walked past me as I went up the block. Then I saw a fella going through the pockets of a man on the ground."

"What did this gent look like? Tall? Short? Fat? Skinny?"

"Slender. Young. Maybe thirty. It was foggy, and he was walkin' fast."

"How was he dressed?"

"Gray suit and top hat. Now let go a' me hair."

O'Gara shoved Doolin's head back and got to his feet, stepping back out of arm's reach. The Irishman sat up, rubbing his shoulder.

"I think you broke it, ye bastard."

"You'll live. I advise you to leave town. Next time I come for you it will be with a gun in my hand."

"Me whole life the law's been against me. For what? Stealin' a sheep when I was twelve. Sent to the penal colonies just for bein' hungry!"

"Stow it, Paddy. Nobody here believes you." The policeman walked to the corner of the room to pocket the derringer. "Don't try to follow us out. Or I'll put a bullet in you."

At the door, O'Gara opened it and motioned with his head for Blake to leave. They pulled the door shut. Walking the unlit corridor, they stepped over the splayed legs of the fat woman who was still sitting, head down, beside her door.

"Think she's dead?" Blake asked.

The detective knelt beside her, putting two fingers just below her nose. "She's still breathing."

"You going to arrest her for assault?"

O'Gara shook his head. "I doubt any time she spent in the jail would change her behavior. So what would be the point?"

Outside, Blake tossed the meat cleaver into the street and re-holstered his revolver. The stories he had heard about soldiers and honest citizens being beaten and robbed in the Barbary Coast were no doubt true, based on what he had just seen. "Doolin didn't give us much to go on," he said. "A man in a suit."

"Well, we know his age roughly and that he dresses well. Looks like you may be right about Finnegan," O'Gara said. "If the killer wasn't after Major Ellis's money, which otherwise wouldn't have been left behind, then he killed Ellis because the major saw something or knew something. Perhaps something about the man who killed him. And you say Hallinan had an alibi?"

Blake nodded. "He was on KP duty the night Ellis was murdered. My commanding officer suggested the theory that Hallinan hired an assassin. But from the look of Hallinan, that seems too elaborate. Besides, he went back and had his way with Janey later."

"Come on," O'Gara said. "Let's go to the Bank Exchange. I need a drink."

* * *

Elena Caltera walked with Santiago Arzaga, her escort, through the grounds of Woodward's Gardens. They had seen the exhibits stored in the Museum of Natural Wonders and the art gallery filled with oil paintings and statuary. They had strolled through the conservatory, viewing dozens of exotic fragrant flowers. Now they walked the grounds beneath the gray skies. They passed a pond with a large circular boat set with benches and six small sails rotating upon the water. It was filled with visitors enjoying the slow-moving ride. Elena had been impressed by the art and found the other sights amusing. Monterey had nothing to compare to such lavish grounds.

"Such miracles the gringos have wrought," Arzaga said contemptuously.

Señor Arzaga was the trusted compadre of Don Carlos Bejarano. Born on the rancho, he had worked for the Bejarano family all his life. He had accompanied Elena north for her visit to the city. She found him a stern, almost spiteful man.

"Can't you just enjoy what you see?" she asked.

"Not when I know that this too was rancho land only twenty years ago."

"Times have changed. California now belongs to the Union."

"*Es verdad*. But the gringos are not *gente de razón*. They have no honor and do not live up to their promises of liberty and equality. Only they are free … to steal our land and murder our people. Do you read *El Mundo Nuevo*? Señor Ramirez is not afraid to speak plainly. He has spoken out against many injustices."

"Can't we talk of something else?" Elena asked.

A group of children ran past them to a small black bear wearing an iron collar that was chained to the trunk of a tree. On the other side of the pine, a man stood by a small cart, selling bags of peanuts for a penny. Two older boys were feeding the bear peanuts from the palms of their hands.

"This ball that you wish to attend tomorrow night—who is giving it?"

"An Anglo businessman, Señor Donahue."

"Will that young soldier be there?"

Elena looked over at Arzaga. "How should I know? I am not privy to their guest list."

The Californio's mouth frowned beneath his bushy mustache. He put his thumbs into the brown sash that he wore. Though many Hispanic men were adopting the frock coats and plain trousers of the Americans, Arzaga always wore the traditional dress of the ranchero—short jacket of dark cloth, a colorful sash, and dark pants with decorative embroidery on the outside of the leg.

"Don Carlos would not be pleased."

"Perhaps. But I am not married yet. I have never attended a ball in San Francisco, and I may never come back here. It is my last opportunity, and therefore I wish to go."

Arzaga nodded. "The problem with you is that you have too much education. Such people are never content. I cannot stop you from attending the ball. But I will go with you, and I am not an old woman who falls asleep."

Elena gave him a resentful look. She walked ahead toward a large pond whose surface was dotted with ducks and a single white swan, the bird's long sloping neck bent downward to nuzzle the water. Elena looked back along the path toward the pine where the small bear sat, wanting to free the poor thing. It should not be chained to a tree, no matter how many children fed it. Arzaga walked slowly toward her, his brown eyes disapproving. She turned to the water and the swan. She wished he would leave, take the stagecoach back to Los Angeles. She wanted to be alone so that she could enjoy her final weeks of freedom.

She glanced back at the bear, hoping that it wasn't kept chained to the tree all night as well. She wondered if it cried out in the dark.

"What troubles you, señorita?" Arzaga asked.

"Nothing," she answered.

Was his intention to make her feel guilty? She had done nothing dishonorable. Well, she decided, if he had to shadow her to safeguard her virtue, then let him earn his pay. She strode ahead, along the edge of the pond, passing a series of carved posts topped with mirror orbs—globes of colored glass. Several young men stood to one side on the path beneath some trees, smoking and talking among themselves. She smiled as she passed them. Two of them tipped their hats to her. Arzaga jogged after her, glaring at the young bucks.

"Señorita, wait!"

* * *

Azariah stood up from the dining room table, dropping his cloth napkin beside his plate. Mary waited by the door of the kitchen to clear the table and wash the dishes. He gestured to the parlor across the hallway.

"Gentlemen, shall we retire to the parlor for cigars and brandy?"

Baugh and Daniels rose from their chairs, leaving their napkins on the table. Their conversation throughout supper had been concerned with local politics and the Yankee occupation of the South. They strolled through the front hallway into the parlor, where Azariah shut the doors and passed around a small wooden humidor of Havana cigars. He poured snifters of brandy from a crystal decanter while his guests took seats around the tea table in front of the couch, then handed out the glasses.

"Wilcox and I meet Saturday to arrange the transfer of the schooner," Daniels said after sipping his brandy.

"Where will it be kept until we're ready to sail?" Baugh asked, lighting a match on the vertical striker of the ashtray on the table.

"A fellow Knight I've contacted owns a private oyster bed down near the hamlet of San Mateo," Azariah said. "He has a dock, big enough to accommodate the ship, which is roughly one hundred feet in length. We'll need to find a carpenter to rename the vessel immediately and several painters to get her colors changed so that she isn't recognizable."

Baugh took the cigar from his teeth. "I know some fellows who can be trusted to do the work and keep their mouths shut."

"We'll need cannon. Some six-pounders with deck carriages. Brass or iron, it doesn't matter," Daniels said.

"How many?" Azariah rolled a panatela between his fingers, sniffing the rich scent of its tightly rolled brown leaves.

"Six would be ideal."

"Someone buying that many might raise a few eyebrows," Azariah pointed out.

"I'll order pairs from three different gun merchants," Baugh said.

Daniels gently swirled the brandy around in the snifter in his hand. "We'll need gunpowder—kegs of it—and cannon balls, ramrods, small arms—"

"What sort?" Azariah asked.

Daniels mused for a moment. "Revolvers and rifles—enough to arm each of the crew, plus extra weapons in reserve. Say, thirty of each. Make the long guns a mix of carbines and rifles—Spencers or Henrys, if you can get them. Single-shot Enfields will do, if you can't."

Azariah spoke. "I know a fellow Knight who has a stockpile of arms he keeps in a warehouse. Or at least he used to. I'll visit him tomorrow to see if he will give us some."

"Fine," Daniels said. "But don't tell him of our plans. Only we should know the whole operation. Tell him the arms are needed by some of our brethren in Mexico."

Exhaling a plume of smoke, Azariah nodded.

Daniels continued. "We'll need to find a crew, experienced seamen, preferably veterans from the Confederate Navy. Any fellows like that around?"

"Hard to say," Baugh said.

"We could put a discreet ad in the New Orleans newspapers," Azariah suggested, reaching for his brandy glass. The liquid was fiery on his tongue after the hot, dry taste of the cigar.

Daniels shook his head. "I'd prefer to use our personal channels. If necessary, one of us can travel to Los Angeles and another to Galveston to see what Southern men are available and willing to join us. We need men who still believe in the cause."

"Should be easy enough to find," Baugh said. "There's only a hundred thousand of them."

All three laughed. Standing, Daniels walked to the fireplace and mantel. He mused for a moment, then turned to face Azariah and Baugh.

"We'll need a contact in the police department or the harbor police," Daniels said, returning the cigar to his mouth. "Someone to let us know if the local law is getting wind of our affairs. Either of you men have a friend in those organizations?"

Baugh picked up his brandy snifter. "I know a fellow who might be persuaded, with enough money, to help us out."

Daniels smiled. "Mr. Baugh, you are most resourceful."

CHAPTER 7

Blake stood in the tall dunes facing the bay, a half mile north of the Presidio Road. In the gray morning light, he paused to pull the envelope from his pocket. Taking out the engraved invitation, he read once again its request of the honor of his presence at the ball to take place in the evening at the Donahue's house on Rincon Hill. Elena would be there. Smiling, he put the invitation away and the envelope back in his pocket.

Admonishing himself to concentrate, he looked at the line of targets arranged in the sand and took the Adams out of its holster, checking that each of the minute metal cones of the cylinder was topped with a copper percussion cap. He aimed the revolver at the targets—an assortment of empty tin cans and driftwood chunks twenty yards distant. As he lined up the revolver's front and rear sights on the first can, he noticed his right hand was trembling. He lowered the Adams.

The bayonet wound in his right shoulder had healed reasonably well. It did not bother him much when he did his floor exercises and punched the bag at the gymnasium. Yet holding a handgun extended in the proper position sometimes stressed the joint, making it difficult to keep his hand steady. Often he fired the revolver with his left, since officers were expected to fight holding a saber in their right. However, he had learned to shoot a pistol with his right and before joining the Army had used it exclusively for handguns.

Blake extended the Adams once again, this time gripping the right wrist with his left hand, which steadied the revolver's front sight. He pulled the double-action trigger halfway back, the hammer clicking as it cocked. He let the sights resettle on the target, then fired. Kicking, the Adams spewed smoke, and the tin went spinning into the air. The small cloud of gun smoke peeled away in the light morning breeze. Blake took aim on the second target in line, again staging the trigger. The Adams roared, and a chunk of wood flipped over on itself. Patiently, he worked his way down the row of targets until the revolver was empty.

Every Saturday morning Blake emptied the revolver for cleaning and reloading, usually practicing for a good hour or two. He had grown up shooting and hunting in the woods near New London. While he was a decent boxer and only a mediocre swordsman, he was, through years of practice, an excellent marksman.

Nudging the pieces back into place with the toe of his boot, he reset the targets and resumed his position back from the line. After taking a powder flask from his pants pocket, he held the Adams by its trigger guard and poured a measured charge into each of the cylinder's chambers. He stowed the flask, then placed a pistol ball from the bullet pouch on his belt onto the mouth of the chamber and pressed it into the cylinder with the loading lever attached to the side of the barrel, repeating the process until all five chambers were loaded. Finally, he took a tin of tallow and beeswax from his other pocket and using the tip of his finger smeared the white grease on top of the bullets to seal each chamber. After wiping his hand on a rag tucked through his gun belt, he recapped the Adams with an oval-shaped brass device.

Elena's face came once again to his mind, and he recalled the tenderness in her eyes as they held hands in the tea room of the Lick Hotel. The memory filled him with yearning. She had dominated his thoughts since the night he had met her. *Was it possible to love someone you had met only twice?* He shook his head, focusing on the revolver in his hands.

Slipping the capper into his belt pouch, he looked at the target line. From twenty yards, he had hit each target, taking his time. He decided to change the drill and walked forward until he was half the distance from the line. He would try again, only this time firing quickly while still aiming. Once the gusting breeze died down, Blake extended the revolver, left hand supporting his right wrist. He sighted and squeezed. The gun recoiled with a sharp report, and the can jumped. Again—sight, squeeze. Again. He missed the second shot but hit the third and finding the rhythm hit the fourth and fifth. The smoking cylinder was empty.

The slow-moving cloud encircling him was carried off by the wind. Blake walked toward the target line, deciding to run the drill again. He dropped the revolver into its holster and went across the sand, resetting the targets.

As much as he was looking forward to seeing Elena at the Donahue's ball, he had to wonder what possible future they could have together. *Would she be willing to leave her family, disobey her parents for him? And what would his father and mother say if he were to bring home a Catholic as his wife?* Blake pushed the last target into place with his boot. Was he only fooling himself? Walking along Kearny Street with her, he had felt so taken, so blessed by her presence, that it seemed insane not to pursue her. He looked at the leaden skies, the wind cold on his cheek. A forbidding omen, he wondered?

"To hell with it," he said defiantly, staring at the clouds.

During the war, he had heard soldiers often voice their uncertainties about the future, about surviving. The first sergeant, a veteran of the Mexican War, had told them the only thing to be done was to look to the present since the future would take care of itself.

Blake went back to his position and started reloading the Adams.

* * *

Detective O'Gara walked along Sansome Street past the Bank of California, crossing Halleck Alley. Just beyond it was the stately edifice of the American Exchange Hotel. As he strolled into the wide lobby, he glanced at the paneled walls of polished, stained wood and the array of comfortable wood-framed couches and armchairs with matching upholstery, crowned with clean white anti-macassars. O'Gara stopped at the large counter where guests signed the registry and received their keys. The clerk, a tall fellow with a trim dark beard, was sorting mail.

"Good morning, Detective."

"How's life, George?"

"Can't complain. What can I do for you?"

O'Gara pushed the brim of his hat higher using the tip of his finger. "We're looking for a man who might have checked in recently … say, in the last two weeks or even a month. I don't have a name, but

I do have a description. He's slender, about thirty years old, and wears a gray suit with a matching top hat. Anyone like that been around?"

George considered the question as he tugged meditatively at his whiskers. "Been a few gents who match that description, but I don't think any of them are still here. You don't have a name?"

"Not yet," O'Gara said. "I'll try the Brooklyn Hotel. Thanks for your time."

George waved and returned to sorting envelopes.

* * *

It was almost noon, and the morning fog had burned off, as Angeline sat in a rented buggy next to Mr. Pettingill. The dappled gray gelding pulling the buggy moved along at a brisk jog, hooves clopping on the black macadamized road of Point Lobos Turnpike. Minutes earlier they had passed the landscaped acreage of Lone Mountain Cemetery, but now they rode through a wasteland of dunes and scrub grass. In the distance, they saw the outer telegraph station perched at Land's End, which communicated information about ships arriving through the Golden Gate to the inner station on Telegraph Hill and thus to the town's merchants.

"This is rather exciting, don't you think?" Pettingill asked, glancing over at her. He was not wearing his glasses.

"You certainly can't go this fast in town," Angeline said. "There's too much traffic."

"Quite so."

A gentleman in a shiny top hat and black suit passed them in a sulky. The man tipped his hat to Angeline, who waved back. The great roan horse pulling the single seat, two-wheeled cart stepped in a lively fashion, just short of a canter.

"Shall we race him?" Pettingill suggested.

"No!" Angeline said, thinking of the deadly accidents that occasionally happened in town, where people were thrown from carriages or horses were killed in the collisions. "That's a racing rig," she added. "He'll be much too fast."

Pettingill looked at her. "Don't like taking chances?"

"Not that kind."

He pursed his thin lips, apparently still considering a race, but refrained from flicking the long whip he held in his left hand.

"I'm surprised at you, Mr. Pettingill," Angeline said. "You don't seem the sort of gentleman who is reckless."

"Perhaps there's more to me than meets the eye."

"I'm beginning to realize that."

Angeline wondered if her mother hadn't been right, thinking of the tiff they had the evening before. Her mother had insisted she have an escort since no one knew this man. Angeline had countered that she was twenty years old and could take care of herself.

The outer telegraph station tower took on size and detail as the buggy approached the end of the turnpike. Seagulls floated on the offshore winds above the rocks. Descending a hill, Pettingill slowed the gray to a walk as they approached a rectangular structure with a sloped roof. The building had tall windows set at intervals in each of its walls, and a broad plank deck surrounded it. A large American flag on a pole topped the building, the star and stripes rolling and snapping in the stiff sea breeze. Above the entrance doors a sign proclaimed it the "Cliff House." To the right of the inn stood a long open shed with a dozen carriages inside it.

A colored valet in a dark uniform and visored cap took hold of the horse's headgear as Pettingill climbed down from the buggy and turned to help Angeline alight. She stepped into the sandy road and taking Pettingill's arm walked up the steps to the establishment. A small group of people stood on the further end of the deck, talking to one another and pointing to the tall, jagged mounds of Seal Rock just beyond in the blue waters.

Heading for the entrance, Angeline caught her reflection in one of the windows, seeing a young woman in a gray dress with black piping. Her blond hair was pinned back and partially covered by a dark woolen snood. Before Angeline had left for the outing, her mother had given her a reluctant smile and told her that she looked very pretty.

Inside the Cliff House, there was a saloon with a mahogany bar on the left and dining rooms on the right. The saloon was crowded with men and only a few ladies. Through its tall windows, the vast Pacific Ocean filled the wide horizon. The dining room had several families and two couples sitting at the linen-covered tables.

"Let's have a drink," Pettingill said, steering her toward the bar.

"But aren't we going to eat? It's noon."

They walked into the noise and smoke of the saloon, stopping by the open end of the bar. A bearded man in a naval-style jacket stood talking to the bartender. He looked over at Pettingill and nodded hello.

"That's Captain Foster. He runs the place." Pettingill motioned to the bartender. "A bottle of champagne, please."

"Oh, we shouldn't. It will make me sleepy. Aren't we going to have lunch?"

"Just a couple of drinks, then we'll dine." He smiled at her.

Angeline frowned, tugging at the palms of her light-grey gloves. Mr. Pettingill hardly seemed like the shy and charming man he had been the day before. Perhaps he felt he needed to appear more masterful, like Mr. Darcy from *Pride and Prejudice*. Men were such odd beings, she mused.

The bartender brought a chilled bottle wrapped in a white towel and two flute glasses. After pouring slowly into each glass, he put the bottle on the counter and moved back down the bar to take care of another customer.

Pettingill handed her a glass and raised his in a toast.

"Here's to new acquaintances."

Angeline clinked glasses with him. She looked out the windows at the sweep of the ocean, the water glistening and blue in the sunlight.

"Isn't it magnificent?" she asked, still staring at the view.

"I think you're magnificent."

Glass in hand, she stared at him, surprised by the compliment. She smiled in spite of herself.

"Mr. Pettingill, we hardly know each other. Your words are very flattering but—"

"But what?" he asked. "Too hasty?"

"Well, yes. It takes time to get a full picture of someone, time to learn to care for them."

Pettingill sipped champagne and smacked his lips. "Then you don't believe in love at first sight?"

"Well, I suppose some women do, but not me."

"What a pity," he murmured.

"Before you came west, what did you do?"

He shrugged. "I was a stage actor for a while, worked at a stock brokerage for a year."

Angeline put her glass down. "You were an actor? Where?"

"It was only for a few months with a traveling troupe out of Boston. Initially I signed on as a road manager but did little parts whenever the stock players fell ill or they needed an extra player."

"But Cousin Sanders told me you were from Illinois."

"Oh, yes. That's where I lived before I came to California." He smiled.

She studied him for a moment, wondering if he could sense her uncertainty.

"Listen, my dear, why don't you see if one of the dining room waiters will give you a menu? Then we can look at it and have already made our decisions."

She nodded and left the saloon.

* * *

When she was gone, Pettingill glanced around to see if anyone was looking at him, then took a small vial from his vest pocket. Pulling the tiny cork from its mouth, he emptied its pale liquid into Angeline's champagne flute. After slipping the re-corked vial into his vest, he topped off the glass with more champagne.

Angeline returned, a printed menu in hand, which she read as she walked.

"There are several things that looking promising," she said.

Pettingill lifted her glass and handed it to her. She gave him the menu.

"Let's finish this bit of champagne and then we'll eat."

She raised the glass to her mouth and sipped the cold bubbling liquid.

* * *

Sanders entered the brokerage of Bronstein & Jones, whose office looked out onto the thoroughfare of Montgomery Street. Being Saturday, only junior employees were working—a good half of the desks were empty. Sanders walked over to where Abram Phillips, one of the regulars at the Occidental's saloon, sat writing in a ledger.

"Good morning!" Sanders took a seat in the chair adjacent to the desk.

His face framed by bushy muttonchops, Phillips looked up from his work. Grinning, he rose to lean over the desk and shake Sanders's hand.

"You're a welcome surprise," Phillips said, resuming his seat. "Come to take me to dinner?"

Sanders pulled a sheaf of stock certificates from the inside pocket of his morning suit. "I'm here to sell these. At par value or better."

After closing the ledger, Phillips pushed it aside to spread out the printed certificates on his desk blotter. He read the face of the first one and then counted them.

"There's ten certificates in $500 denominations," Sanders said. "What are they going for these days?"

"I'll look up yesterday's closing price," Phillips answered distractedly as he studied the face of the first certificate. He rose and walked into a back office. In a moment he was back, holding a blank stock sheet from the Ophir Mining Company. He sat and compared the blank to the ones Sanders had handed him.

"What is it?" Sanders asked.

Phillips opened a desk drawer and took out a magnifying glass. Holding it over the paper, he leaned forward to examine Sanders's document.

"These are good. These are very good."

Concerned, Sanders stared at his friend.

"These are the best fakes I've ever seen," Phillips said, continuing to study the paper. "Where did you get these?"

"Fakes? Are you sure?"

Phillips straightened, placing the glass on his blotter. "Yes, there are engraving details missing on yours that are on this blank original. If you look along the borders—"

Sanders rose to his feet but staggered suddenly as though struck. "Impossible! Fakes!"

Phillips nodded, his eyes worried. "Who sold you these?"

"I'll kill him!"

"Sit down, Sanders. We'll notify the police. Don't go to pieces."

"That son of a bitch! I'll put a pistol ball right between his eyes!"

Muscles tight with rage, Sanders strode rapidly out of the office and down the street. At first he walked, but then he broke into a sprint, moving along the sidewalk, dodging slow pedestrians, heading for his hotel. He was going to load his derringers and find Pettingill.

* * *

"Now we can eat," he said, putting down his empty glass.

Angeline had only drunk half of hers but already she felt a steady purling at the back of her head. "Yes, I'm starving."

Pettingill motioned to the bartender to get his attention. "Have the waiter bring this bottle to our table."

The bartender nodded.

Pettingill offered Angeline his arm. Putting down her glass but retaining the menu, she placed her gloved hand inside the crook of his elbow and walked with him across the hallway. Just as they were about to enter the dining room, she tripped and almost fell. She gripped his arm, dropping the menu. Her knees wouldn't hold her weight.

"What is it?" Pettingill asked.

"I don't know, I can't …"

The maitre d'hotel came out of the dining room. "Is anything wrong?"

Pettingill gripped Angeline's waist as she leaned against him. "The young lady is not feeling well. A private room, quickly!"

"I'll see if any are available."

Pettingill placed a gold half eagle into the man's hand. "See that we get one."

"Right away."

Pettingill walked her to a bench seat next to a tall grandfather clock and sat with her. Angeline's head rested on his shoulder, her eyelids drooping. He gazed at her fine features, focusing on her mouth. He had to force himself not to smile.

* * *

Angeline stirred, feeling pain. As her eyes opened, she saw the ceiling of a narrow half-lit room. She was on her back against a hard surface, hands at her sides. Her legs were in the air, dress gathered at her hips, her thighs bare. Something was stabbing her repeatedly in the groin, and Pettingill's red convulsed face was between her knees.

She tried to speak, to shout "No!" yet she heard only an agonized moan. She tried to lift her hands, but they wouldn't move. Her eyes closed as dark waters rose over her again, pulling her back into their drowning depths.

* * *

It was the bouncing movement of the buggy that woke her. Opening her eyes, Angeline saw they were traveling back toward the city. The sunlight was bright on the sand dunes, making her squint. Her head throbbed. A sour taste filled her mouth, and when she felt the soreness between her thighs and their sticky wetness she knew she had not been dreaming. Pettingill sat next to her, a short cigar clenched in his teeth, driving the horse at a vigorous trot.

He glanced over. "Feeling better?"

She said nothing, staring at him in disbelief. Her hands began to tremble. She clasped them together to hide their shaking.

"I shouldn't have let you drink that champagne on an empty stomach. You fainted in the hallway."

She looked away, tears trickling down her face. She wiped at them with the back of her glove.

"You shouldn't cry, my dear. It had to happen sooner or later."

Keeping her eyes on the road ahead, she willed herself not to sob. Yet drops still escaped and ran down to her chin. She wanted to scream but her head was aching so painfully she knew she would faint if she did.

"In a few days, it will all be forgotten."

When they reached Market Street, Pettingill had to stop the buggy to wait for a teamster's wagon to pass. Angeline climbed down.

"Don't you want a ride to your front door?"

"Not with an … animal like you. If I have my way, you'll spend the rest of your life in San Quentin Prison."

"Because I took what you willingly offered?" he asked.

"Liar."

She walked away, moving as quickly along the wooden sidewalk as her unsteady legs could carry her. She saw him drive past, heading downtown. She stopped at a cab parked by the curb, the driver reading a newspaper.

"Are you for hire?"

"Yes, miss."

"Then please take me home."

* * *

Sanders, a loaded derringer in both his pants pockets, walked into the saloon at the Occidental. Floyd was on duty behind the long gleaming bar. There were only a handful of drinkers among the plants, marble, and brass. The sidewalks beyond the tall windows were bright with afternoon sunshine and crowded with Saturday pedestrians.

"Have you seen Pettingill lately?" Sanders asked.

Floyd put down his polishing rag, frowning with thought. "You mean the sorrowful feller you was drinking with the other day?"

"Precisely."

Floyd shook his bare, scarred head. "He ain't been back."

Sanders slapped his hand on the bar in frustration. "Know where he might be staying? He's not registered here. I've already checked."

"He never said nothing to me," Floyd replied. "Take a look over at the Lick House. He might be there."

"An excellent idea," he said, pointing his finger at the barman.

"Don't you want a drink?"

"Later. After I've found Pettingill."

Sanders turned to head for the lobby doors.

* * *

Three hours later, he trudged up the stairs of his aunt Martha's house along outer Washington Street. Though lower in the sky, the sun was hot on his dark clad shoulders. He had taken off his cravat and loosened the collar of his shirt, which was damp with perspiration. Pettingill was nowhere to be found.

Manipulating the iron knocker mounted on the middle of the stout door, Sanders waited until a maid opened it to admit him. The inside of the house was cool and its familiar décor something of a comfort. The maid showed him to the parlor, where his aunt sat by the window with a teacup in hand, staring across the room, her face frowning with concern.

"Hello, Auntie," Sanders said, standing in the doorway, thrusting his hands into his pockets, where he felt the curved wood of his derringer grips.

"James, please come in and sit down. Would you like some tea?"

At forty-five, Martha Whitfield was still a striking woman. She had once been beautiful, but now her face was marked with lines around the mouth and eyes. Her thick blond hair was threaded with gray. She poured tea into a cup from the ornate silver teapot. Sanders took the cup and sat in the chair opposite her.

"I'm very worried about Angie. Since she got home today, she's been sobbing in the bathroom with the door locked. I think she's in the tub because every once in a while you can hear splashing. Something's terribly wrong."

"I'll say it is." Sanders drained half his cup in one sip. "It's been the devil of a day. I've been defrauded of a large sum of money."

She looked at him. "How so and by whom?"

Sanders slapped his hand against his forehead, then pushed it through his hair. "This man, Pettingill. I met him in the Occidental's saloon. He sold me bogus stock certificates! I'm out over three thousand dollars!"

Martha's eyes were angry as she spoke. "The very same man drove Angie out to the Cliff House for lunch late this morning. He's done something terrible. When she got home, she went straight up to her room and then into the bathroom."

"What?" Sanders said. "I didn't realize she was walking out with him."

"Who is this Pettingill?"

"I thought I knew. But it's obvious he is a fraud. I've been looking for him all afternoon, but I had no idea he … had outraged Angie."

"Well, it's time to involve the police. Chief Burke was a friend of your late uncle. Seek him out and tell him what has happened. I'm sure we can rely on his discretion."

"I hope so. If my name gets bandied about, I'll be humiliated."

"Go now, James."

Sanders nodded. "I'll go talk to Angie and see if she wants to join me."

* * *

He stood outside the locked bathroom door in the hallway of the second floor and knocked on the painted wood.

"Angie? Are you all right? Your mother is worried. Aren't you coming out?"

"Go away." Her voice was nearly unrecognizable—weak and full of misery.

"I'm on my way to see Police Chief Burke. Pettingill is a criminal. The stock he sold me is counterfeit. Do you want to go with me?"

"I'm … I'm not feeling well."

"Did he hurt you?"

"I can't talk about it."

"You don't want to go to the police with me?"

"No."

Sanders made a fist. *Pettingill, you son of a bitch!* His stomach churned as he recalled the carriage ride where he had introduced Angeline to the blackguard.

With an angry sigh, he took a last glance at the bathroom door, then strode the corridor to the stairs. He could walk to the Hall of Justice in ten minutes. Leaving the Whitfield house, he vowed that he would not rest until Pettingill was caught and punished.

Chapter 8

Lamplight gleamed along the parquet floor of the Donahue ballroom beneath two large glittering chandeliers. A six-piece string orchestra played from a small stage at the end of the long room. At the opposite end, two white-gloved servants poured drinks from a cut-glass punch bowl and from bottles of whiskey and claret. Out on the floor, couples moved in graceful spirals to a waltz. Lieutenant Blake stood near the entranceway, a new red silk sash knotted about the waist of his best uniform. He looked at the guests, ladies in fine gowns and gentlemen in white tie and tails standing along the golden-stained wainscoted walls. Blake did not see Elena among the dancers or the people along the periphery. He walked to the refreshment table to ask for a whiskey and soda, feeling uncomfortable, very much wanting to see Elena and yet nervous about seeing her at all.

"Is this what love feels like?" he muttered.

As he sipped the bubbling drink, he saw a fellow Army lieutenant enter the room with a maiden on his arm. It was Martin Tevis, whose dark blond hair hung over his collar, long mustache drooping over his mouth. Having served in the 1st Michigan Cavalry under Brevet General Custer during the war, Tevis was now assigned to the quartermaster's depot just down California Street from the inspector general's office. Blake did not recognize his female companion. Tevis nodded to him, and Blake raised his glass in response. Tevis led the young woman out onto the floor to join in the dancing.

Blake moved back toward the entry, drink in hand, continuing to look among the guests. He recognized only a handful, a consequence of having attended so few dances since arriving in the city. He watched the dancers, disappointed that his lady was not among them. But then a gloved hand slid into the crook of his arm, causing him to turn. Elena smiled at him. She wore an elegant burgundy gown, and her sable hair was pinned up. He returned her smile, relieved to find her at last, and captured once again by her presence.

"You look lovely," he said.

"My chaperon thinks I'm in the ladies' room. Let's dance."

Blake set his drink on a nearby table. Clasping hands, they walked out and began stepping to the music. His eyes locked on hers, his nervousness lessening. In time with the music, they glided across the smooth floor. As they danced, he became aware of her slender body moving beneath the hand he held at her waist. It filled him with excruciating desire. Looking into her warm eyes, he knew he would sacrifice the good will of his parents, his military career, everything he had, if only she would be his.

The music ended after far too short a time. The dancers stopped, returning to the groups gathered along the walls. A few hopeful couples stayed out on the floor. Blake noticed a short, broad-shouldered man in fancy Californio clothes staring at him from the entranceway. Elena saw him as well and leaned toward Blake.

"Meet me out on the balcony in three minutes," she whispered.

She bowed to him in a curtsy and walked away. Blake stood alone on the dance floor, watching as Elena walked past the Californio and into the interior of the house. The man turned his head as she went in, then followed her.

Blake strolled to the refreshment table and asked for another whiskey and soda since he hadn't finished the first. Drink in hand, he went to the French doors that led out onto a stone balcony and slipped into the cool night air, closing the door behind him. He thought about the chaperon that Elena's family had sent along, knowing that Spanish tradition required it. But he wondered whom it was they did not trust—Elena or a young man she might meet. Or possibly both. Her Spanish heritage bound her to tradition, just as he, being of old New England stock, was expected to follow the societal norms of his Puritan ancestors. *What chance did they have of fighting it? What narrow chance did they have of winning?*

He sipped the whiskey, feeling a sudden surge of despair as he looked at the dark sky. The stars were faint overhead, nearly lost to the lights of the city. The balcony doors opened, and a young man and lady stepped out. The orchestra began playing a Virginia reel. The closing doors muted the music. Blake finished his drink, looking out at the lights scattered across the dark land. He glanced at the couple who had moved to the far end of the balcony and were embracing. Not wanting to pry, he returned his gaze to the landscape. Footsteps brought him around to see Elena walking toward him. Her face was solemn.

"Don't tell me," he said. "You have to leave."

"No," she replied, stopping before him. "But I had a row with Señor Arzaga, my escort. I told him to wait for me by the front door if he was going to be rude and stare at everyone I danced with."

"What did he say?"

"He warned me not to dishonor his patron."

"You think he would give a lady the benefit of the doubt," Blake said.

"What are we going to do?" she asked, her dark eyes searching his.

"Live in the moment." Blake took her gloved hand in his. "It's all we have."

She touched his shoulder with her other. "I wish that I were free. That we had met under different circumstances."

He nodded, pulling her close. "I'm in hell … I love you, and I want you. And I cannot—"

She put her fingers against his lips. He took her hand in his, bending his head toward her. She raised her mouth to his. As the kiss deepened, she pressed against him. When their lips parted, she rested her head against his chest.

Suddenly, a hard hand gripped his shoulder and spun him half around.

Arzaga backhanded Blake across the face. *"Cabron!"*

"Stop it!" Elena sought to step between them but was held at the elbow by another vaquero.

Stepping away from Arzaga, Blake raised his hands, expecting another punch.

"In the name of Don Carlos Bejarano, I will have satisfaction," Arzaga said.

"I have done nothing—"

"You will fight, señor. Tomorrow at five a.m. Name your weapon."

"Listen, you fool, I will not meet you. I haven't done anything—"

"*Cobarde!* You have lain hands on Don Carlos's betrothed. That demands blood. Nothing else will wash away the insult. *Comprende?*"

Elena spoke in Spanish, her words too quick for Blake to follow. He caught only one phrase: "*Castigues me, no este hombre.*"

"*Callete!*" Arzaga told her, then turned back to Blake. "Name your weapon, señor."

"No. I will not—"

"Then I will. Knives. The beach on the south side of Mission Creek. Tomorrow morning at five. If you have no seconds, then I will bring one for you."

"Don't fight him, Liam. He grew up with a knife in his hand. Don't—"

Arzaga gestured for the vaquero to take her away. He pulled Elena along as he moved around the corner of the balcony to another set of doors. Blake started after him, but Arzaga stopped him with a push.

"You have done enough to disgrace her."

Blake raised his clenched fists. Arzaga stepped back in a smooth balanced motion, opening the distance between them. He held his hand at the small of his back where he undoubtedly had a weapon.

"Save your strength, gringo. You will need it for the morning."

Blake could only stare as Arzaga retreated then ducked around the corner of the house.

"Blake!"

Tevis strode toward him, his lady standing back at the doors to the ballroom.

"What was that all about?"

He shook his head. "The lady I was with … is engaged to another man. Her escort insists I have insulted the family and is demanding satisfaction."

"A duel?" Tevis asked. "Jesus Christ! Are you going to fight him?"

"Of course not. This is impossible … What in God's name am I going to do?"

"Personally, I think you should kill the son of a bitch. Teach him not to lay hands on an officer of the US Army. You can do it. I've seen you shoot."

"We're supposed to fight with knives."

"Hell and tarnation, that's completely different. You should have demanded sabers."

"I was too shocked. He broke in on us so unexpectedly. What in the devil am I going to do?"

Tevis looked at him, his expression grim. "Well, if you don't want to leave town, you're going to have to face him."

* * *

The eastern sky was pale with the coming light as a cold breeze from the bay blew in fitful gusts. Small waves lapped at the sand on the edge of the creek where it emptied into the wide circle of Mission Bay. Blake stood in his blue greatcoat and kepi, staring out at the changing color of the bay waters. He felt weary, having been unable to sleep, unable to stop thinking about Elena or Arzaga.

At four a.m. he had met Tevis on Sacramento Street in front of the What Cheer House. Tevis had brought two saddled horses. With little talk, they had ridden in a brisk trot out to the creek.

Tevis finished tying the reins of the mounts to a large hunk of driftwood. He pulled the tab loose on his holster flap and checked his pocket watch, showing the dial to Blake. It was 4:52.

"Wonder where they are," the cavalryman said.

"Perhaps waiting to rattle our nerves ... or my nerves," Blake replied.

Through his fatigue, he felt an edginess—a roiling mix of resentment, anger, and regret. The growing morning light on the calm water was the very picture of serenity, which was a bitter irony.

"I wish we had some coffee," Blake said.

The sound of horses made them turn. Cantering along the trail that led to the beach, Arzaga and two other vaqueros moved toward them. Tevis looked at Blake, who took off his greatcoat and slung it over the saddle of his horse. He began unbuttoning his wool vest. The Californios halted their mounts, swinging down from their saddles.

"Buenas dias, amigos."

One vaquero held the horses' reins as the other stepped forward to consult with Tevis. Arzaga stood apart, stripping off his short jacket and then his sash. Blake put his kepi into the saddlebags and took out an Ames knife, its blade a foot long—standard issue to mounted troops. He had borrowed it from Tevis. Blake noticed his hands were steady, but his heart was beating fast. He turned to face Arzaga across the sand and waited. The Californio held a long dagger in his hand and wore a red kerchief tied over the crown of his head, which would keep any sweat from his eyes.

Blake knew his best chance was to end the fight as soon as possible, before Arzaga's experience could be brought to bear. Tevis went through the formalities, asking if the duel could be avoided and satisfaction had some other way. The vaquero acting as Arzaga's second smiled, shaking his head.

"Are you ready?" the cavalryman asked loudly.

His heart pounding, Blake nodded. Arzaga, ten feet away and looking into Blake's eyes, gave his consent. Both men crouched, intent on the other, closing the distance between them. Blake lunged forward, blade flicking for Arzaga's face. The Californio parried and countered, but Blake evaded the thrust. The sand underfoot made moving treacherous. Blake had almost lost his balance on his first strike. The blades chimed briefly in the murderous exchange as Arzaga attacked and Blake parried, giving ground. He circled to the right, away from his opponent's weapon, then lunged in, slapping aside Arzaga's blade with his own and slashing. The tip of the knife caught the man just below his left eye. Arzaga skipped back, wiping at the blood with his free hand. Blake moved in, stabbing. The Californio parried as he slipped in the sand, cutting Blake across the thigh. Blake stumbled back, blood starting down his pant leg. Arzaga regained his feet, still crouching. Smiling, he began passing the knife from his right to his left and back as blood trickled down his unshaved cheek. Blake waited, watching intently. Arzaga feinted, Blake jerking back a step.

"Scared, gringo?" Arzaga asked, breathing heavily.

The knife went into his left hand. He lunged, blade flashing. Blake sidestepped, throwing his left arm over the extended limb. He jerked Arzaga to him, stabbing with his right. The man cried out as Blake's steel punched into his back. Shifting the dagger to his free hand, Arzaga twisted, driving the point for Blake's neck. But he caught the descending wrist with his left.

Blake thrust again with his right, only to be trapped by Arzaga's other hand. They stood locked together, feet shifting for leverage, breathing in ragged gasps. The Californio was too strong for Blake to manhandle, and the wound in the man's back seemed to have no effect.

Blake stepped suddenly rearward, pulling Arzaga off-balance and hurling him to the sand. Going to one knee, Blake drove his knife deep into the leg closest to him. Arzaga stifled a scream. Blake's hand slipped from the hilt as he tried to pull the blade free. He pushed himself to his feet, ready to lunge for the revolver in his saddlebags. Yelling in Spanish, Arzaga's compadres gestured for him to rise. But the Californio was not able to lift himself from the sand. Twice, he sat up but then collapsed. Blake looked at Tevis, who was watching the wounded man. The cavalryman lifted his eyes, their look intense as he nodded to Blake.

Arzaga's second stepped in front of him, his palm on the pistol butt protruding from his sash.

"Señor Arzaga is unable to continue. The match must be postponed."

Blake's hands were shaking. He clenched them into fists to hide it and backed up toward to his horse, watching the vaqueros. The sock in his right boot was wet, squelching softly as he moved. Standing by his mount, Blake felt blood trickle inside the sleeve of his shirt along the forearm. He did not remember being cut there.

Arzaga's men bent over him, tending to his wounds. Tevis grinned at Blake as he approached.

"You did it, you lucky bastard."

Blake stayed silent, relieved the duel was over but feeling it was all for nothing. From his saddlebags he pulled his gun belt out and strapped it on. He looked at his vest draped over the seat of his saddle. Not wanting to soil it with blood, he folded it gingerly and stuffed it into the saddlebag. Tevis stepped close to him and began tying a bandage around Blake's forearm. The trooper held a handful of bandages he had wisely brought along.

"We'd better look at that leg."

He inspected the gash while Blake waited, the cold bay wind cool on his damp face. The cavalryman pressed a folded bandage to the wound and wrapped another around Blake's thigh and tied it to hold it in place. Tevis pulled the greatcoat off the rear of the saddle and held it while Blake slipped his arms into the garment.

"Can you ride?"

"Let's go."

Putting his foot into the stirrup, Blake climbed into the saddle. Tevis mounted his horse. Steel scraped as the cavalryman drew the saber from his scabbard. The Californios looked up from their work.

Solemnly, Tevis brought the saber up to his face in salutation, then swung it away in brisk slash.

The sun's molten eye had risen above the hills to the east, pouring light across the land. They turned their mounts and rode along the sandy trail. Blake kicked his horse to a gallop, shouting wordlessly, his angry voice carried off by the rushing wind.

* * *

The doorway of Mission Dolores church was crowded with people from the Mass just ended. Holding up her black skirt and petticoats, Elena picked her way along the muddy lane through the crowd. Carriages and buggies blocked the street as the parishioners climbed into their vehicles to drive home for breakfast. Don Miguel Noe closed the door of the family carriage and waved the driver on. He turned to Elena, who looked at him quizzically. He offered his arm to her and they walked over to a cabbie seated on a landau with enclosed passenger seats waiting just beyond the crowd. He helped Elena into the compartment and climbed in, closing the door behind him. He took the seat across from her, rapped his knuckles against the roof, and the carriage swayed into motion.

He looked at Elena silently for a moment. She began to fidget with the ring on her finger.

"You have behaved very badly, Cousin. And the consequences have become quite serious. I believe you know a duel was fought early this morning between Señor Arzaga and this *Americano* soldier you have chosen to consort with."

Elena lowered her eyes, nodding. She had been up all night worrying and praying. Dawn had brought no relief. She wept as the growing light brought color to the leaves of the garden trees beyond the windows of her room, thinking Liam might now lie dead.

"You should know Señor Arzaga is not expected to live. By witness accounts, he fought valiantly to rectify the dishonor you brought to his patron, Don Carlos. What have you to say for yourself?"

"I did n-nothing ...." She lost her voice as emotions took hold of her. She lifted her palm to her face. "I did not want them to fight. I ... I'm so very sorry."

"At least you realize what you've done." He handed her a clean white handkerchief.

Taking it, she wiped her eyes and waited for him to continue, hopeful that Liam still lived and anguished that Arzaga would not.

"Your punishment is this. You will go back to the house and pack your things. You will write to your parents to say that you are coming home early, that you miss them too much and are anxious to begin your new life as Doña Bejarano."

Elena stared at her cousin, holding the handkerchief to her mouth. She closed her eyes, knowing she had no choice. Feeling she was losing everything, she nodded her consent.

"*Bueno.* And there is one more thing. If this duel had gone the other way and the soldier had lost, I would have been able to suppress the matter. But with Señor Arzaga dying, I will not be able to keep it from Don Carlos. He will want to know why his most trusted friend did not come home."

"Yes," she said in a small, tight voice. "I understand."

"I think you know none of this brings me any pleasure."

She looked at him, hoping for a gesture—a forgiving smile or conciliatory nod. But his face remained set, his eyes stern. She lowered her head.

Don Miguel settled back into the padded leather seat, looking out the window.

* * *

Blake had his right arm slung around Tevis's shoulder as he limped down the hallway to his room in the What Cheer House. His right leg had stiffened, and the stitches in the wound were stinging beneath the bandages, visible through the stained slash in his trousers. They reached his door, Blake leaning against the wall while he handed Tevis the key. The cavalryman opened it and helped him inside to the bed. After tossing the key on Blake's dresser, he closed the door.

"Have anything to drink?"

"There's a pint of bourbon in the top right drawer of the dresser."

Tevis retrieved the bottle and poured whiskey into a tumbler from the tray on Blake's night stand. He swirled it around in the glass, then took a sip.

"Want one?"

"No." Blake's head was aching. Riding back, they had passed Tevis's pocket flask of malt whiskey between them, celebrating. Once in the city again, they stopped at a physician's house across Third Street from the oval lanes and elegant homes of South Park. The doctor was an old man with a bald head and a white beard. He had put Blake under, using an ether mask, while he washed the lieutenant's cuts with water and sutured them closed.

"The kitchen is sending up some eggs, bacon, and biscuits for you," Tevis said, pouring himself another shot.

"I'm famished, and my head is splitting."

Tevis removed his hand from his trousers pocket, placing a small brown bottle on the nightstand. Blake, resting on his pillows, looked over at it.

"What's that?"

"Laudanum. The doctor gave it to me, in case you can't sleep over the next few nights. He said you were to take two teaspoons full. And no baths. He said you shouldn't get your wounds wet until he removes the stitches, which will be in two weeks."

"Anything else, Clara Barton?"

The cavalryman put his glass down to shake his finger at his injured friend. "You owe me, partner. You left my knife stuck in that greaser's leg."

Blake looked away toward the windows. The city was lit with sunshine—it seemed too nice a day for recent events.

"There's one more thing I need from you," Blake said.

"Name it."

"I don't want Elena's name bandied about. You mustn't tell anyone what you know or saw."

Tevis stared, his mouth open. "Are you joking? You fight a duel and want me to keep silent? I have no problem not mentioning your lady, but you redeemed the honor of the Infantry this morning and taught that bastard a valuable lesson. You expect me not to relate the affair to our brother officers?"

"Please," Blake said. "Not a word."

Tevis shook his head. "It's going to be all over town anyway."

"Damn it, Martin! Swear that you won't talk about it!" Blake started to get up, but his leg was burning. Grimacing, he fell back onto the mattress.

"Please."

Tevis made an impatient gesture. "I won't mention her name, but if people ask—"

"Tell them you can't talk about it."

Blake's friend stared at him. "All right. I'll keep my mouth shut, but it won't matter. People are most likely already discussing it. Hell, it will probably be in the papers by evening. You need to think about what you are going to tell Wagner. Carving up civilians is generally frowned on, although he can't fault you too much since you got the better of the Mex."

"I have no idea what I'm going to say to him."

"There's something you can tell me," Tevis said. "Where did you get that move? Where you drew him close and drove the knife into his kidney?"

Feeling weary, Blake paused before answering. "It's a sparring ploy. I learned it back in Washington with the last boxing professor I studied with. I've used it more than once at the Olympic Club. But I didn't plan it today. The opening came, and I reacted. It was just instinct."

"Nonetheless, I'll have to practice that one." Tevis ran a hand through his thick hair. "I'm going back to my room. It's been a long night. I'll check in on you later."

After the cavalryman had left, Blake stared out the window, thinking he had to get in touch with Elena. Perhaps he could get a note to her by paying one of the boys who sold newspapers on the street. He tried to sit up, but the pain in his temples spiked, forcing him to lie back against his pillows. Maybe after he had eaten.

CHAPTER 9

Azariah Dekker pulled on an old ragged sweater over his long-sleeved undershirt. Wearing faded canvas pants and scuffed brogans, he studied himself in the tall oval freestanding mirror in the corner. He looked like any of the dozens of bummers who lounged on the city docks begging for pennies and rolling cigarettes. He found the outfit distasteful but knew the clothes to be necessary. Wilson and his cutthroats were handing over the schooner at midnight.

He glanced at the weapons on top of the dresser: his .31 Colt, long-bladed dagger in a leather sheath, and the sawed-off shotgun. A man his age could only question what he had gotten himself into. Daniels was very capable but more than a little mad. Still, Azariah had taken an oath when he joined the Golden Circle, which he was duty-bound to honor.

He left his bedroom and walked the short hall to his wife's room. The door was open and the lamp lit. Larissa was upright in bed, reclining against the pillows placed against the headboard. Her gray hair was pinned into a bun. Her hazel eyes stared vacantly at the white embroidered coverlet atop her slender legs. She had had a stroke four months earlier that left her catatonic and had lost considerable weight.

Azariah would often sit by her and read aloud from Thackeray, Scott, or Dickens. Other times he would talk to her, rambling on about his thoughts and reminiscences, sometimes speculating why their son never returned from the war. He had gone missing at the second Manassas. Azariah had wondered if he might have deserted but reckoned that, in all likelihood, he had been killed.

He sat in the wooden chair by her bed and watched her. She would be frightened if she knew what he was involved in. With Lee's surrender, Davis's capture, and Yankee armies occupying so much of the South, the cause seemed irrevocably lost. Daniels's intention to revive the struggle was just so much hubris. Most likely they would end up shot or hanged. Who would care for her then?

For years he had written editorials defending the Southern way of life and believed the rhetoric he used in his arguments, published in the *Democratic Press*. He had willingly paid for his son's trip to Texas to join a regiment and had been both proud and fearful when he watched Samuel leave. While Azariah had chosen to use a pen instead of a sword to advance the interests of the South, he had given as much as he thought the situation required. But neither the pen nor the sword had proved enough. *What difference would further sacrifices make at this point?* he asked himself.

Hearing footsteps, he looked to the doorway and saw Mary enter.

"I'm just going to tuck her in for the night, Mr. Dekker."

"Very good." He stood and went back to his room.

Checking his pocket watch, he saw that it was time to depart. He rolled the shotgun in a length of sacking and snugged his other weapons into his waistband, reaching for his coat. He had to trust that

some good would come of this venture and that God had not turned
His back on them.

* * *

In her home on Stockton Street, Martha Whitfield waited at the
bottom of the wide carpeted stairway leading to the second floor. She
stared up at the landing, biting her lips. A door closed softly above
and the floorboards in the upper hallway creaked beneath the runners
as Mrs. Dunbar came into view and descended the stairs. When she
reached the bottom, Martha gestured for her to follow her into the
parlor. Once inside, she shut the doors, turning to her guest.

Mrs. Dunbar was a plain woman with long dark hair that she
wore tied back with a single blue ribbon. She was a midwife and had
worked as a nurse in Mississippi during the war.

"How is Angeline?" asked Martha. "Has she been—?'

"I gave her some medicine to make her drowsy, and then I examined her. She was assaulted. She should be examined by your doctor
when she is up to it."

Martha nodded, frowning, the news as bad as she had expected.
"I'll see to it."

Mrs. Dunbar reached out to touch Martha's shoulder, looking at
her with sympathetic eyes. "You must rest yourself."

"Thank you. However, I'm fine. Can I offer you some coffee?"

"No, I should be on my way."

"Please take this." Martha pressed a half eagle gold piece into Mrs. Dunbar's hand.

"It really isn't necessary."

"I insist. We can rely on your discretion in this matter, I pray."

"Absolutely, Mrs. Whitfield. This is a most alarming occurrence. No woman should suffer as she has. You must remain her support. She is not to blame for what happened. I've seen other women who have suffered through this in Vicksburg—Southern women violated by Southern soldiers, no less. This sort of thing can drive a woman to despair, if she has no one to turn to."

"Angeline is my life. I would never abandon her."

"Of course. I must leave. I told the cabriolet driver to wait. But if there is any further service I can render, please let me know."

Martha led her to the front door. They shook hands, and Martha watched her leave. Once the cab had pulled away, she shut the door. She walked to the back of the hallway where her late husband kept his office. She lit the oil desk lamp and sat, taking a piece of note paper from the drawer. Dipping a pen in the inkwell, she wrote to her nephew, James Sanders, requesting that he visit her and report on his meeting with Chief Burke. Martha was going to see to it that her daughter had justice and that this blackguard, Pettingill, paid for his crimes. Had her husband, Richard, been alive, he would have loaded his 10-bore fowling piece and hunted Pettingill down. Martha had no knowledge of guns, but she had other resources and she was going to make good use of them.

* * *

The pier was quiet and dark. Branching out from the Mission Bay Bridge, it pointed east toward the Oakland shore, which was marked by tiny gold lights. The bay waters splashed softly against the pylons. The night air smelled of brine, tar, and sun-bleached wood. It was cold by the water. Azariah huddled in his wool coat, standing between Daniels and Baugh. Dressed in rough garb and holding repeating rifles, a half-dozen other men waited in the shadows around them. The men were acquaintances of Baugh and all sworn to the cause. The rest of the pier was deserted, and there weren't any lamps. Wilcox had chosen the rendezvous point well.

"Azariah, you take the money, and once they're in sight walk back along the pier about halfway. Have two men go with you and use one of the miner's lamps. We'll send Wilcox and his gang up to retrieve their funds after we've taken possession of the ship. Keep your shotgun ready, in case they try any mischief." Daniels pulled a cloth sack from his pocket, which clinked, and handed it to the older man.

Twelve-gauge cradled in his arm, Azariah took the heavy sack with his free hand and stowed it in his coat pocket. Baugh peered at the timepiece in his palm. Muttering, he gave his Henry rifle to Daniels and crouched. He pulled a match from his pocket and struck it along the rough wood of the rail at his feet. It flared, illuminating the watch's white dial. He shook out the lucifer.

"Eight minutes after the hour."

"Wilcox is generally late," Daniels said.

"Do we have any sailors among us?" Azariah asked.

"Several, including an oyster fisherman who knows the San Mateo shores well," Baugh answered. "They will do the sailing, though we may have to lend a hand."

Daniels spoke. "Once the schooner docks, Mr. Baugh, you take three of our brethren and search the boat for any surprises, human or mechanical. Nothing happens until she's been cleared. When that is done, we'll send Wilcox and his pirates up the pier to you, Azariah."

"And if they try any mayhem?" Baugh looked at the Georgian.

"I assume your rifle is fully loaded?" Daniels handed back the long gun. "Then take cover and pick your shots. However, four hundred dollars is a lot of money to sacrifice for the sake of revenge. If I had to guess, I'd say Wilcox cares more for the almighty dollar than he does about avenging any insults to his pride. We will, however, stay alert."

Minutes passed. A quarter-moon was straight overhead but nearly smothered in a thin veil of clouds. The night breeze gusted fitfully as the water glistened in the darkness. The cold wind against Azariah's cheek felt like a malevolent omen, warning him off.

From the muted splashing along the pier another sound emerged—water slapping against wood but yards away from the dock. Out of the darkness, just north of the pier, pale shapes floated above the glinting black sea. For a moment, Azariah had the impression they were wraiths of drowned sailors. But the shapes took on detail, forming themselves into billowed sails. The long lines of the schooner's hull lurked beneath the tall canvas.

Baugh whistled a sharp note. Placing a miner's lamp atop a mooring pylon, he struck another match and lit the lantern. The schooner sailed slowly past and began to turn toward them, heading into the wind as she approached the pier. Lamps appeared along the schooner's gunwales. As the ship drew near, mooring lines were cast fore and aft to the men standing on the dock. When the schooner was secured, the slight figure of Wilcox opened a doorway in the railing to step onto the dock. Daniels looked at Azariah, who headed back up the pier. Baugh spoke softly to two others who followed the older man away from the boat.

Wilcox, holding a long-barreled Colt revolver by his leg, walked up to Daniels.

"'Ere's your ship. Where's me money?"

Daniels gestured with his thumb. "Back up yonder along the pier. You can have it once we've cleared the ship."

Wilcox smiled, showing dull teeth. "Blimey, you think of everything."

Baugh and the others went on board. Wilcox turned to the schooner, cupping his free hand to his mouth.

"Look lively, lads! Off the boat! No tricks! Let the toffs 'ave 'er!"

Slowly, eight men moved in the lamplight, passing through the portal in the ship's rail. Facing them were Daniels and a fellow Knight, their repeating rifles at port arms, ready to be shouldered and fired.

"Easy does it, lads. Once they're sure we hain't scuttled her, then it's a short walk up the pier to our money."

After several long minutes, Baugh and his crew appeared at the rail. "She's clean."

Wilcox shoved the Colt through his belt. "If I'd 'ave wanted to ram boat-hook up your arse, I'd 'ave left a powder keg in the bilge with a five-minute fuse."

He waved along his thieves. "Off we go. Our work is done."

Daniels, Baugh, and their men watched them leave, holding their firearms uneasily, waiting for them to be gone.

As the harbor pirates approached, Azariah pointed to the sack he had left several yards further up the pier as he and his cohorts backed away toward the boat. Wilcox picked up the bag, shaking coins into his hand.

"Nice doin' business with you bastards!" he called.

Azariah strode hurriedly to the boat, handed over his shotgun to Baugh, and climbed aboard. Two others cast off the mooring lines, tossing them onto the deck and scrambling over the railing as the schooner floated free of the dock.

"What's our heading?" asked the man who took the ship's wheel.

Azariah walked to where he stood, seeing a broad-chested man with dark wavy hair that was nearly to his shoulders. He had a full mustache and a gold hoop earring glinting in one earlobe.

Baugh, standing by, gestured to the steersman. "Azariah, this is Frank Corso, our pilot."

Corso held out a hand as he steered with the other, glancing briefly at the older man as they shook. He had big hands and a crushing grip that made Azariah wince.

"What's our heading, Mr. Dekker?"

"The dock of Cicero Madison on the San Mateo shore. He owns large oyster beds down that way. Do you know the place?"

Corso's face looked troubled, but he nodded. "I can find it."

* * *

The quarter-moon was lower in the sky. The clouds had fled, and the ancient drooping orb shed its pale light across the obsidian bay. They sailed on light winds, the schooner gliding through the water, which hissed along the sides. Azariah stood at the rail near the ship's wheel, looking out at the dark flat of the land, lit here and there by specks of light. The landscape and its silence were spectral, as though the boat were not full of privateers but dead men. The black waters were not the bay but the river Styx and the boat that of Charon.

Azariah was startled by the hand that clapped his shoulder. Daniels smiled at him.

"What do you think of her?"

"She sails well."

"Whose dock are we taking her to?" the Georgian asked.

"His name is Cicero Madison," Azariah answered. "He's a sworn Knight like us. He owns extensive oyster beds and farmlands in San Mateo County. A gentleman farmer, formerly of Virginia."

Daniels turned to the man steering the vessel. "How long till we reach Madison's dock?"

"Four, maybe five minutes. We're very close now. You'd better tell the men to put out the running lights. That way Mr. Madison should mark us. Someone should stand in the bow to greet him. Else they might take a shot at us," Corso said, an uneasy look in his eyes as he gave the wheel a few spokes to port.

Daniels went forward, giving orders quietly. A green lamp was hung on the starboard rail and a red one used to light the port side. Azariah walked toward the bow. Ahead, a pier extended out over the dark water, lit by a sizeable lamp at its end. The schooner began to move away to port so that Corso could round her up into the wind. As the vessel turned, the bow swung to north, the sails going limp then luffing slightly in the breeze as the lines went slack. The schooner floated toward the pier where the half-lit figures of men were visible in the lamplight. Hawsers were cast to the landsmen and secured to the pylons. The ship stopped moving, and the men from the pier clambered aboard.

Azariah saw a stocky gentleman with long white hair, slicked back, step through the opened doorway in the railing and recognized Madison as he approached to shake hands.

"Mr. Dekker, a pleasure to see you again, sir!"

Madison wore a light-brown frock coat with matching trousers. He had a strong face etched with lines. In a red sash he carried a Volcanic Repeating Pistol.

"Welcome aboard," Azariah said. "We've brought two men with us who are carpenters. They'll be staying to work on renaming and refitting the vessel."

"Good. Two six-pounders were delivered to my house just this morning."

Madison looked around, his eyes resting on Corso, as the pilot walked away from the ship's wheel. Madison stared as though trying to recall something. He gestured toward Corso, who busied himself at the rails, loosening the lines for the sails, while others did the same.

"Who's that?"

"Our pilot, a local fisherman," Azariah answered, wondering what Madison was on about.

"You there! What's your name, sir?" Madison called.

The older man walked over and laid his hand on Corso's shoulder. The fisherman stared directly into Madison's face.

"By God, it's you!"

Madison stepped back, pulling the Volcanic pistol from his sash. "Seize him! The man's a damned oyster pirate!"

Madison's men circled Corso, whose hand closed over the hilt of the knife sheathed on his belt.

"What do you think you're playing at?" Daniels demanded.

"This man has been raiding my oyster beds for years, even killed one of my night watchmen. What's he doing here?"

Baugh spoke. "I recruited him. He took the oath, once he was paid. But—"

Cocking the hammer, Madison leveled the Volcanic and fired. The concussion was startlingly loud, smoke and flame spearing from the muzzle. Corso stumbled back, falling to his hands and knees. He collapsed onto his side, face grimacing. The onlookers stared from the fisherman to the patrician with ringing ears, the smell of spent powder in the air. Daniels's men spoke out in protest.

"I won't have it," Madison said. "I won't have a thief and murderer of honest men on my property."

"Damn it, man! You can't just execute a compatriot. It has to be discussed and decided, the man's character and actions judged." Daniels held his own revolver at his side.

"I won't have it, I tell you. A man like that is not worthy to serve with us. Treacherous dog."

Azariah, tension in his neck, stepped close to Madison so that he could whisper. "If we don't work together on this venture, we will all hang. What we are attempting to do is too important to let personal matters interfere. Are you with us or not, Cicero?"

The planter stared defiantly. "I'm sworn to the cause. But I will have my say in important matters. Had I been consulted on Corso's recruitment, I would have condemned it. Furthermore, I will let no man steal from me and get away with it."

Baugh joined in. "How do you know it was Corso filching from your oyster beds? How do you even know what he looked like?"

Madison turned his head to answer Baugh. "His depredations irked me so much I hired a detective to track him down. When the detective had done so, I rode up to the city to have a look at Corso. I confronted him on Commercial Street near the Central Wharf and told him if I caught stealing my oysters again, I'd see him strung up on his own mast and riddled with bullets."

"And?" Baugh asked.

"He stayed away for a few months, preying upon other owners, then started in again on my beds. His boat is well-known to my watchmen."

Daniels and Baugh exchanged glances. Azariah stood uncertainly to one side, fearful more violence would occur, but relaxed when he saw Daniels's face soften.

"All right," Daniels said. "You shot him; you bury him. Back to work, boys."

Madison turned to one of his men. "Ride back to the house and fetch a wagon. Then take this man up into the hills and bury him in an unmarked grave."

A fellow who knelt beside Corso looked up. "He's hurt bad, but he's still breathing."

Madison waved a hand at the oyster pirate whose eyes were pinched shut in pain. "Most likely he'll be dead by the time you get him up into the woods. If he isn't, hit him in the head with a shovel and then bury him."

"There's only one problem," Baugh said, stepping closer. "Corso was our pilot, the man to sail the schooner out of the bay. Now we have no one who knows the waters and the shoals."

Madison cast a disgusted glance at the dying man. "No matter. I know several retired captains. Replacing this blackguard won't be difficult."

"We need patriots, Cicero. Not just any man will do," Azariah said. "There's too much at stake."

"Don't you think I know that? Are we going to stand here and jaw or get on with our work?"

"Strike the sails, Mr. Baugh," Daniels said, looking at Madison with gauging eyes.

The patrician pointed to two men standing by. "You fellows carry him ashore. The wagon will be by for him directly."

CHAPTER 10

Lieutenant Blake limped down the marble-floored hallway to the door of the inspector general's office, using a silver-knobbed cane borrowed from a fellow boarder at his hotel. After opening the door, he hobbled inside to find Schaeffer at work. The aging lieutenant ceased his writing to stare at Blake. While hanging his jacket and pistol belt at the coat rack, Blake saw that Colonel Wagner's office door was closed, indicating he was already at work.

"The old man's in a temper," Schaeffer warned. "He's knows about your—"

The colonel's door opened to reveal the man himself, looking stern.

"Mr. Blake, in my office, now."

"Right away, sir."

Blake hurried, wincing as he put too much weight on the leg. Inside the chamber, he stood at attention in front of the senior officer's desk, holding the cane close to his leg like a sword. The colonel shut the door, walked to his chair, and sat. He picked up the pipe from his blotter, testing the tobacco cake inside with a fingertip. With the briar in his mouth, he puffed ominously, gazing at Blake.

"I had thought better of you, Lieutenant. You don't seem to be a hothead, but this incident over the weekend is unacceptable. I heard about it at my club last night from the provost marshal. So far, no one has preferred charges against you, but that is only because no one has come forward."

"Yes sir."

"How's the wound?"

"Better, sir. A first-rate physician stitched it closed. He also sutured the one on my forearm."

"Good. Now tell me, what the hell were you thinking?"

"The man left me no choice, sir. He even struck me across the face. I didn't want to fight him, but he wouldn't back down. Lt. Tevis with the quartermaster's depot witnessed most of it. He'll back me up. I had two choices: leave town or fight the bastard."

"Knives, I heard."

"He chose the weapons, sir."

"What was this over?"

Blake frowned. "A young Californio woman. I met her at the Selby's party just last week."

Wagner nodded, exhaling smoke. "I recall you talking to a lovely señorita. So what happened?"

Blake's leg was smarting. "May I sit, sir? My leg is—"

The colonel waved his hand toward the chairs facing his desk. Gratefully, Blake eased himself down. He stared for a moment at the corner of the room.

"I've only known her a few days, but damned if I haven't fallen in love with her, sir. And to make matters worse, she's engaged to be married. Some wealthy ranchero down south. One of these arranged marriages."

"I see. And the young woman? What were her intentions?"

"She felt the same as I. We were sharing an intimate moment on the balcony of the Donahue's house when this escort of hers interrupted us. He claimed I had insulted his patron, the man Elena is to marry. He insisted on satisfaction." Blake paused, feeling very discouraged. "You know the rest."

Wagner shook his head. "And the young lady? What's become of her?"

"I don't know, sir. I paid a newspaper boy to carry a letter to her, but I don't know if she received it."

Wagner brooded for the better part of a minute as he smoked, finally taking the pipe from his lips. "I'm willing to let this go, but a word of warning. No more fighting for whatever reason. I'll do my best to shield you if anyone brings charges, but there will be no more interactions with any of these Spanish hotheads. You'll learn as a soldier that it's best not to involve yourself in local affairs. Unfortunate as it is, you are going to have to put your feelings aside. If this young lady is slated to marry, you had better not meddle. It's too damned dangerous, and I will not have soldiers under my command engaging in illegal actions—dueling has been outlawed. Is that understood?"

"Yes sir."

Wagner's stern expression softened. "Go back to your hotel, Lieutenant. Get some rest. I'll expect to see you in the office in two days."

"Yes sir."

"That's all."

Chastened and yet relieved, Blake stood to salute, then limped out of the colonel's office.

* * *

Francis Pettingill stood in the narrow lobby of a cheap hotel on Commercial Street, watching as two drayage workers carried the crate that contained his portable printing press out to their wagon, where an old draft horse with long fetlocks waited patiently, its hammer head drooping.

"Make sure that it gets on the steamer for Los Angeles," Pettingill said as the men maneuvered their way through the lobby door.

"Yeah, yeah," one answered, without bothering to look back.

The clerk at the counter watched in silence. Behind him, a Whitney revolver hung from a nail above the small pigeonhole box where the guests' keys and mail were kept.

"It's only a block to the wharf," the clerk said.

Pettingill looked over at him, made no reply, and left. Moving along the wooden sidewalk, he carried a carpetbag that contained two folded shirts, a pair of clean underwear, and the $3,750 he had taken off Jim Sanders. Pettingill began whistling "When Johnny Comes

Marching Home," not because he had any particular sympathy with the South but because it was the most cheerful song he knew. The sun was breaking through the clouds, illuminating the sandy unpaved lane. Pettingill turned at Davis and headed toward California Street. He tipped his hat to a woman in a dark dress with a matching hat and carrying a parasol. She regarded him suspiciously and kept walking. He smiled, recalling his recent amorous moments with Angeline. He hailed a taxi and told the driver to take him to the train depot at Townsend Street. Minutes later, he climbed a small set of stairs and approached the ticket window of the depot. On the tracks, a panting locomotive and coal car waited in front of a string of passenger cars.

"That the train to San Jose?" Pettingill asked, taking the wallet from his inside breast pocket.

"Leaves in three minutes," the clerk said.

"One ticket, one way south," Pettingill stated, laying down a five-dollar bill.

After receiving his ticket and change, he carried his bag down the steps, glancing at a gent in a suit leaning against the building and reading a folded newspaper, which obscured his face. Pettingill stepped down onto the sandy flat alongside the waiting train.

"There you are, you son of a bitch!"

He turned to see Jim Sanders glaring at him from the side of the depot building, tossing aside the newspaper. Grabbing the brim of his hat, Pettingill ran out of the yard, the carpetbag banging against his leg, clutched by his other hand. He crossed Townsend Street, dodging between passing wagons, and headed for an alley that intersected the boulevard. Knees pumping, he glanced over his shoulder as he sprinted into the alley, seeing Sanders chasing after him. The few pedestrians along the street had paused to watch.

"Stop, thief!"

Exhaling in rapid gusts, Pettingill kept up his pace, passing a series of old barrels filled with stinking refuse. A pistol report split the air, a board splintering on the building as Pettingill ran by it.

"Stop, you bastard!"

He turned into another alley, knowing he had to act. He stopped in the middle of the lane to draw a pocket revolver from beneath his coat. He cocked it as his pursuer came around the corner. Sanders skidded to a halt, aiming a derringer. Both men fired. The noise was painful in the confines of the alley. A twisting cloud of gun smoke obscured the air. The two men lost sight of each other for a moment until the breeze dispersed it. Sanders was crouched, holding the derringer, seemingly unhurt. Pettingill, unaware of any wound, cocked his revolver for a second shot. His face alarmed, Sanders ran out of the alley.

Pettingill de-cocked the revolver, waited a moment to see if Sanders would reappear, then stowed it back in a coat pocket. Breathing hard, he walked quickly to the opposite end of the alley. He followed the street back to the train depot. Passengers were climbing into the ends of the cars, the conductor calling out the "all aboard" warning. Jogging past the depot building, Pettingill reached the back of the last car and leaped onto the rear platform. An older man, going through the door, turned and held it open for him.

"You almost didn't make there, young fellow," the man commented.

"Indeed, sir, it was a close one." Pettingill smiled, still trying to catch his breath.

He entered the car and found an empty seat on one of the wooden benches. Sitting by the window, he looked for Sanders as the train pulled out of the station but did not see him. *Frisco's too hot for me now*, he mused, *but it has been a very profitable visit, all the way around.*

* * *

Blake sat on his bed in his shirtsleeves, trousers, and stockinged feet. A book lay beside him atop the coverlet, but he stared out the window. A knock came from the door. On the nightstand next to Blake lay his loaded revolver.

"It's open," he called.

The door swung inward, and Inspector O'Gara peered around it. He stepped into the room, closing the door behind him.

"I went looking for you at your office. They told me you were here. What's happened?"

"You mean you don't know?" Blake asked, sarcasm in his voice. "I thought it was all over town. I got mixed up in a duel yesterday. Over that young lady I was seeing. Regrettably, she is engaged to another man—a ranchero. His lackey claimed I had insulted the ranchero's honor by … paying such close attention to the lady."

"Are you hurt?"

"A cut across the leg, one on the arm—both seen to by a doctor. The colonel sent me back here to recover. Two days of furlough."

"What about the other fellow?" O'Gara asked.

"I wounded him pretty seriously, but I've had no news on him. Listen, Tom, I need you to do me a favor. Will you go to the Noes' home and slip a note to Elena?"

"Yeah, I guess, but if this other fellow is dead … Dueling is illegal. I'll have to arrest you for murder."

"He challenged me. I have witnesses."

"But you met him at a place other than where he challenged you?"

"Of course."

"Then you can't claim self-defense," O'Gara said. "I might have to take you in, until the matter can be decided by a police court judge."

Blake sat silent for a moment, biting his lower lip. He scooted off the bed, then limped to the table across the room and picked up the small envelope lying on top of it. He held it out to O'Gara.

"Take it to her. If Arzaga is dead, I'll go with you willingly once I know she has the letter."

O'Gara took the envelope, then slipped it into his coat pocket, his eyes on Blake.

"This could compromise our investigation of Major Ellis's murder."

Blake folded his arms across his chest, leaning against the table behind him.

"I have to get word to her."

O'Gara nodded. Walking to the door, he opened it, then paused.

"I'll be back in a couple of hours. I expect to find you here when I get back."

"Understood."

O'Gara went out, shutting the door behind him. Blake stayed against the table, wondering if he would ever see Elena again.

* * *

Martha Whitfield sat on the loveseat in her parlor, working on a needlepoint pattern. Angeline stood by the curtained window, looking out at the street, her eyes pensive. They were waiting on their midday meal. Martha had noticed how quiet Angie was since she had emerged from her room.

"We should have the carriage readied and take a drive out to the Presidio Reservation. The fresh air would put some color in your face."

Angeline moved her head in a half nod but said nothing, seeming too deeply trapped in thought to reply. Martha frowned with concern.

The maid appeared in the open doorway. "Mr. Sanders is here, ma'am."

Sanders strode in, gesturing with his fist. "I had him! I had him!"

Martha put aside her needlework and stood.

"James, what on earth are you talking about?"

"Pettingill. I saw him not an hour ago at the train depot. I chased him down Townsend Street."

"You saw him?" Angeline turned from the window.

"I chased him into an alley and fired my derringer as we ran but missed. Then I cornered him, and we exchanged shots. But damn the luck I think I missed again! The derringers must not be properly sighted. I didn't have any other guns on me, and so I had to beat a retreat as he drew aim a second time. He had a revolver."

"James, there's blood on your cuff," Martha said, alarmed.

He raised his left hand, the shirt cuff enclosing his wrist stained crimson.

"Yes," he said gallantly. "I was grazed by Pettingill's bullet. The policeman I found noticed the hole in my coat sleeve. We searched for Pettingill; only, he must have made it to the train before it pulled out. I told the patrolman all about it as he walked me to a doctor's office."

Martha took him by the elbow, leading him to a couch. "Do sit down, Nephew. You're sure you are all right?"

Sanders nodded. "A flesh wound. The doctor tended and bandaged it. I'll be fine."

Angie, her face pale, dark half-circles below her eyes, sat next to him. "What about Pettingill? Was he shot as well?"

Sanders frowned. "I don't think so. Of course, I might have hit him, but I didn't have the chance to see. I ran for a policeman, and it took some minutes to find one. He followed me back to the depot, but the train was gone by then and Pettingill with it."

Angeline looked down for a moment, then raised her head. "You were very brave, Jim."

"The man defrauded me of a small fortune. And … treated you insultingly. I was going to have his blood."

Mrs. Harrington, the housekeeper, entered the room. "Will Mr. Sanders be staying for dinner?"

"I'm too excited to eat," Sanders said. "But I'll have some coffee, please. And some brandy if you have it."

Mrs. Harrington was a stout woman in her late thirties. Her face was serious as she regarded Sanders. "There isn't a drop in the house. Mrs. Whitfield won't have it. God bless her."

"That will be all. Thank you, Mrs. Harrington," Martha said.

She stared at her nephew and took a deep breath. It was a good thing that Jim's mother was no longer living. She would have fainted at the news her son had been wounded in an exchange of pistol fire in an alley. Wondering what society was coming to, Martha announced that she would see another place set at the table and left the room.

Watching his aunt go, Sanders sighed his disappointment "A shot of brandy is exactly what I need."

"What will happen next, concerning Pettingill?" Angie asked.

"The policeman said he would wire ahead and have him arrested in San Jose, where the train stops."

"And what will you do now?"

"Go see if the police have arrested the blackguard ... after I have a drink or two. Do you want to go with me?"

She shook her head. "I don't want people to know."

Seeing the fear on her face, Sanders nodded slowly. "I wish for your sake that I had killed him."

Angeline attempted a smile but shook her head again as if to imply that was not her desire. "I wish I had never met him."

Sanders touched her shoulder, and she clasped his hand with her own. The sorrow in her blue eyes was humbling.

* * *

At the terminus point of the Market Street & Mission Dolores Railroad, O'Gara descended from the passenger car onto the sand of Valencia Street, passing the huffing steam engine oddly fitted with a square wooden frame, which made it look like the longer passenger cars. From where he stood he could see the old mission church, only two blocks away. He walked along Valencia, which was sparsely occupied—empty lots between the houses and businesses that had sprung up in the last six years since the railroad had begun operations, making the areas beyond the town accessible to those without horses. He wasn't sure how far it was to the Noe residence, and the June sunlight was hot on his jacketed shoulders. Deciding it would set a better impression to arrive by carriage rather than walking and sweaty, he hailed a cabriolet. Telling the driver his desired destination, O'Gara climbed in.

A short ride later, the cab halted in front of the Noe residence. It was large two-story structure of mastic-covered brick, with a series of tall windows bordered by wooden shutters on both floors. A row of California oaks had been planted along the sidewalk close to the street. Standing by one of the trees was Don Miguel, smoking a cigar and talking to another Californio man in a tan suit, a sombrero on his head. O'Gara handed up the twenty-five-cent fare to the unshaved cab driver and walked over to where the men stood. They stopped their conversation to regard him.

"Don Miguel, I'm Inspector Tom O'Gara." He offered his hand.

Noe studied him for a moment, then shook his hand. The don nodded to the Californio gentleman, who said adios and left. Noe puffed his cigar, his dark eyes on O'Gara.

"What are you here for, señor?"

"I'm making inquiries into a duel that took place yesterday between an Army officer and a vaquero. I heard the vaquero was injured. Can I speak to him?"

Don Miguel took the cigar from his mouth. "That will not be possible. The vaquero's lung was punctured, and the doctor unable to stop the internal bleeding. Señor Arzaga died last night."

Notebook in hand, O'Gara started writing, thinking Blake was in serious trouble. "Will you be preferring charges against the soldier?"

"That remains to be seen. The vaquero was not one of my servants. He belonged to Don Carlos Bejarano, who resides near Los Angeles. It is up to Don Carlos. I have, however, had the body photographed and had our lawyer depose the two vaqueros who were with Arzaga when he was stabbed by this lieutenant."

Impressed, O'Gara nodded. "Very careful of you, Don Miguel."

"My family has learned the hard way concerning Yankee lawyers and the due process of American courts," Noe said. "If Don Carlos wishes to proceed legally against this lieutenant, then we will provide sufficient evidence. From what I have heard, this *soldato* behaved shamelessly and took advantage of a girl's innocence, as well as besmirching the honor of an old and noble family. Society will be better served if the lieutenant hangs, but I don't hold out much hope for that, knowing the court system. However, perhaps he will be disgraced and forced to resign his commission. It is only just, don't you think?"

"I can't say, not knowing all the facts," O'Gara replied, making another note. "Can I speak to the young lady in question?"

"That is not possible either, Inspector."

"And why is that?"

"She left this morning on a coastal steamer, along with an escort. She is on her way back to her family in Los Angeles, to marry Don Carlos."

Thinking of Blake's note in his coat pocket, O'Gara slipped his pencil into his vest and tucked away the notebook. "Thank you for your time, Don Miguel."

The Californio made a dismissive gesture with his hand.

"Please let me know if Senor Bejarano decides to pursue criminal allegations against the lieutenant," O'Gara requested.

"I will see that you are among the first to know."

* * *

It was a few minutes past noon. The sun was bright as Azariah and Daniels stepped down from the car of the Omnibus Railway. They had caught the train for the city at the San Bruno depot, got off at the terminus at Townsend Street, and walked two blocks to catch the Omnibus north to Market Street. They strolled along Market to the plaza between Battery and Front Streets. The sidewalks were busy with pedestrians, the streets cluttered with wagons and carriages. Though he had fallen asleep on the hard wooden passenger seat during the train ride, Azariah still felt done in. After several hours of working on the schooner, Cicero had invited the pair of them back to his house for breakfast and a campaign strategy session. It had been a long night.

"Let's meet this evening and go talk to that friend of yours to see if he will come through with the small arms we've asked for."

Azariah nodded. "There's something else we need to discuss."

Daniels regarded the older man with tired eyes. "What's that?"

"When you go to sea, I can't go with you. My ... my wife is an invalid. If I leave, she will have no one to look after her. I hope you won't take this as deserting the cause."

Daniels looked down at the worn boardwalk, then nodded. "I heard from Baugh that you lost a son in the war. Have no fears, my friend. You have served admirably and made some of the greatest sacrifices a man can. Furthermore, I will see that you get a share of the spoils, which, hopefully, will be significant."

Azariah relaxed, taking a deep breath. "Thank you. That is most generous."

"My old friend Captain Raphael Semmes used to take the chronometers of the ships he captured. I intend to settle only for gold, or a useful cargo that can be easily sold. Shall we say seven o'clock this evening?"

"Fine."

Daniels patted the older man on the shoulder and turned away, heading for his hotel. Azariah watched him merge into the streams of pedestrians, then lost sight of him. Dekker eyed the cabman parked at the curb, waiting for a fare, but reminded himself he had to conserve funds, even though Daniels had given him three hundred dollars to settle his outstanding debts and live on. Wearily, he started walking up Market Street, the bundled shotgun in the old blanket held in his hand.

* * *

Entering the chief of police's office, Jim Sanders stopped in front of the desk of the chief's secretary—a slender-faced man in a black suit who wore pince-nez spectacles propped on the end of his nose. Parted in the middle, the man's hair was slicked with pomade, which gave off a faint, pleasant scent.

"Yes?" he inquired, looking up at Sanders.

"I have a matter to discuss with Chief Burke. You may remember, I spoke to him on Saturday afternoon. I have more information."

"Are you Pettingill?"

"No," Sanders answered. "I'm the aggrieved party. James Sanders."

"Ah, yes. Well, the chief has referred the matter to Capt. Lees. His office is down the hall."

"This is very delicate," Sanders insisted. "I thought the chief would handle it personally."

"I can assure you, sir, that Captain Lees is very discreet and utterly capable. Quite frankly, Mr. Burke has other weightier matters to see to."

"I don't like your inference," Sanders said.

"Nonetheless, for further action, you must speak to Capt. Lees."

"Damned bureaucrat."

Sanders left with a malevolent glance over his shoulder, but the secretary had returned to his paperwork. Down the hallway, which was murmurous with voices, he found the detectives' room. Recognizing the famous Capt. Lees, Sanders strode up to him as the man stood in the doorway chatting with another detective.

"Captain Lees?" he asked. "Jim Sanders. I believe you are handling this matter of fraudulent stock certificates I was sold, as well as another issue regarding Miss Whitfield, my cousin."

Lees looked at him, the detective's blue eyes thoughtful and kind. "The chief asked me to handle it personally."

"I saw Pettingill this morning at the Townsend Street train depot. I chased him, and we traded pistol fire in a nearby alley. I received a slight wound but was forced to retreat, having fired both my derringers."

"Yes, the officer you enlisted for help made a full report to me just an hour ago."

"Very good. Did you wire ahead to San Jose to have Pettingill arrested?"

Lees gave a slight shrug. "I tried, but at the telegraph office I was told the wires were down. Apparently, there is a break in the line somewhere south of the city. Crews are out searching for the break."

Sanders stared in disbelief. "You mean he might get away?"

Lees frowned. "I left orders with the operator to wire the message through just as soon as the line was repaired."

"Damn the man and his infernal luck! This is outrageous!"

"Have no worries, Mr. Sanders. Men like Pettingill are always caught sooner or later. I speak from experience."

Sanders turned away, cursing beneath his breath. He wandered out into the hall.

"I'll let you know as soon as anything develops," Lees called out.

Sanders waved his hand in acknowledgment but didn't look back. If only his pistol ball had hit Pettingill between the eyes! He should have taken just a second more to be sure of his aim. Feeling ill, he walked to the entrance doors.

* * *

Blake moved slowly down the board sidewalk toward the What Cheer House, using his borrowed cane and wearing the black suit he had worn to class while attending university. When Lee's invasion of Maryland was in the headlines of all the newspapers and Northerners feared the worst, he had left college to join a company of volunteer university students. He shook his head at the brave naïveté they had all shared and their blind confidence in thinking they could save the Union. Blake passed a liquor emporium and the Original House Hotel, advertising baths for twenty-five cents on a sign hung in front of the glass fanlights of its entranceway. Out on the sidewalk, by the gas lamp painted with the What Cheer name, Detective O'Gara stood, scanning the passing pedestrians, an angry look on his face. He caught sight of Blake.

"Where the hell have you been? I told you to stay put."

"Relax, Officer. I just went to my tailor's to order another pair of uniform trousers. The pair I wore during the duel was ruined. It's just a block away. I didn't go far."

O'Gara's glaring eyes softened only slightly. "You have trouble, my friend."

Blake leaned against the cane, taking the weight off his injured leg. "What is it?"

"That vaquero you fought, Arzaga, is dead."

Surprised, Blake took a weary breath, glancing at the crushed cigarette butts and flattened bits of paper strewn randomly over the worn sidewalk boards. "I'm sorry for that."

"If the vaquero's patron decides to file charges against you, it won't go well. The matter is still being decided."

Blake raised his head. "He challenged me. Couldn't it be argued that I was merely defending myself since he had a knife as well?"

O'Gara shrugged irritably. "Depends on the judge and jury. Worry about that later. The other problem is your lady has left town. Gone home to Los Angeles to marry her betrothed. I wasn't able to give her this."

The detective handed him the envelope. Holding it, Blake stared at the paper, his hopes crushed. He put it into his coat pocket and turned away, limping toward the door of the hotel. O'Gara called out.

"What about the Ellis investigation? We still haven't found the man in the suit. The one Paddy Doolin saw."

Blake stopped, looking over his shoulder. "We'll talk about it later."

CHAPTER *11*

Jim Sanders opened the glass-paned door of the Callard Detective Agency and stepped into a single room with a desk against the wall. A heavyset man turned in a swivel chair to face him. The vest of his suit bulged from the paunch behind it. An aging top hat sat at a rakish slant on his head. His face was wide and outlined with a full grey beard. One of his eyes was marbled and blind, while the other was clear and blue.

"Can I help you?" the detective asked.

"Are you Mr. Callard?"

He nodded. Sanders stepped forward to introduce himself, avoiding the man's disconcerting stare. Callard stood, shaking Jim's hand in a strong grip, gesturing to the wooden armchair next to the desk. The office smelled with stale cigar smoke. Pale light streamed in from the windows beside the desk. Sanders lowered himself into the hard seat and glanced at Callard, uncertain where to begin.

"I was going to go to the Pinkertons, but I found out they don't have an office in town. I ... need an agency that's professional and discreet."

"Discretion is my watchword, sir. I used to be a Pinkerton myself, back in Chicago before the war. I worked on many a case with Mr. Allen himself. We sort of created the business together. Now, how can I help you, my friend?"

Sanders looked from the man's hairy-cheeked face down to the tips of his own shiny polished boots. "A man named Pettingill sold me several thousand dollars' worth of counterfeit stock certificates. He … also forced his attentions … on my female cousin. He fled town yesterday, headed south. The local police haven't made much effort on the matter. I caught him myself, and we shot it out in an alley off Townsend Street. I received a flesh wound in the skirmish but had to retreat, having emptied my derringers. I know from the ticket agent Pettingill caught the train to San Jose. From there, who knows?"

Callard nodded as he listened. "I assume you want me to track down this rogue and see him brought to justice."

"Precisely. Most importantly, I want the money returned. I lost $3,750. For my cousin's honor … I would see him hanged, but his offenses against her are not such that will earn him a death sentence by our laws."

The detective shrugged. "Once caught, he could be made to suffer."

"How so?"

Callard gave him a sly look. "A jailer could be enlisted to make the man's life unpleasant. Most jailers know how to use a truncheon to great effect. Ten dollars or so would probably be enough. I know of a criminal who urinated blood for a month after his going-over. Could well happen to this man, Pettingill, if you catch my meaning, sir."

Sanders fingered the soft brim of his hat. "It sounds exceedingly cruel, Mr. Callard, but perhaps not without merit."

"The world is a harsh place. It would be merely one way for him to pay for his crimes."

"I will meditate upon it. In the meantime, how much is it to engage your services?"

Callard hooked a thumb in his vest pocket. "Five dollars a day with reimbursement for any expenses. But if this man, Pettingill, is still in the state, I will find him."

"That's rather expensive," Sanders said, hesitating.

The detective smiled at him in a fatherly way, despite his ghastly stare. "The Pinkerton's motto may be that they never sleep, which isn't true. But mine, sir, is that I never quit. I'll catch this blackguard for you and see him in custody. What happens from there is your decision."

Sanders nodded. "All right."

"I'll need a twenty-five dollar retainer fee upfront and a thorough description of Pettingill."

Sanders took out his leather billfold and counted out the money.

* * *

The dining room at the What Cheer House was crowded with midday diners and clamorous with voices. Still wearing his old suit, Blake sat at a small table with Tevis, who was in uniform, his wide yellow-embroidered collar nearly touching the soldier's jaw. The meal finished, they lingered over their coffee.

"Wagner went easy on you, I'd say," Tevis commented. "Any word out of the Noes?"

"Nothing beyond Arzaga's death. Charges may be filed, but it remains to be seen. I haven't been able to get word to Elena."

"And she's left town."

Blake nodded, his eyes downcast.

"Well, you certainly have the respect and admiration of your fellow officers. Your reputation has gained gravitas."

"You sure you don't mean infamy? It wasn't my intention to kill the man."

"Nonetheless, the soldiers around you, below rank and above it, will know you are not one to be trifled with."

"I don't give a damn about that. I've lost Elena for good."

"I hate to say this, brother, but she was never yours to start with."

Blake stared at his friend. "Spare me your clear-sightedness."

Dropping his cloth napkin onto the bare tabletop, Tevis stood. "I don't intend to argue with a fool in love. Let me give you a word of advice: this town is full of young maidens."

"Isn't it time you got back to the quartermaster's?"

Tevis smiled. "Let me know if you need help drowning your sorrows."

Blake waved good-bye as he sipped his coffee. Placing his kepi on his head, Tevis turned and walked out. When he had finished the coffee, Blake signed a chit to have the meal added to his bill and left the dining room. Limping back into the lobby, he headed for the stairs, still using the cane. The clerk at the counter called out to him, holding up a letter. Taking it, Blake saw it was written in Elena's hand. He hobbled over to an armchair to sit. Using a penknife, he slit the top of the envelope and took out the folded page to read the flowing script.

Dearest Liam,

My heart is so full that I do not know where to start. I prayed for you all night after the dance, and my prayers were answered when I learned that you lived. I know you were injured, but I hope that you will heal quickly. My family is sending me back south, where I must wed Don Carlos. But my love is with you. I will treasure the time we spent together. It will be a secret garden I visit whenever I am lonely or sad. And though we may never see each other again, I will always remember how I felt when you held me in your arms.

All my love,

Elena

He refolded the note and put it back into the envelope, blinking his wet eyelashes. He stood and moved slowly toward the stairs. The climb was difficult.

* * *

Azariah stood in the shadowed interior of a warehouse on Falcon Street, its air cold and redolent with machine oil. In the entranceway a rented wagon and two draft horses stood facing the street. Baugh and Daniels loaded crates of small arms into the wagon, grunting with the weight of them. The unmarked crates were filled with Remington revolvers and Enfield carbines. Azariah closed the rear gate of the wagon, dropping the pins into their latches as Daniels stowed the wooden handcart used to move the crates. Azariah waved to Hiram Guthrie, owner of the warehouse, who was standing in the office. The old Scot was another displaced Southerner, who had lived in Nashville for thirty years before the war. They had told him the firearms were being shipped to Mexico to a company of ex-Confederates who were waiting to take up arms again for the cause.

Climbing onto the wagon, Azariah sat next to Baugh, who held the reins with one hand and settled a wool cap on his head with his other. Daniels looked up at them.

"There's another problem we need to deal with," Baugh said. "One of the ship's crew—Hopkins. He wants out. It seems he's done of fair bit of oyster-filching in the past, and he's scared of Cicero."

"Does Cicero know who he is?" Daniels asked.

"I don't think so. But Hopkins left yesterday afternoon, just before I came back myself."

"What's his address?"

"I'm not sure. I met him through one of our fellow Knights. But he swore to the oath."

Daniels nodded. "I'll see if I can find him. Get him to reconsider. If not, I'll pay him off."

"Hopkins knows a fair bit about boats. Try the water-front boardinghouses."

Daniels nodded. Baugh slapped the reins against the horses' rumps, and the wagon rumbled forward. Out in the daylight, Azariah squinted even though the sky was overcast. The wind, whipping along the sandy street, made him turn up the collar of his old wool coat. Baugh turned the wagon at Folsom Street to head south.

"What do you think our colleague meant by 'pay him off'?" the older man asked.

Baugh shrugged. "It means either bank notes or a bullet. We can't afford to have any loose tongues at this point."

* * *

It was the third saloon along East Street that he tried after beginning his search. Daniels walked into the warm dimness. The interior smelled of new sawdust and sour beer. Half full of dock loafers, idle stevedores, and unemployed seamen, the taproom was murmurous with their coarse voices. Stopping at the bar, he ordered a steam beer and after a few sips asked the bartender if he had seen Elihu Hopkins about.

"The oysterman?" asked the bartender, who had suspicious, half-lidded eyes. "Not today."

"He owes me some money," Daniels said nonchalantly.

"Hopkins owes everyone money."

"Don't know where I could find him, do you?"

The bartender had to think for a moment as he wiped at the worn wood of the counter with a rag. "I've seen him coming out of that boardinghouse just across from the Clay Street Wharf. What's it called?"

"The Newcastle," said a toothless red-bearded loafer, standing nearby. His coat had holes at the elbows, his boots were scuffed, and the hems of his trouser legs frayed.

The barkeep nodded. "That's it."

Daniels slid his schooner of beer down to the loafer. "Thanks, fellers."

* * *

When she opened the door to his rooms, Sally found Jim Sanders sitting in the darkened parlor. The heavy curtains were drawn and backlit from the daylight at the windows. Unshaven and in his shirt-sleeves, Jim looked up from the couch where he sat, his stocking feet propped on the table next to a whiskey bottle. He held a glass in his hand.

"James, what's wrong?" Sally asked, taking off her hat.

"I hired a detective today."

"Whatever for? I haven't heard from you in days. I thought you might be ill."

"I am," Sanders said, taking a sip of bourbon.

"What is it?" Sally sat down next to him, placing her hat on the table.

"That son of a bitch Pettingill. He's ruined my life and my cousin's."

"That man you had a business arrangement with? The one that was going to make you so much money?"

Sanders looked at her with sullen eyes. "Cheated me and he raped Angie. She won't say it, but I know that's what happened. I should have killed him."

"He did all that?" she asked.

Sander nodded, placing his glass on the table. "I introduced them. The three of us took lunch together. It's broken her spirit, and it's my fault!"

Putting down his glass, Sanders sobbed, his face convulsing. Sally embraced him. She was speechless, having never seen him this way in all their months together. He was always the devil-may-care bon vivant.

"Calm yourself, my darling," whispered Sally. "Calm yourself."

He snuffled, wiping his sleeve across his nose and mouth. Composing himself, he glanced at her then picked up his whiskey for another swallow.

"This private detective assured me he would find Pettingill and that he would be brought to justice. He even implied that for an extra fee Pettingill could be given a proper beating for his crimes since he certainly won't hang for them."

Sally stared at him. "Are you going to pay the money?"

"I haven't made up my mind."

"But it's horrible," she said. "It goes against all morality."

"By not turning the other cheek? He's a criminal and deserves punishment! Angeline will never see him prosecuted. She couldn't face the shame of people knowing what he's done to her. Nor can I blame her. Hell, the fault is mine. If only I hadn't missed! If my derringer had fired true, then he would be dead and her honor avenged. And I'd have my money back."

"Let's not talk of this anymore. It's too horrid."

Jim stared her with brooding eyes. "Yes, we'll let it go."

He let her take the whiskey glass from his hand. As she placed it on the table, he thought that ten dollars was not a lot of money for the satisfaction it would bring.

* * *

Elihu Hopkins unlocked the door to his room in the Newcastle Boardinghouse and accidentally kicked the folded note on the floor. It skidded across the uneven planks. He stepped back into the hallway, looking back and forth. It was empty -- whoever had left the note was gone. Shutting the door and locking it, he walked over to pick up the paper. After unfolding it, he squinted to make out the tightly penciled script.

"Word has it," he read haltingly aloud, "you wish to leave our or-gan-i-za-tion. Meet me … at Yerba Buena Cemetery … this evening at dusk … Will have money for you … and a contract of … silence to sign. Daniels."

Hopkins ran his callused hand over his dark thinning hair. This could mean real trouble after seeing how Corso had been dealt with. He sat down on the blanket of his sagging mattress to think. He pulled the little money he had from his pants pockets: two dollars and seventy-eight cents. It wasn't enough to buy a gun. The only weapon he owned was a belaying pin he sometimes carried inside his coat, but he would need more than that. The single other choice would be to disappear—ship out on the next clipper sailing for China. He looked out the speckled window to the gray bay waters, which appeared cold and miserable. Sailing would mean fifteen-hour workdays and months of bad food. He had sworn to himself he would never ship out again.

He rubbed his stubbled jaw, considering his meager options. Rising, he knelt by the sea chest at the foot of his bed, taking out the belaying pin to slip it into an inner pocket of his woolen coat. He stood, walked to the door, and unlocked it. He knew one or two fellows on the docks who owed him favors. It was time to call in the markers.

* * *

The clear sky was colorless now that the sun had disappeared beneath the foothills to the west. A petulant breeze blew in intermittent gusts, raising grit from the soil. Daniels stood by the iron gates of Yerba Buena Cemetery, at the southeast edge of the town. Row upon uneven row, wooden crosses and small headstones marked the dead interred in this desolate place. However, whole sections had been emptied—the shallow holes half-filled by the drifting sand—giving the cemetery a vaguely ghoulish air, as though an army of grave robbers had been through the place. Daniels had read in the local papers that the city planned to convert the cemetery into a park; however, corrupt politicians were continually making off with the funds set aside for the effort.

Stunted pines stood here and there among the markers like gnarled mourners. Patches of scrub grass grew between some of the plots. As Daniels entered the unlocked gate, he saw a man standing by one of the pines some fifty yards away. He walked through the graves toward the lone figure. As he drew closer, he recognized Hopkins as one of the crewmen who had helped sail the schooner to San Mateo. Tall and slender, Hopkins watched as Daniels approached. The failing light was still enough to discern the brown of Hopkins's wary eyes. Daniels stopped a few yards from the oysterman.

"Where's the money?" Hopkins asked.

"Here in my pocket," Daniels said. "But I'm hoping you will reconsider. We need every good man we can get."

"Not after watching Corso get slaughtered like a hog. I'll take that money now."

"First things first," Daniels replied. "The contract of silence."

Hopkins grinned malevolently. "I knew it. Fellows—now's the time."

Two men stepped out from behind a nearby pine tree. Both of them held thick ax handles. Hopkins pulled an old pepperbox pistol out of his coat. Growling, Daniels took his hands from his pockets, a cocked derringer in each. He fired at Hopkins, the small gun impossibly loud. Aiming with the second pistol, he shot the man to his left.

Wreathed in smoke, Daniels dropped both pistols as he knelt by a wooden headstone to pull the Le Mat from its holster. The last man hesitated, terror on his whiskered face. He threw the ax handle at Daniels, who ducked the spinning missile. Daniels thumbed back the Le Mat's hammer and shot the thug as he turned to run.

Ears ringing in the vibrant silence, Daniels slowly stood up, his pulse racing. Cottony smoke peeled away in the breeze. He caught movement in the corner of his eye. Hopkins was crawling away. Cocking the heavy revolver, he walked over to the wounded man.

Daniels shot him in the back of the head, the concussion rolling across the hillside. Hopkins sprawled in the sand, his head a butchered ruin. Daniels strode to the oysterman's partners. The first one lay on his back on the ground. He was alive, but the derringer ball had taken him at the base of the throat, which was dark with blood. He would not live long.

Daniels moved on, past the tree to another row of markers. He saw the final thug slumped over a plot. Moving toward him, Daniels held the Le Mat ready. The man's face rested against a sandy mound. Nearly black in the waning light, blood streaked his chin. His eyes were glazing.

"No reason to waste a bullet on a dying man," Daniels said to his victim.

He holstered the Le Mat and walked away to retrieve his derringers.

CHAPTER *12*

The stage had been rolling all night. Pettingill sat on the cramped padded bench between an old Wintun squaw whose clothes reeked of wood smoke and a drummer who sold paint. Across from them was a family—a father, mother and two small children—all asleep. They were well dressed and had said very little. Carpetbag on his lap, Pettingill drowsed, waking briefly whenever his head fell forward. Cool morning air blew past the tied-down leather shades. Vaguely, he was aware the coach was climbing a hill, feeling gravity press him against the seat, and hearing the sharp commands of the driver. As the stage crested the hill, it stopped. Rousing, Pettingill squinted at the sunlight as he peered past the shade. They stood on a sparsely-wooded hillside. He thought that the driver was resting the horses.

"Everybody out, Goddamn it!"

The door jerked open. A man in a white duster, wearing a mask, motioned with a shotgun for the passengers to step down.

"Now, Goddamn it!" he ordered.

Frightened, the passengers stumbled out onto the dirt road to find three men in dusters. One trained a Colt revolving rifle on the driver. The other held a shotgun and the third a handgun. All three wore sacks over their heads with eyeholes cut in them.

"We want the Wells Fargo box," said the man with the rifle.

Hands lifted above the shoulders of his blanket coat, the driver spoke. "There ain't one. Which is why there's no shotgun messenger with me."

"Give us the mail pouch then."

Pettingill glanced from one road agent to the next. With no money box, they would undoubtedly rob the passengers. He held his satchel clutched to his chest, his gun inside the bag. The driver threw down the mail pouch. All three robbers had their eyes on it as it thudded to the ground.

Pettingill lunged, shoving the road agent closest to him. The man fell in a sprawl, losing his revolver. Pettingill sprinted for a clump of oaks at the side of the road, his hat flying off as he ran. The rifle thundered, echoing off the hills.

* * *

Through the tall bay windows, morning light filled the inspector general's office as Blake sat down at his desk, seeing an envelope on top of the blotter. Schaeffer was at his desk, working, as were the other two officers, both captains. Wagner's door was open—the colonel in his office, smoking his pipe and writing. Blake slit the envelope with a brass letter opener and took out a telegraphic summary report. It was from Washington's Department of Records, the response to his inquiry regarding Major Ellis. He skimmed the first few lines, then his eyes stopped.

Ellis wife known secessionist sympathizer. Ellis seen with CS spy, Thaddeus Daniels, on one occasion. No collaboration confirmed. Ellis first-rate QM officer according to fitness reports.

Rising, Blake limped into Wagner's office. The colonel looked up, taking the briar from his mouth.

"Good to see you back, Mr. Blake."

"Sir, here's Major Ellis's record summary. It states he was observed with a Confederate spy." He handed the paper to the senior officer, who scanned the writing.

"My police contact said Ellis was killed for something he knew or saw, since the valuables were left on Ellis's corpse. Could it be he recognized this spy?"

"Yes, but why bother to kill Ellis? The war is over."

"Perhaps there was some personal treachery involved."

"Not according to this record," Wagner said, putting the paper down.

"Or maybe this spy has some devious business afoot here in San Francisco. There're many Southerners who have been reluctant to accept the peace. Look at all the trouble in Texas."

"We don't have enough information to assume anything at this point." Wagner picked up his pipe and resumed smoking. "Wire the Secret Service in Washington to see what you can find out about

Daniels. Unless we know he's in town, we'll end up chasing our tails, and if he is in town, we need to find out why."

"Yes sir."

"Carry on, Mr. Blake."

Blake saluted, which brought a wry smile to Wagner's face. The colonel returned the salute with a cursory two-fingered wave. After limping to the coat stand for his jacket and gun belt, Blake headed for the wire office.

Twenty minutes later, Blake made his way down the corridor to the detectives' bureau, still limping but no longer needing a cane. O'Gara stood in the doorway to the office, his hat on his head. Schmitt was behind him, putting on his coat.

"I've got news," Blake said. "Ellis's service record noted he had an unconfirmed connection to a Confederate spy by the name of Thaddeus Daniels."

O'Gara stepped past the lieutenant but turned and stopped. Schmitt walked by with a silent, unfriendly look at Blake.

"You think this Daniels may be the killer?"

"Could be." Blake shrugged. "The obvious question is why kill anyone now that the war is over?"

"I have to go. Let's meet up at the Bank Exchange at seven this evening."

"All right," Blake said. "What's going on?"

"Three men were shot dead at Yerba Buena Cemetery. We're going over to have a look before they remove the bodies."

"Tonight then," Blake said.

He watched the two men walk quickly away toward the bright glass-paned entrance doors. Slowly, he followed, wondering if the new information would lead to anything.

* * *

Pettingill lay in the warm dust of the sun-lit road. He was bathed in sweat. Or blood. He was unsure. Hot on his face, the sun filled his squinting eyes with fiery light. The raucous voices of the road agents were a confusing babble, excited by the money in his bag. He heard them tramp off, voices dwindling. He was uncertain how many times they had shot him after rolling him onto his back.

Pettingill's chest and stomach were spiked with pain. Groaning, he turned onto his side and then his stomach. He tried to move his legs but could not. Using his hands, he crawled toward the shade of an oak, cursing his weakness. He moved only inches before he stopped, his dripping face falling against the dirt. When he came to, someone was tugging on his arms. Pettingill saw his own boot heels plowing furrows through the dirt. Something firm lodged against his back, and the driver's face loomed before him.

"They've done for you, pard. There's nothing I can do. I've got to get the others to safety. You'll be more comfortable here in the shade. It won't be long now."

Pettingill tried to raise his hand but couldn't. He opened his mouth to plead with the man, to not leave him behind, yet he only managed a groan. He saw the driver walk away as the passengers climbed into the coach. His head fell back against the hard trunk, staring as the coach rolled away, his panic subsiding into fatigue. His eyelids drifted down despite the pain in his torso, bringing darkness.

* * *

Daniels stood at the foot of the wooden staircase leading up to a two-story Italianate house along Dupont near Post Street. Baugh had told him it was one of the better sporting houses in the city. He put his hand on the railing and started to climb the steps but stopped. It had been months since he had lain with a woman. In the few times he had done so since Jeannette, he found the experiences disappointing—the women too coarse in their looks or manners. Yet he had neither the time nor the patience to court any maidens.

He ascended the staircase to the landing and knocked on the door. It was opened by a Negress dressed in a servant's uniform. She showed him into the parlor, taking his hat. A middle-aged man with graying hair and mustache leaned on the mantel of the fireplace, in a black morning suit, looking at a folded newspaper. On the couches surrounding him were several young females in frilly undergarments. The bulge of a holstered firearm was visible beneath the man's cutaway coat. He had a proprietary air and after a moment looked up from his paper.

"Good afternoon, sir." The man stepped forward to shake Daniels's hand.

"Thomas Jackson," Daniels replied, using his favorite *nom de guerre.*

"It's five dollars an hour, Mr. Jackson. For that you can have any girl you wish. Girls, stand up for Mr. Jackson."

The four ladies present stood, hands behind their backs, chests arched. Each wore colorful silk stockings on her legs.

Daniels looked at them, then turned to the proprietor. "Any French girls here?"

The man smiled. "*La femme fatale.* Yes, we have one."

He spoke to the black maid. "Show Mr. Jackson up to Monique's room."

"Yes sir."

Curious, Daniels followed the maid out into the corridor and up the stairs to the second floor. She stopped at a door in the middle of the narrow corridor and knocked.

"Miss Monique, you've got a visitor."

* * *

Daniels lay back on the sheets, catching his breath, staring at the plasterwork fretting along the ceiling and upper walls. Standing naked at the washbasin by her dresser, Monique finished cleaning herself and left the cloth by the bowl. She ran a hand through her red hair, fingering her scalp, and glowered at him.

"I never 'ad a man do that to me before," she said. "Mount me from behind and pull my 'air like I was *un cheval.*"

"Some women like it," Daniels replied, having enjoyed the encounter more than he expected. "Besides, you're not just a horse, you're a filly."

"*Vous êtes l'animal.*"

Smiling, he sat up to clasp his arms about his knees as he regarded her. She was pretty, though not beautiful. Her dark eyes were angry, her full lips pouting. She had freckles on her cheeks and must have worked in the sun at some point in her life.

"Where are you from in France?"

"Rouen," she answered.

"Where you used to work in the fields."

"*Oui*. I came to *Amérique* for an advertisement seeking wives for French miners *en Californie*. Money was sent for my passage, and when I am arriving, M. Josiah met me at the docks and brought me 'ere."

"Where he makes you work until you've paid for your passage."

"*Oui*. I did not come here to be *une prostituée*—a whore."

"The world is full of stories like yours."

"You don't care."

"Why should I?"

He lay down again, reaching for the small cigar he had left on the stand next to the bed. Firing a wooden match on his thumbnail, he lit the cigar and exhaled smoke. Blowing out the match, he dropped it in the ashtray on the stand. He thought of the cemetery yesterday, the moment etched in his memory—the roar of his derringers, their jerking recoil as he shot Hopkins and his henchmen, cool wind on his cheek, smoky stench of burnt powder, men collapsing in the fading light. He understood now why some soldiers got to liking war. The other killings he had been involved with had been quick and brutal—the Yankee informant he executed in Liverpool, the woman he caught skulking outside the Maryland barn where he rendezvoused with two of his agents, the Yankee major from the El Dorado Saloon, and the Swedish hooligan with Liverpool Wilcox. But the cemetery was different—it energized him, made him feel alive. He drew on the cigar and carefully exhaled smoke rings.

"Cigar smoke *est viliane*," Monique said, waving her hand where she stood.

She put on a blue silk robe, hiding her small, round breasts from his view, and sat at her vanity table to frown at herself in the silvery mirror, brushing at the hair on her forehead with her fingertips. Daniels went back to his brooding. He would stay until he finished the cigar.

* * *

Angeline sat with her mother on the parlor sofa as they took tea from the family silver service. In an armchair across from them, Police Captain Lees sipped from a bone china cup. The sunlight through the curtain-framed windows was mellow with the lengthening afternoon. Angeline thought the policeman's features to be homely rather than handsome, but his eyes were kind. He was quiet and respectful.

"More milk, Captain?" Mrs. Whitfield asked.

He raised his hand. "No, thank you."

"What progress have you made on apprehending this dreadful man Pettingill?"

"Initially, the telegraph lines were down between here and San Jose, but once the wires were restored, I sent a cable to the sheriff in San Jose. He detailed a deputy to make inquiries. We believe Pettingill boarded a stagecoach for Los Angeles."

"And will you have him arrested in Los Angeles or somewhere in between?"

"I have wired the Los Angeles constabulary. An officer will meet the stage when it arrives, which should be Friday, I think."

"That's not for two days, sir. What if he gets off the stage before then?"

Lees hesitated as though caught off guard. He started to fiddle with his teacup, then put it aside on the small table next to his chair.

"Well, ma'am, even if he should do that, the driver will be questioned as to where and when Pettingill made such a move."

"And if this odious Pettingill does, it sounds rather likely that he will escape. All he has to do is to get a hold of a horse and he's gone over the Sierra Nevada, with my nephew's money."

Lee's mouth pursed in a frustrated line. "Let me assure you, Mrs. Whitfield, he will be taken into custody. I doubt he knows that word has made it to Los Angeles ahead of him. He will be caught and brought back to San Francisco to stand trial."

Angeline looked at her mother, feeling a stir of panic. Martha raised her teacup, pausing to speak.

"Tried for swindling my nephew?"

"Of course."

"The offense he committed against my daughter must remain a secret."

"Certainly," Lees said, standing. "If you will please pardon me, I must get back to work."

Mrs. Whitfield put down the cup. She rose and escorted the captain to the front door. Angeline stayed seated, staring at the chair Lees had occupied. She closed her eyes, wishing she could go back in time. *She would tell Mrs. Harrington let Pettingill know she was not feeling well and would be unable to join him on the excursion to the Cliff House. If only things could be different.* Yet she knew life did not make such allowances. She damned him, whispering the curse aloud. It was most unfortunate that Jim had not killed him. Then she could have at least had that small satisfaction.

* * *

"Well, we've tried half a dozen hotels. What's next?" Blake said as he followed O'Gara along California Street. The sun had disappeared behind the tall hump of Fern Hill to the west. The sky was pale, its light waning. The gas lamps along the street had yet to be lit.

"Shall we try the Russ Hotel or the Brooklyn House?" Blake asked.

"The American Exchange is closer. And this time I have a name to go with the description."

O'Gara led the way, Blake lagging a half step behind. The smell of cooking food came from the restaurants scattered among the office buildings they passed. The wooden sidewalks were mostly empty except for the few workers heading home.

"Any word from your señorita?" the detective asked, glancing over at Blake.

"I received a letter, but I doubt I'll ever see her again."

O'Gara shrugged as he walked. "Perhaps you can find comfort in the arms of that lovely Negress Janey. She seemed to like you."

Blake shook his head. "A woman like that is not for me. Slow down a bit. My leg hasn't healed yet."

The detective eased his pace. "No Janey? Why not?"

"It would be a betrayal," Blake answered.

"Certainly, the señorita wouldn't hold you to any sort of promise, implicit or otherwise, if she's marrying another man."

"It doesn't matter. I haven't the eyes for any other woman, nor the heart …"

O'Gara looked at him. "I wonder if I was as romantic at your age. How old are you?"

"Twenty-five," Blake answered, annoyed.

"Have you even had a woman?"

"A gentleman doesn't talk about such things," Blake said.

O'Gara laughed. "If so, you're probably the first. Hell, Liam, relax. You're among friends. So you're a virgin, right?'

"There was a girl back in New London, the daughter of the Irish servants who worked at a neighbor's house. Her name was Caitlin. She preferred adventuring in the woods and hunting to sewing or taking tea. I was fifteen and she a little older when we … Never mind."

The detective stopped at the corner as a wagon rattling with empty beer barrels passed through the intersection. "Where is she now?"

"I intended to marry her once I had finished school, although I found the prospect of marriage daunting," Blake said. "She died in a typhoid outbreak back in '57. That seems like a very long time ago."

His eyes solemn, O'Gara nodded. "I guess you will need some time. Let's see if we can find Daniels."

They walked into the lobby of the American Exchange, which was buzzing with voices. Men in suits and women in lavish dresses occupied many of the couches and chairs. Blake and O'Gara approached the desk where the tall, bearded clerk stood watching over the room.

"Hello, George. I'm back about that fellow I'm looking for," O'Gara said. "His name is Thaddeus Daniels."

George nodded. "I believe I saw him this morning. Slender fellow, gray suit, mustache. But it's not Daniels. He's registered under the name of Thomas Jackson."

"What room is he in?"

"Number 213."

"Is he in now?" O'Gara glanced at Blake.

"No. His key is in the mailbox." George gestured to the wide wooden pigeon-holed mail and key box on the counter behind him.

"Give us the key. We'd like to take a look at his room."

The clerk retrieved the key and handed it to O'Gara, who held it up.

"I owe you one, George."

Blake and O'Gara went up the broad carpeted stairs leading to the upper floors. At the second landing, they moved quietly down the gas-lit corridor until they came to the right room. Unclasping his holster,

Blake drew his revolver. O'Gara unlocked the door and pushed it open. The room was spacious. A large double bed with brass head and foot railings sat against the wall, facing the windows. A marble-topped teak bureau with inset mirror stood between the bed and the door. On it was a decorated porcelain bowl and a matching ewer, with hand towels folded neatly next to it. A leather and wood trunk sat at the foot of the bed. On the opposite side of the room was a small fold-down desk, set between the windows. In the corner by the door, a tall stained oak armoire stood with closed doors.

"You take the trunk. I'll search the armoire and desk," O'Gara said.

Holstering his weapon, Blake crossed to the trunk and stiffly knelt. The trunk was unlocked. He lifted the lid and began shifting through the items in the wooden top tray. There was a bone-handled razor; a handful of black, blue, and gray silk cravats; and a leather-bound book. He picked up the book to flip through the pages. There were entries, but they dated back to the war. After lifting out the tray, he searched through some folded clothes.

"Not a goddamned thing," O'Gara cursed softly, standing over the desk's writing board and its bare contents.

The detective stepped over to the armoire but found the doors locked. He glanced at Blake and grinned. Taking a ring of keys out of his pocket, he selected one and inserted it into the lock, but it failed to turn. He tried another, and this time the lock clicked. He opened the door and searched the shadowed interior.

"Liam." O'Gara held up a Spencer carbine. He opened the breach partway, then closed it.

"It's loaded." He put it back inside and began checking the pockets of the clothes hanging there.

"I've got nothing so far," Blake said.

The door to the room creaked as it was pushed wide. Dark-haired and mustached, a man in a gray suit stood the doorway, his eyes angry. O'Gara stepped back from the armoire.

"You! Daniels! Stay put!"

O'Gara hurled himself through the doorway as Daniels turned to run, grabbing Daniels's shoulder. Clinching, they spun in a circle. Pushing himself up, Blake pulled out his revolver as he moved across the room. The two men grunted and snarled, struggling. Daniels had his hand on the policeman's throat. The blast of a pistol shot filled the corridor.

O'Gara fell to the floor, gray smoke roiling above him. Lifting the Adams, Blake aimed to fire. But Daniels ducked beyond the door frame just before the gun went off. Then he leaned back into view, cocking his weapon. Blake flattened himself against the armoire. Daniels's gun roared; a window shattered inside the room. Two more shots thundered, Blake feeling the slugs strike the side of the armoire. The sharp scent of spent powder tainted the air.

"Come on, Billy Yank!" Daniels shouted. "Let's fight!"

Shifting the Adams to his left hand, Blake snapped off a shot as he leaned out. The corridor was hazy with smoke, Daniels's outline elusive. The response was a rebel yell.

Blake pulled back. Two more shots slammed the edge of the armoire, spraying splinters. He crouched to glance out, searching the sulfurous fog, handgun ready. He fired at a shadow, hearing after the loud concussion what might have been a grunt of pain.

Shouts sounded down the corridor, accompanied by the pounding of boots. Blake glimpsed a figure bolt from the eddying smoke, heading in the opposite direction. Rising, he went over to O'Gara. His leg pulled against its stitches as he knelt. The policeman was curled in a fetal ball amid the lingering brimstone.

"Get help!" Blake yelled as George and other men came to a thudding halt around him. "Get a doctor! On the double! Move, damn it!"

Two men pulled away and ran back up the corridor. Ears echoing from the gunfire, Blake put a shaky hand on O'Gara's head. The detective opened his eyes for a moment, then closed them, his face grimaced. Blake felt the stir of panic. He had seen such a look among the wounded in the war. Most of them died.

* * *

Azariah sat in the parlor of his home, sipping brandy from a snifter and reading the newspapers. With the liquor's tang in his mouth, he scanned the headlines and saw nothing unusual other than the discovery of three men killed in a shooting affray at the old Yerba Buena Cemetery. There was no mention of the stolen schooner—now being repainted and gun ports cut in its gunwales—or the men being assembled for its crew. Daniels was meticulous, and so far his planning had proved faultless.

A cabriolet pulled up outside, where a man stepped down and paid the driver. Azariah stood to get a better view, but the street was dark and the gas lamps not much help. The man threw open the picket fence gate and walked quickly to the front door. Azariah went into the entranceway, the Colt five-shot in hand. Outside, the visitor pounded on the door. Holding the small revolver behind his leg, Azariah opened the portal. Daniels pushed his way through, an urgent look on his face.

"What is it?" Azariah asked, shutting the door.

The Georgian drew a sharp breath. "In the parlor."

Once they were behind closed doors, Daniels dropped to the couch, checking the blood-soaked kerchief he pressed to his side.

"Good God, you've been wounded!" Azariah stared, feeling consternation.

Daniels spoke, his voice edged with pain. "Two men were going through my room at the hotel. I was just getting back from supper and noticed the key missing from my box in the lobby. The clerk was helping someone else, so I slipped up the stairs and found them. One was a big fellow, who grabbed me. He might have been a policeman. I had to shoot him to break free. Then I exchanged fire with the other, a Yankee soldier. The sumbitch hit me."

Gathering his wits, Azariah poured a shot of brandy, handed it to Daniels, and left the room. He went into the kitchen, where Mary was cleaning up. Taking a dish towel from one of the cupboards, he told Mary to get her coat and fetch the doctor immediately.

"Right away, sir." Mary began untying her apron.

Azariah went back into the parlor and closed the doors. He heard Mary leave the house, the front latch clicking audibly.

"How bad are you hurt?"

Daniels hadn't touched the brandy on the lamp table beside him. "Hard to say. It's keeps bleeding, and breathing is painful. But there's no bloody froth, so I don't think the ball entered my lung."

"Take this." Azariah held out the cloth. "You know a lot about wounds."

Grasping the towel, the Georgian pressed it to his side. "I read medicine in London for two years before I left school for the Continent."

"I've sent for a doctor. He lives only a few blocks away."

Azariah watched Daniels lift the brandy glass with an unsteady hand. He drank half the glass, then put the snifter down.

"Do you think the police know about our venture?" Azariah asked.

The Georgian shook his head. "I can't think that they know anything. We've been very careful. And I silenced Hopkins before he had a chance to talk, or at least I assume so. However, this bodes ill."

Daniels paused, face clenching. "I don't know why they would be looking for me, or how they could have traced me to my hotel."

"Do you think Wilcox betrayed us?" Azariah hesitated, unsure whether to sit or stand. He remained on his feet.

"Perhaps," Daniels said, wincing again. "But I rather think the Harbor Police would have been waiting for me rather than some Yankee officer. It … might have to do with a man I came across by accident soon after I arrived. I believe his name was Ellis, a major with the quartermaster's department, if memory serves. I approached him during the war about shipping information—his wife was a known sympathizer of Richmond—common enough in capitol society. He ignored my overture."

"Wasn't he was the Army officer found dead near the Barbary Coast last week?"

Daniels's face was pale, his brow glistening with perspiration. "He recognized me in a crowded saloon. But how did the police … ? Must have been a witness I didn't see. Damn it all."

Azariah stared across the room, wondering how much was known of their plan to resurrect the war. He started to speak but stopped. Daniels had lain back on the sofa with his eyes closed.

CHAPTER *13*

Chief Burke stood behind the desk in his immaculate office and bade them sit in the four chairs in a half circle facing the desk. Blake took the seat next to Colonel Wagner while Lees and Schmitt took the other two. Short and barrel-chested, Burke addressed them with a sober look on his bearded face.

"Gentleman, I view the death —the murder—of a police officer in the most serious terms. This maniac, Daniels, will be brought to justice, and, if I have my way, sentenced to hang. It is imperative that we coordinate our efforts and work together."

Years away from his native England had softened Burke's British accent, but it gave his voice a formality that Blake thought matched the man's dark well-tailored suit.

Burke sat. "I have gone over what we know so far with Captain Lees. We believe Daniels is responsible for the murder of Major Ellis, and we know that he killed Detective O'Gara. He was a spy working for Richmond in the late war and perhaps is engaged in some nefarious activity here in our city. We must find him and what he is up to and stop him. Now, I believe you soldiers are not from the provost marshal, is that correct?"

Wagner spoke. "We are from the inspector general's office. However, Lieutenant Blake has the full authority of the provost marshal in this matter. We are ready to commit whatever resources are necessary."

"Very good, Colonel. However, perhaps we should make young Blake here a member of the Special Police to add civil authority to his part of the investigation. Captain Lees, tell us your plan of action."

"I've gone through the few things that were found in Daniels's room at the American Exchange Hotel. There's nothing there to indicate what he is involved in. I intend to check with my informants to see what they may have heard. We do know that he has been at the hotel for the past two weeks. But who he might have been associating with remains unknown. However, we will interview the entire staff." Lees interlaced the fingers of his muscular hands and rested them in his lap.

"Did you get a good look at Daniels?" the chief asked Blake.

He nodded. "Yes sir. He's about five feet ten. Dark-brown hair, slim physique, wears a mustache. He had on a gray suit. He used a Le Mat revolver to kill O'Gara, and in our exchange of gunfire he was recklessly brave."

"Which will require utmost precaution on our part," Burke responded. "Detective Schmitt, have you anything to add?"

The scarred policeman stared at Blake. "Only that if I had been with O'Gara, this Daniels would be dead or in custody."

"Have you seen the armoire in Daniels's room, you arrogant bastard?" Blake said.

"Lieutenant," Wagner cautioned.

"I suggest—no, I insist—that you, Schmitt, make your peace with young Blake here," the chief ordered. "You will be working together. Is that understood?"

Schmitt said nothing for a moment, then nodded.

"All right. A description will be given to all police officers to be on the lookout for Daniels. You three will be the spearhead of the investigation, with whatever assistance from the rest of the force that you may require. Schmitt, you and Lt. Blake are under the direction of Capt. Lees. I expect results, gentlemen, and daily updates on your progress, which I will receive from the captain. Are there any further questions or matters to be discussed?"

The four seated before Burke shook their heads.

"Then let the hunt begin."

* * *

Blake and Col. Wagner left the City Hall, walking along the wooden sidewalks toward California Street. Traffic was brisk along Kearny, wagons and buggies rattling by over the paving bricks. The senior officer moved at an easy pace that Blake could keep up with despite his injured leg. The streets were bright with sunlight, though the air was still cool.

"You look tired, Mr. Blake," the colonel observed.

"It was hard to sleep last night, sir. I rode with Detective O'Gara in an ambulance wagon to the hospital. He quit breathing long before we got there."

"Not an easy thing to do—watch a man die."

"No sir. I kept thinking that if I had acted differently … if I had jumped in while O'Gara was struggling with Daniels and hit the bastard with my gun, O'Gara might still be with us."

"Or Daniels might have shot you both."

"Still, it's hard not to—"

"Lieutenant." Wagner stopped, turning toward him. "You've been in battle. You know how chaotic and relentless it is, and that when a man's time is up, nothing short of a miracle will save him."

Blake nodded, looking out from under the bill of his kepi.

"O'Gara's time was up. Nothing you think or say can change that."

"Yes sir," Blake said.

"Go back to your hotel, son. Get some sleep. Come back to the office after lunch. Things can hang fire for a few hours."

Blake nodded. "Thank you, Colonel."

Minutes after leaving the colonel, Blake made his way along the plank sidewalk of Clay Street to a brick building with a large sign above the doors: Wilson & Evans Gun Makers. Inside the shop, the air was cool and smelled faintly of gun oil. Wood-framed glass display cases divided the front of the room from the back, which had a walk space and built-in shelves full of goods—cans of powder, boxes of paper cartridges, and tins of percussion caps neatly arranged. A No Smoking sign was tacked to the back wall. A stocky man in a blue work shirt and brown canvas apron stood behind the counter, the sleeves rolled up on his muscular forearms. A deep, crooked scar went from his brow down to his cheek.

"Can I help you, Lieutenant?" the man asked, glancing at the gold bars on Blake's shoulders.

Blake scanned the rows of revolvers in the cases as he unclasped his holster and lifted out the Adams, holding it by the trigger guard.

"I need a better weapon."

"The Adams is a fine revolver," the man said, taking and placing the weapon on a small leather mat atop the glass counter.

"Yes, but it's only a five-shot .36. I went up against a man with a Le Mat recently, and I was quite overmatched."

The gunsmith nodded. "A fearsome weapon, the Le Mat. Unfortunately, I don't stock them."

The man looked at the selection of blue-steel revolvers, opened up the case, and removed a Remington .44. He placed it on the mat next to the Adams.

"The finest revolver made, in my opinion. Powerful and accurate, more durable than a Colt."

Blake frowned as he picked up the long-barreled gun. "Too big. I need something I can conceal easily under a coat."

The gunsmith searched the cases again. He moved to another case and took out a pair of Colt Army .44s. They had been modified— the barrels shortened and the grips smaller than factory issue.

"Did the work on these myself for a local gambler. He sold them back to me before leaving town a few weeks ago." He placed the pair on a separate mat.

Blake picked one up. It was heavy but compact. He aimed at the wall and noticed he could hold it steady, even with his right hand.

"I cut the barrels down to five and a half inches, shortened the loading levers, and soldered on taller front sights so that they hit dead center at fifty feet. The grips are from a set of Colt Navys. The Le Mat carries nine rounds. These two will give you twelve. With forty grains of powder under each ball, you'll have some real firepower."

Blake nodded, holding one in each hand. "These will do nicely."

The gunsmith pursed his lips. "All right, then. Since I'm a veteran myself, of the Long Walk down in Mexico, I will make you a deal. I'll take your Adams in trade and charge you fifteen dollars for the Colts. How's that?"

"Perfect." Blake placed the revolvers on the mat and pulled the wallet from his trouser pocket. "I'll need a pair of holsters."

The gunsmith gestured toward the street. "There's a leather goods place just across the way. He can make a pair to your specifications."

"I'll need round-ball .44s and percussion caps."

"You want a bullet mold?"

Blake shook his head. "Maybe later."

The gunsmith wrapped the Colts in paper and bundled them with several tins of caps and small cartons of .44 bullets. He wrapped it all together with more paper and tied it with twine. Blake handed him fifteen dollars in bank notes.

The gunsmith placed the money into a partitioned drawer. "Of course, the thing you have to watch out for on a Le Mat is that second, shorter barrel that the cylinder rotates around. It's a twenty bore. Filled with buckshot, it will kill you and your neighbor. Perhaps you should consider a rifle as well."

Blake gave him a grim smile. "I've just acquired a Spencer carbine, which used to belong to the fellow who carries the Le Mat."

"Well, then, good luck, son."

* * *

Azariah carried a tray with biscuits, eggs, bacon, and coffee into the spare second-story bedroom, which faced the backyard. Daniels was still asleep. The doctor had given him a dose of laudanum to ease his pain. Azariah placed the tray on the wooden dresser adjacent to the bed. As the floorboards creaked under Azariah's shoes, Daniels jerked awake with an anguished cry. He clutched the swath of badges about his ribs, wincing as he slowly sat up.

"Easy, hoss," Azariah said. "You've been asleep for ten hours."

Daniels put a hand to his forehead. "I was dreaming—nightmares—of drowning at sea, the way my lady died."

"You're safe for now. I brought you some breakfast. Better eat it while it's still warm." Azariah placed the tray in Daniels's lap, then stacked the beds pillows behind him.

The Georgian picked up a fork and began slowly working on his eggs. Azariah sat in a chair by the windows, watching his guest.

"You're going to have to leave town, you know," Azariah said. "I'm sure Cicero will put you up. It's in the morning papers. That detective you shot died on the way to St. Mary's Hospital. The police will be looking for you."

Daniels chewed and swallowed, then shook his head. "I'll be more effective if I stay in town."

Astonished, Azariah stared. "Have you lost your mind? You could jeopardize the whole plan. You killed a detective. The whole force will be searching for you, and they know what you look like!"

Daniels lifted his coffee cup carefully. He sipped, then spoke. "I've played cat-and-mouse with the police before—when I was operating in Liverpool. I'll change my appearance. Let my hair get long, grow out my beard. It's worked before."

"You're serious, aren't you?"

"Of course I am." Daniels ate another forkful of eggs and picked up a piece of bacon.

"It's too risky."

"Nonsense," Daniels replied. "I'll dress like one of those dock loafers, and no one will know the difference. Besides, all my clothes are still back at the hotel."

Azariah shook his head. "Well, I hope you will at least rest here until your wound has begun to heal."

Daniels smiled. "As for that, I'm afraid you're stuck with me for a few days. What will you tell the maid?"

"That a friend was injured by a Barbary Coast ruffian and is staying here until he is well enough to go home."

* * *

A steady breeze moved along the terraced lanes of Lone Mountain Cemetery. Marble headstones and stout white crosses were laid out in orderly rows and sections, with decorative plots of grass and flowers between them. Macadamized roads wound through the many land-scaped acres. Jim Sanders stood to the side, hat in hand, while Martha and Angeline said a final prayer at the grave of Richard Whitfield, husband and father. Martha knelt to place a bouquet of flowers into a metal holder that was mounted at the foot of the headstone. They walked quietly back to the Whitfield carriage, where Jim held the door and handed the ladies up into the vehicle. The sun was lost momentar-ily behind a tattered band of gray cumulus clouds staining the clean blue skies.

Climbing in, Jim shut the carriage door and settled into the padded leather seat, opposite his aunt and cousin. The carriage began to roll along the smooth cemetery road.

"I heard that Capt. Lees came to tea the other day. Did he have anything useful to relate about the investigation?" he asked.

Martha glanced at him, an introspective expression on her lined face. "He made a lot of excuses and some unfounded assurances that the man would be caught."

Jim smiled wryly. "I had a similar experience with the police myself. Damn little information and damn little effort. So I decided to take matters into my own hands again."

Angeline looked up at him, the dark bonnet she wore shadowing her face. He saw the interest in her eyes.

"I've hired a private detective to track down Pettingill, to see him brought to justice."

"What did you tell him?" Angeline asked.

"That I had been robbed of a small fortune … and that Pettingill had acted inappropriately with you. I did not elaborate."

Angeline sat back, her face displeased.

"Do you really think this private detective will find the man?" Martha asked.

"He has more incentive than our local constables: five dollars a day, plus expenses. He took the train to San Jose yesterday morning. Or so he said in a telegram I received last night. The man is a former Pinkerton agent. I think he will deliver the goods."

Martha stared at her nephew. "If this blackguard is found and tried, there must be no mention of Angeline."

"Understood," Jim said. "When he's caught and brought back to the city, I'll see to it that he suffers for what he did, even if he's found innocent. Though I don't see how any judge or jury could."

"Suffers how?" Angeline asked.

"You needn't concern yourself, Cousin. Suffice it to say, he will weep with regret for what he has done."

* * *

It was early afternoon when Blake entered the inspector general's office and found Detective Schmitt standing in the doorway to Wagner's office, talking with the colonel.

Blake wore his dark school suit and a new hat with a creased crown and a medium brim. Beneath his coat at the small of his back, he carried the Colts in new holsters. He had managed a few hours of sleep and was stopping to report in before heading over to the Hall of Justice.

"Well, Lieutenant, you're finally back," Schmitt said.

Glancing at the policeman, Wagner stepped out of his office. "Mr. Blake, why are you out of uniform?"

"Sir, the uniform marks me. Daniels will see me coming a hundred yards away. In mufti, I'll be less discernible."

"Good point," Wagner conceded.

"That's a mighty stylish hat," Lt. Schaeffer said, smiling.

Blake gave him a stern look, which made the older man smile all the more.

"There's work to be done." Schmitt nodded to the colonel and headed for the door. Blake gave the senior officer an informal salute and followed the policeman down the marble corridor.

Out on the street, Blake tried to keep up with Schmitt as they walked down California Street then turned at Front, heading north.

"Can you ease up? I still have stitches in my leg," Blake said to Schmitt's back, who was two paces ahead.

The detective turned and stopped. "Sure thing, soldier boy. Let's get a few things straight while we're at it. When we're working together, I run the show. You do what I tell you to, savvy? You're the greenhorn; I'm the detective. As far as I'm concerned, you got O'Gara killed and let this Daniels get away. You've got a lot to make up for."

Blake stood, hands clenched into fists. If he hadn't been under orders to work with Schmitt, he would have punched him in the face. Instead, he nodded while his jaw muscles flexed.

"All right. Where are we going now?" he asked, keeping his voice neutral.

"Lees and I interviewed most of the hotel staff, but turned up nothing. There's a dock loafer I want to talk to. He can usually be found around the Vallejo Street Wharf."

"Does he have a name?" Blake asked.

Schmitt looked at him but did not answer. He started walking while Blake tried to keep pace.

Blake was damp with perspiration by the time they reached the busy dock of the Vallejo Wharf. Hawsered to the pylons, tall-masted ships lined the wharf, many of their cross-trees still hung with half-furled sails, which moved lazily in the breeze. Off-loaded bales, barrels, and crates crowded the broad planks of the dock. Stevedores loaded mule-drawn wagons and carts with the goods as sailors watched from the decks of the creaking ships. Seated along the low railings and on piles of unused nets, bearded loafers sat watching the action, smoking cigarettes, and looking out from beneath battered hats with eyes that missed nothing. Halfway down the pier, Schmitt walked over to a dark-skinned man in frayed clothes seated on a short keg. He had brown eyes, a pointed beard, and unruly hair, topped by a sun-faded sea cap. His massive shoulders strained the fabric of his worn work shirt. Taking the blackened corncob pipe from his mouth, he nodded to Schmitt.

"Juan Serrano, meet Mr. Blake. He's with the U.S. government."

The loafer's eyes shifted to Blake and he nodded again, replacing the pipe to his lips.

Schmitt placed a silver dollar on the wooden rail next to Serrano and covered it with his booted foot. "We need information, amigo.

Have you noticed anything lately, heard any scuttle-butt in the local saloons?"

Serrano took the pipe from his mouth, glanced at the small char of tobacco, and slipped it into the pocket of his shirt. "Like what?"

"Anything. Whatever the locals are jawing about."

Serrano squinted up at the detective. "Lots of wharf rats are talking about the schooner that went missing. It just vanished one night last week. Could be the owner sailed her out through the gate; only, it was reported stolen in the papers."

"What else have you got?"

Serrano folded his thick forearms across his chest. "There's talk about Hopkins, the oyster pirate, turning up dead. Word has it he was helping refit a ship. The two Flannery brothers were with Hopkins when he was found."

"We're already working on that one. What else?"

Serrano shrugged. "There was a dead body lying in the sand under the piers over by Pacific Street. Looked to be a sailor from his clothes. Had his head stove in."

"I'll let the Harbor Police handle that one."

Serrano looked up, squinting again. "So, have I earned the beer money?"

"No," Schmitt said, but he lifted his foot from the rail, exposing the coin. "Keep your ears open. We're looking for anyone who knows or heard anything about the fellow who murdered O'Gara. Get me information on that, and I'll give you a half eagle."

"All right." Serrano picked up the silver dollar and pushed it into his pants pocket. Blake noticed the thick handle of a Bowie knife sticking up from the belt around Serrano's hips.

"Let's go," Schmitt muttered.

The two men walked back up the pier while work continued around them.

"Think the stolen sloop might be significant?" Blake asked.

Schmitt looked at him with scornful eyes. "I don't see any connection to the son of a bitch who shot O'Gara."

"Then Serrano wasn't much help."

"He's had better information. The dollar was a down payment."

"What do these dock loafers do all day?" Blake asked.

"Most of them are petty thieves and drunks, begging for pennies. Sometimes they run errands for the sailors and ships' officers. Can't figure Serrano though."

"How's that?"

"See that knife on his hip? He's known as the best knife fighter along the wharves, carved up plenty of men foolish enough to take him on. What I don't understand is why he isn't running a gang of toughs."

"Maybe he is."

"What would you know about it?"

* * *

Azariah and Baugh entered Daniels's bedroom after briefly knocking on the door. They took the chairs on each side of the bed while Daniels sat up, grimacing with the effort. Through the window looking onto the backyard, the evening shadows had gathered over the city.

"I wanted to see how you were faring," Baugh said, whose work clothes were dusty.

The bandages wrapped around Daniels's chest were spotted with blood. He looked down at them. "I suppose I was lucky."

"The doctor said the other fellow's powder must have been damp. Otherwise a ball at close range would have perforated the lung," Azariah said.

"Anything among your possessions that would tip the authorities to our little secret?" Baugh asked.

Daniels shook his head. "I learned long ago not to write anything down. How are things going in San Mateo?"

Baugh sat back, running a hand tiredly through his hair. "Things are busy, but there's still a lot more to be done. The carpenters have changed the name of the boat to the *Massauga*. It was Cicero's suggestion. We need an extra set of sails to be made. And we still need a pilot to sail her safely out of the bay, as well as someone who knows celestial navigation. The cannons have arrived with fifty shells for each, but we need more gunpowder. At least another thirty kegs. And Cicero's insisting that we have cutlasses and pikes."

Daniels smiled. "Does he want a black wig and a tri-corner hat so that he can dress as Blackbeard?"

The Texan made a dismissive gesture. "He's an arrogant son of a bitch, that's for sure. He wants boarding weapons."

"Well," Daniels said, "once I'm back on my feet, I'll see if I can't find some."

"Meanwhile, Mr. Baugh and I can start looking for a pilot and a mate." Azariah folded his arms. "We should change your bandage."

Daniels nodded. "I wouldn't mind something to eat first."

"Aren't either of you concerned about the police? They'll be as eager as bloodhounds to find our friend here. We've got to stay ahead of them." Baugh leaned his elbows onto his knees.

Azariah looked at Baugh. "Don't you have a connection, someone on the force who can keep us apprised?"

"Yes, but it will take money. More than I have at the moment, not having sold any work for the last two weeks."

"How much?" Daniels asked.

"That's a good question," Baugh answered. "Offering too much might imply collusion or guilt."

"Why not ask him outright?" Azariah suggested. "Tell him you are working on a story for the *Morning Call*. If the fellow refuses to talk, offer him ten dollars. Tell him you're hoping to scoop the other reporters."

"And if he still refuses, offer him more," Daniels said. "Make it known that you're willing to pay for information."

Baugh shook his head. "We have to be very careful with this. One of their own has been killed. The wrong word and we could have the whole force on top of us."

"Still, knowing what they do will be invaluable," Daniels said.

"Working as a news reporter following up on the killing of this detective is the perfect guise," Azariah said.

"Well," Baugh sighed. "Let me see what I can do."

* * *

In his shirtsleeves, Blake sat at the table in his gas-lit hotel room. A tumbler and a pint bottle of Cutter's Whiskey stood on the table, the glass almost empty. An ink pot, a steel pen, and a sheet of paper were in front of him. On the paper, he had written the words: *Dearest Elena.* Staring at the blank page, he took another sip of the whiskey. He picked up the pen, held it uncertainly, then put it down, covering his face with his hand.

A knock sounded at the door. He looked up, thinking it somehow might be her. Rising, he moved quickly to the door.

"Elena?" he said as he opened it.

Captain Lees nodded hello from where he stood.

"Come in," Blake said, stepping back, crestfallen.

Lees glanced at Blake as he entered the room. "Are you all right?"

"Just tired and a little drunk."

"I was on my way home," Lees said. "I found this tucked into one of Daniels's folded shirts."

Lees pulled a photograph from his pocket. Framed in pressed cardboard, it contained a sepia-tinged image of a young man dressed in a white tie and tails, seated in a chair, a beautiful dark-haired young woman standing next to him, her hand on his shoulder. She wore a splendid gown that displayed her smooth shoulders and a saucy bit of cleavage. The picture had a hallmark in the lower corner from a Parisian studio.

"Is that the man who killed O'Gara?" Lees asked.

Blake nodded. "He's older now and sports a mustache. But that's him."

The police captain smiled in a feral way. "We've got the bastard now. I'll have copies made and distributed to everyone on the force."

Blake handed back the picture. Lees studied him, concern in the detective's eyes.

"Go easy on the bottle, Lieutenant. I need you to work tomorrow."

"Understood."

"Try to get some sleep. Good night."

Blake shut the door as the policeman left. He walked back to the table and sat, staring at the paper and pen.

Chapter 14

Colonel Wagner strolled down the hallway to the office. He had his kepi in hand and was unbuttoning his tunic in preparation for the day's work, yet his mind kept going back to the formal dinner he attended the night before. Seated next to the elegant wife of a local alderman, he had spent most of the meal talking with her when she surreptitiously placed her hand on his thigh under the table, smiling as she looked at him. Shaking his head, Wagner entered the office. Schaeffer and Blake were at their desks, but the two captains were not in yet.

Blake approached him, a serious look on his face. "Sir, I've got the Secret Service report on Daniels," he said, handing the document to the colonel. "He's a very dangerous man, as we already know."

Wagner scanned the written words.

Known member of the Knights of the Golden Circle. Implicated in murder of US Consul informant in Liverpool shipyards. Left England in May 1863. Known to have run spy ring in Maryland from 1863 to 1865. Believed to have assassinated Union female operative in October 1864. Not seen in Washington environs since July 1864. Known to have close ties to Capt. Bulloch, CSN, and other CS naval officers.

He looked up from the report. "Who are the Knights of the Golden Circle?"

"I'm afraid I don't—" Blake started to answer when Schaeffer spoke up.

"They are a secret society of Southern men, sir. Before the war, they intended to conquer various lands around the United States, such as Mexico and Cuba, and bring these territories into the Union as slave-holding states. There was a book about the Knights published a few years back. I read it."

"Tell us more, Lieutenant," the colonel said.

Schaeffer put down his pen. "Besides colonizing various Latin countries, they intended to establish a monopoly of certain vital commodities: tobacco, cotton and sugar. And as the territories became states, the South would have more seats in Congress."

"Sounds a little farfetched," Blake said.

"Perhaps, but they were in deadly earnest. The members swear an oath on penalty of death to advance this cause. Certainly you've heard of William Walker, the filibusterer who conquered Nicaragua. I believe he was one of them."

"I'll be damned," Wagner muttered as he entered his office, a meditative frown on his face.

After hanging up his coat and cap, he sat at his desk, staring at the report as he filled his briar pipe with tobacco. Blake stood in the doorway.

"Sir, Daniels seems to have ties to the Confederate Navy. Perhaps he's planning some sort of naval operation. There was a ship that went missing recently. Schmitt and I talked to an informant down on the docks. Schmitt dismissed it, but I'm not so sure we should."

"You say a boat went missing?"

"A schooner. Stolen off Meigg's Wharf last Sunday. I looked up the article this morning."

"Interesting coincidence. I think you should show this report to Captain Lees. Perhaps Daniels is in town to engineer some sort of outrage with the help of local Confederate sympathizers. Maybe Daniels can be found through one of the locals," Wagner said, handing the report back to the lieutenant.

"I'll take it to Captain Lees right now." Blake folded the sheet into thirds.

"Let me know what the captain decides to do, Mr. Blake."

"Yes sir."

* * *

Blake found Capt. Lees and Schmitt at a small restaurant along Portsmouth Square, idling over their coffee. The establishment was nearly empty. Several of the waiters stood talking among themselves by the kitchen doors. Blake approached Lees's table and handed him the report.

"We've just received this from the Secret Service in Washington. It concerns Daniels."

Blake remained standing. Schmitt glanced up without greeting him. Lees tugged musingly at his chin whiskers as he read the report. When he finished, he looked up.

"I've had dealings with the Knights of the Golden Circle before," Lees said, frowning. "With the Chapman affair."

"Daniels has ties to the Confederate Navy, and a schooner was stolen last week. Of course, Auguste Dupin over there"—Blake gestured to Schmitt—"dismissed it when an informant brought it up yesterday."

Lees glanced over at the detective. Schmitt's face looked irritated.

"If we want to find Daniels, shouldn't we start questioning known Confederate sympathizers?" Blake asked.

"Don't tell us our job, sonny—" Schmitt began.

Lees held up a hand to stop him. "The lieutenant is right. We'd better bring in all the local Copperheads. I'll make a list and so should you, then we'll combine them. We should talk to the other detectives as well to see if we've left anyone off. Then we can start bringing them in."

Lees dropped his napkin onto the table and stood. "Lieutenant, this will take us an hour or so. Can you stop in at the provost marshal's office to see if they have a list of suspected Confederate spies or supporters—locals they might have had watched?"

"I'll see what I can find," Blake answered.

"Meet us back at our offices once you have anything."

Blake nodded and turned to leave. He smiled as he went out the door, savoring the angry look on Schmitt's face when Lees had silenced him.

* * *

Azariah had just sat down to his midday dinner, when someone knocked roughly on the door. He hesitated a moment, feeling uncertain, then put his napkin on the table and called to Mary, who was working in the kitchen, saying that he would get it. He walked into the entryway and opened the door. A man in a suit stood on the wooden porch next to a uniformed policeman with a visored cap.

"Mr. Dekker?" asked the detective. "Can we come in?"

* * *

Daniels woke as voices carried from the hallway on the first floor. He scrambled out of bed, his pulse surging in his temples. Wrapping a flannel robe over himself, he jerked open the drawer of the nightstand to snatch up the Le Mat. Heart hammering, he softly opened the door and slipped out into the hallway. Pressed up against the wall, he moved forward until he was able to see into the front hall, where Azariah stood facing two policemen.

"What is this about?" Azariah asked.

"We are making inquiries into a recent incident, and we're hoping you can shed some light on it for us," the detective answered.

"I doubt I can help you. My wife is an invalid. I spend my time caring for her."

"Still, if you would accompany us to the headquarters."

"I don't see why."

"You used to be the editor of the *Democratic Press*, a newspaper that was outspoken in its support of the Confederacy in the recent war of rebellion. Isn't that true?" the uniformed officer stated.

The detective shot a reprimanding look at the constable. "We just want to ask some questions. Would you like to get your hat before we go?"

"I've just sat down for my dinner. Come back later."

"Get your hat," the detective said.

"Now, you secessionist son of a bitch," the constable added.

Daniels hooked his thumb over the hammer of the Le Mat. If they laid hands on Azariah, he would open fire. But, injured as he was, he doubted he could kill both men before one of them escaped out the door.

"All right." Azariah reached for the low topper hanging on the wall rack beside the door.

"Is there anything wrong, Mr. Dekker?"

Daniels recognized Mary's voice. She must have emerged from the kitchen but stayed by the door, as Daniels couldn't see her.

"No. I'll be back in a few hours. Save my dinner for me."

Before she could respond, Dekker walked out of the house, hat in hand. The two policemen followed him out, closing the door behind them. Daniels released his breath in an agonized sigh and let his head fall back against the wall. His racing heart slowed while he took deep breaths. He stayed against the wall for a moment, then walked back to his room. Something had to be done for Azariah. Daniels put the revolver down and started to dress, moving carefully to avoid aggravating his wound.

* * *

Blake followed as Capt. Lees walked toward the open loading bay of the Isle of Skye Warehouse on Falcon Street, leaving the landau and its driver waiting at the curb of the boardwalk. A warehouse man in a leather apron halted them at the door.

"What is it you want?" he asked.

"We're here to see Mr. Guthrie," Lees answered.

"He's busy right now."

Lees opened his coat to show his police badge pinned to his vest. "Will he come to the door, or do we go to his office?"

The warehouseman turned and called to another man moving some crates with a handcart. "Hey, get the boss. There's some gents want to see him."

Lees turned to Blake while they waited at the warehouse door. "O'Gara's funeral is tomorrow at St. Mary's. Will you be there?"

Blake nodded, troubled by his memories.

"It's a hell of a loss for the department. We're taking up a collection for his widow and orphan, if you want to contribute."

Blake mused for several seconds. "Is twenty dollars enough? I'm a little short of funds this week."

"That will do just fine."

Mr. Guthrie was a small, slender man with a fine white beard. He wore a dark-brown suit and a narrow-brimmed hat.

"What do ye want?" he asked in a Highlands accent.

"Your name has come up in the course of an investigation. We would like for you to accompany us downtown to discuss the matter," Lees said.

"Am I under arrest?"

"No. But if you refuse to cooperate, I will arrest you."

Guthrie snorted dismissively. "I've naething to hide."

"Then if you would step into this carriage, we will be on our way."

The aproned warehouseman appeared in the doorway, a wooden sledge handle gripped in his fist. "Any trouble here, Mr. Guthrie?"

"There is nane. Go back to werk. I'll be along."

Guthrie opened the door to the landau and climbed in. Lees followed, as did Blake, who kept his eye on the man in the doorway until he was in the carriage.

* * *

Henry Baugh climbed the staircase inside the boardinghouse where he lived on Trenton Alley, a block past Chinatown. He untied his cravat as he walked down the hall and stopped as he saw Daniels leaning against the wall beside the door to his room. The Georgian's face was pale and tired.

Baugh hurried the rest of the way. "What are you doing here? You should be in bed."

Daniels gave him a pained smile. "I found it expeditious to leave my former quarters."

Henry unlocked the door, pushing it open for his companion to enter.

Once inside, Daniels sat on the neatly made-up bed while Baugh closed the door. Taking off his hat and coat, he hung them on the door pegs.

"The police took Azariah away an hour ago, for questioning," Daniels said. "As to what, they didn't say, but mentioned his being the editor of *The Democratic Press*."

Baugh turned the chair at his small desk so that its back faced Daniels and sat down. "I was at police headquarters this morning. Something's going on, but the flatfoots wouldn't say what."

"Were you able to contact your connection there?"

"I was asked to leave."

"What are we going to do about Azariah?"

"Hire a lawyer and get him released," Baugh answered. "I'll handle that. Meanwhile, you need to find quarters somewhere. I used to work for *The Democratic Press*, so they may come looking for me here. I may be arrested as well."

Daniels frowned, irritation in his voice. "Damn it all. Things were going fine until those idiots showed up at my hotel room."

Baugh stood, taking his coat from the door and putting it on. He pulled the cravat from his pocket and began re-tying it as he looked in the mirror above his dresser.

"Stay here and rest for a half an hour. I know a lawyer I can engage for Azariah and for myself, if necessary. As for new rooms, I'd stay away from the hotels by the wharves. They're dives and probably being watched by the police. Try a boardinghouse. There's several good, respectable ones over by Second Street. You can use me as a reference."

Daniels sat holding his hand to his vest where his wound was. "All right. I'll send word once I'm settled in my new surroundings."

Baugh opened a drawer of the dresser and retrieved a slender squared-toothed key. He handed it to Daniels.

"It's my spare. Turn the lock on your way out and slide it under the door."

Taking his hat, Baugh opened the door, glanced at Daniels, and left.

* * *

Dark and crowded, the holding cell reeked of urine from the slops bucket in the corner. Azariah leaned against the wall while others sat on the filthy floor. Most of the men in the cell were old acquaintances, and none knew why they had been picked up. One inmate, in slovenly clothes, slumped in the corner opposite the bucket. His back was against the wall, his face resting on his forearms laid atop his knees. A battered hat covered his head. Azariah had to wonder why the man didn't move.

Through the cluster of muttering men, Mr. Guthrie approached him. They shook hands.

"D'ye know what this is about?" the Scot asked.

"I haven't the foggiest."

"Perhaps those guns—"

Azariah made a cutting motion with his hand, which stopped Guthrie. He tipped his chin toward the man in the corner.

"Oh," the warehouse owner said. Then he whispered, "An informant?"

Azariah nodded in a slight motion.

"Aye."

They regarded each other silently, then Mr. Guthrie walked on. A half an hour passed, and conversation among the prisoners waned. Keys jangled outside, the lock clicked, and the door opened.

"Azariah Dekker. Front and center," the guard ordered.

A uniformed policeman led him up to a room on the first floor just past the detectives' office. The room was windowless, not much bigger than a closet, and lit by a single gas jet. It held a small wooden table separating three chairs. On one side of the table sat a young man in a suit and a stocky fellow Azariah recognized as Capt. Lees. The table surface was scarred and darkly spotted in places, which looked like dried blood. Hesitantly, Azariah took the single seat while the uniformed officer shut the door.

"What am I being charged with?" Azariah asked.

"Nothing yet," Lees replied. "You've been detained for questioning."

"Regarding what?"

The policeman stared at him, then finally spoke. "Do you know a man named Thaddeus Daniels?"

Azariah thought for a moment and shook his head. "I do not."

"What about the Knights of the Golden Circle? I believe you once belonged to the organization."

"That was before the war."

"And now?" the young man asked.

"What would be the point? General Lee surrendered a year ago," he replied. "The Confederate government collapsed shortly thereafter."

"Others may not have given up. This man, Daniels, killed a policeman recently. He is known to be a Knight. Perhaps he has contacted you."

"He has not. As I said, I do not know the man."

"Yet, you support the goals of the Golden Circle," Lees said.

Azariah regarded the policeman with steady eyes. "The cause was lost at Appomattox Courthouse, sir. There would be no point in taking up arms again. Besides, my way of supporting the cause was not with the sword or the musket but with the pen and the printing press. But when my offices were smashed by rioters last April with the news of Lincoln's assassination, I gave up the struggle. I lost a son in the war. I've lost my position and occupation. I'm through with making sacrifices. If others are still striving, then they are fools."

Lees nodded, though his eyes looked unconvinced.

"A schooner went missing recently. Know anything about that?" the young man asked.

Azariah shifted his gaze to the gent's face. "I don't follow waterfront matters. My days are taken up with caring for my invalid wife."

The young man glanced at Capt. Lees.

"If there are no more questions, I would like to go home. I have things to do," Azariah said.

"I'm afraid that won't be possible, sir," Lees said. "I don't believe you when you say you know nothing of these matters."

* * *

It was late afternoon when Baugh entered the German Saloon. The establishment had only a scattering of patrons. Baugh saw the man he sought sitting at a table close to the bar, eating a sandwich and drinking from a stein of beer. He had heard rumors about Schmitt—that he did favors for money. Baugh knew a pimp whose girls worked along Belden Alley, who said he paid Schmitt regularly to leave him and his soiled doves alone. Taking a chair at the table, Baugh smiled while the detective regarded him with wary blue eyes.

"What do you want?" Schmitt asked.

"Henry Baugh," he said. "I'm writing for the *Morning Call* these days."

"I know who you are."

"I'm following up on the murder of Detective O'Gara. Has there been any progress?"

The detective gazed at him, a look of ironic amusement on his pitted face. "We're following some leads. Talking to people who might have information."

"So no real progress yet?"

Schmitt picked up his beer to take a long sip, then put the mug down. "I have to wonder why you're asking."

Baugh lifted his palms. "I'm following the story. O'Gara is news."

"There's list of people to be questioned regarding O'Gara's murder. Your name is on it."

"Why would my name be on it?"

Schmitt leaned forward. "You tell me."

"How the Hell would I know?" Baugh said.

The detective sat back, picking up his beer again. "We know who killed Tom O'Gara. It's just a matter of finding him."

"Can you tell me who this man is?"

Schmitt stared at him.

"Look, this story means a lot to me," Baugh said. "I haven't been producing much lately. I was down with a fever for a couple of weeks. My editor told me my job is in jeopardy. I can pay for information if I have to."

Taking another swallow of beer, the detective set the mug precisely atop the wet ring on the table. "How much?"

Baugh shrugged. "Ten dollars?"

"You're wasting my time."

"That's all I can afford right now," he said. "Can you tell me who else is on the list?"

"I might … for ten dollars. But you couldn't print the information. On second thought, forget it."

"How about twenty-five?"

"I thought ten was the limit," Schmitt said.

"Well, it would be all of my rent money but—"

"Let's see the cash."

Baugh took out his wallet and placed ten dollars in bank notes on the table. He dug another fifteen in half eagles and silver dollars out of his pockets. Schmitt drank more beer, his eyes patient and scornful.

"There's a few other names you might recognize on it besides your own," the policeman said. "Your old editor, Dekker, for one. W. O. Biddle is another. Jonah Farnum. But you can't print any of this."

Baugh frowned. "I should have kept my money. You've told me nothing. None of those men are killers."

"*Caveat emptor*," replied Schmitt, sweeping the coins into his palm and picking up the bank notes.

A waiter approached the table, but Baugh waved him away. He stood, pushing in his chair, looking angrily at the detective, then he strode toward the door.

"Nice doing business with you." Schmitt laughed.

* * *

It was early evening when Azariah stepped through the doors of City Hall. Relieved, he inhaled the fresh, cool air. His head ached, and he was brutishly hungry. The lawyer who had seen to his release had told him Baugh was waiting to speak to him across the street in Portsmouth Square.

Azariah checked the street for traffic and crossed the cobbles to the broad incline of the plaza, which was surrounded by an iron grille fence. He passed through the open gate, walking along the sandy ground past triangular lots of shrubbery and trees. He saw his bene-factor leaning against a short decorated iron post. Baugh's hat was pushed back on his head.

"Are you all right?" Baugh asked.

Azariah stopped beside him, sighing wearily. "I don't know how many hours they had me boxed up, answering questions, but it felt like an eternity. I denied everything, but they wouldn't let me leave until your lawyer, Drake, showed up. Good lord, I'm famished."

"There's a restaurant just across the street. Let's get some supper." Baugh stood.

Azariah looked at him. "Thank you for getting me out of there."

Baugh smiled. "I paid the lawyer a retainer and then got cleaned out greasing Detective Schmitt's palm. However, his information was useless. He said they know who killed O'Gara and that they were work-ing from a list of suspects. Apparently both our names are on the list. Supper's on you, by the way."

"Gladly. Is Daniels still at my house?"

Baugh shook his head. "After the police brought you in, he showed up on my door. I sent him off to look for rooms elsewhere."

"We've another problem. Guthrie's in custody. If he talks, we're doomed."

"Do you think he will?"

"I doubt it, but nothing is certain. If they find out about the guns, it would be very damning for us."

Baugh pulled his hat lower. "I'll see if I can find that attorney and get Guthrie released. I'll meet you in the restaurant in a half an hour or so. If I don't show, then I'll have been arrested and you'll know Guthrie's talked."

Azariah watched uneasily as the Texan walked back toward City Hall, admiring the man's calm courage.

CHAPTER 15

Blake dismounted from his rented horse and tied the reins to a section of wooden fence that stood abandoned in the dunes past Washerwoman's Lagoon. He had ridden straight from O'Gara's funeral service at St. Mary's Church, having no interest in the wake. Strong afternoon sunlight made the grayish-white sand luminous as he walked toward the distant blue bay waters. Try as he might, he could not rid himself of the sight of the lacquered wood coffin before the candle-lit altar and the anguished gasping of O'Gara's widow.

Yards ahead, a bleached hunk of wood sat upright in the sand. He took the Colt revolvers from the holsters at his back, their weight pleasing in his palms. He cocked, aimed, and fired the one on his right. The concussion was sharp in his ears as the Colt recoiled, wreathed in gray vapor. Splinters jumped from the wooden target. Alternating right and left, he continued shooting. The .44s were alive in his hands, spitting fire, smoke, and death. The driftwood jerked and spewed chips. When the Colts were empty, he stared at the splintered and pocked target, the bay breeze cold against his face and ringing ears. He prayed God would grant him one last encounter with Daniels.

* * *

Jim Sanders stood at the bar of the Occidental Saloon, staring at the dark gleaming wood. His whiskey and soda fizzed, the glass beaded with condensation. *You can't undo the past,* he told himself. A hand touched his shoulder, causing him to start. The old detective, Callard, stood next to him—the man's worn top hat at a jaunty slant.

"Did you find him?" Sanders asked, glancing at the man's face and looking away from his grisly eye.

"Yes, I did," Callard said. "But not above ground."

He pulled a newspaper clipping from his pocket. Sanders took it from him, feeling puzzled. It read:

MURDERED. *Francis Pettingill was killed by road agents during a stage coach robbery north of San Luis Obispo. Three men halted the coach and were set to rob the passengers when Pettingill broke and ran. The robbers fired their weapons, bringing down the unfortunate man. Four bullets found their mark, and Pettingill breathed his last.*

Jim looked up from the clipping in his hands. "You're sure of this?"

The detective nodded.

"And my money?"

"Gone," Callard said. "I spoke with the coach driver and a drummer who was present. Pettingill ran but was brought down by an outlaw's rifle. In his flight, he knocked another thief flat, who then got up and shot Pettingill three more times as he lay in the road. They went through Pettingill's bag, which had the money stowed in it. The road agents fled and the coach went on its way. When it got to San Luis, the driver alerted the marshal. He rode out to recover the body along with some deputies assigned to trail the outlaws. The deputies had just returned empty-handed when I arrived."

"Damn it," Sanders muttered. *Nearly four thousand dollars!* He closed his eyes.

"At least Pettingill got his just reward."

Sanders nodded, looking at the detective. "Drink?" he offered.

Callard smiled. "Don't mind if I do. Scotch whiskey, Bartender, with just a bit of ice."

When the glass was placed in front of the detective, he raised it to his employer and sipped. Sanders picked up his but paused to speak.

"It's good Pettingill is dead, but I rather wish he weren't so that he could be made to pay more thoroughly for his crimes."

"Four bullets aren't a comfortable exit."

"Still," Sanders said. "I had come to like your idea of the bastard getting a good going-over with a truncheon. Make him suffer for days, even weeks, rather than minutes."

Callard looked at him with his unnerving gaze. "Fortunes of war, my friend. Perhaps not a perfect resolution but a just one nonetheless. Your retainer covered all my work on this case, but I have a list of expenses that I'll need reimbursing for."

"Send the bill to me care of the hotel."

Callard finished his drink, left the glass on the bar, and turned to Sanders, extending his thick hand. They shook.

"You're young yet, Mr. Sanders. You've plenty of time to make more money."

He watched the detective leave, thinking he did have time but he would never be able to give Angeline back all that she had lost.

* * *

The afternoon was windy and bright—the sky soft and blue, a scattered flotilla of cumulus clouds sailing on high as stately as schooners. Azariah walked along the weathered planks of Meiggs Wharf, a lone pier extending out over the bay, close to the north end of Powell Street. Passing the waterside drinking and eating establishments, he headed for the far end of the wharf. Here and there along the dock, gray-haired seamen smoked pipes, tattoos visible on their bare forearms and necks, as they sat on benches yarning about old voyages and past adventures. Azariah glanced back along the dock, making sure he was not being followed. He saw Henry Baugh standing by a lamp, his hands in the pockets of his coat. Next to him was a ruffian in a faded jacket with the collar turned up and a cap low over his eyes.

"Here he is now," Baugh said, reaching out to shake Azariah's hand.

The ruffian in the cap looked over at him. It was Daniels, his lower face covered with the wiry beginnings of a beard. He smiled at his cohort. "I'm glad you got those two policemen out of the house. I was getting ready to shoot them."

"I thought you might be up to some mischief. Getting them away was the best solution for all of us."

"Any more trouble from the police?" Baugh asked.

"No," Azariah answered. "But the house is being watched. I was careful to make sure I wasn't followed here. We need to see about Guthrie. Is he still in custody?"

Last evening after his release, Azariah had finished his supper and was on his second cup of coffee when Baugh finally showed up at the Portsmouth Square restaurant. He had been unable to find the lawyer, Drake, at City Hall or at his office on Montgomery Street.

"Guthrie was released late this morning. Drake told me when I went to his office earlier today," Baugh answered.

"Can we assume that he didn't talk?" Daniels asked.

Baugh shrugged. "Probably. If Guthrie had, I imagine the police would have re-arrested Azariah and brought me in as well."

"Unless they are waiting for something else. Me, perhaps," Daniels said. "The *Massauga* will be ready to sail within the month, correct?"

Baugh nodded. "That's what Cicero told me a few days ago."

"Then we've got to be extra cautious. Perhaps it's too risky to let Guthrie live."

Azariah and Baugh stared at the Georgian. He stood, firmly meeting their eyes.

"But we don't know if he's talked," Azariah said. "Angus Guthrie is a staunch Southern patriot. I can't see him telling tales."

"Why was he released then?"

"Drake filed a writ, or Guthrie had his own lawyer free him," Baugh answered.

"And if some lawyer didn't get him released? We have to be certain. The best way may be a bullet, unfortunately."

"Let me talk to Schmitt first, sound him out," Baugh said. "He took money for information just yesterday. He thinks I'm working on the O'Gara murder. He also told me my name was on a list of people to be questioned, though he wouldn't say why. He did say they knew who killed O'Gara, which means they must know who you are." Baugh's eyes were on Daniels.

* * *

Jim Sanders sat with Sally at a table in the dining room of the Occidental Hotel. Around them, numerous other couples and parties were at early supper before taking in various evening performances. Jim and Sally were headed to the Academy of Music to hear a program of music by Beethoven and Handel. The air in the dining room was filled with conversing voices and clinking cutlery. Sanders took a bite of his *coq au vin* and chewed distractedly. He washed it down with a sip of wine and noticed Sally watching him.

"You're unusually quiet this evening," she said.

"The detective I hired returned with news today."

"Did he find that terrible man?"

"Pettingill. Yes, he found him—buried in a pauper's grave. He was killed during a stagecoach holdup down south."

"Aren't you pleased?" she asked.

Sanders shook his head. "My money was stolen by the high-waymen. Pettingill got off too easily. But what galls me most is poor Angeline. She's ruined."

Sally cut another piece from her *steak au poivre*. She lifted it to her mouth, then paused. "The only thing for her to do is marry."

"Who would have her? She's … damaged goods," Sanders said.

Sally chewed and swallowed, then took a sip of wine, putting her glass carefully down on the linen table cloth.

"You could marry her."

Sanders stared at the woman as though she had thrown her wine in his face. "Have you lost all sensibility? I cannot marry her. She's my cousin."

"First cousins can marry, though I hear doctors do not advise having children."

"Angeline's like a sister to me. I have no amorous interest in her."

Sally shrugged. "It would be the surest way to prevent any scandal."

"Nonetheless," Sanders said, shaking his head, "I can't marry her. I'm not ready to settle down. I may never settle down."

"I see." She looked at him, her face both handsome and serious.

"Besides," Sanders added, "I enjoy being with you."

"But you have no intention of marrying me."

"I didn't say that …. Look, can't we just drop the subject?"

"Perhaps we should," she agreed.

Sanders picked up his wineglass. *Did women have any idea how exasperating they were?* He took a long sip.

* * *

It was past nine o'clock and fully dark as Baugh entered the Bella Union. Inside there was a barroom manned by two husky fellows with pomaded hair, tending to the needs of several patrons standing at the long polished counter. Through a wide curtained doorway music and singing carried from the theater beyond. Baugh stopped at the bar to speak with one of the bartenders.

"Where would I find Detective Schmitt?"

The heavyset man smirked. "Cozying up to Nellie Durand, the new girl. She's singing on stage now."

Baugh nodded and walked over to the curtains and into the theater. A small orchestra played in the pit below the stage lamps. On stage was a blond girl in a low-cut chemise, white corset, short red drawers, and white stockings with pink garters. She sang in a clear voice about a sailor she loved as she stepped gracefully around a single wooden chair, striking brief poses—one foot lifted to the seat of the chair to give the audience full view of her half-bare thigh and rounded hip, then spinning to sit and cross her shapely legs. Meanwhile the male audience whistled, calling out to her.

Baugh went down the side aisle and through a door on the left, which led backstage. Closing the door, he smiled at the bouncer standing in the darkened hallway.

"I'm here to see Schmitt," Baugh told him.

The broad-chested brute nodded up toward the stage wings and let Baugh pass. Climbing the stairs, Baugh approached Schmitt, who had his back to him as the detective leaned against a section of stage wall watching the young woman perform. Baugh tapped the policeman's shoulder. Schmitt looked over, annoyed.

"What do you want?" he hissed below the music.

"I need to talk."

"Get out of here!" he whispered.

The song hit a crescendo and stopped abruptly, with Nellie standing with her back and pert rump to the audience, looking over her shoulder. The house roared with applause and lewd whistles. The curtains dropped as she came scampering off the boards toward Schmitt. He glared at Baugh, then caught her in his arms, spinning her. They kissed emphatically.

"Wait for me. I may be a while, darling," the detective said.

Nellie glanced at Baugh, offering him a brief smile as she walked by.

Beyond the stage, the orchestra began playing a melodic interlude. Schmitt turned to Baugh.

"Let's go."

"We can talk here."

"You got a hell of a nerve, searching me out when I'm off duty. We'll talk all right—at City Hall. I'm running you in."

"What for?" Baugh asked, lifting his hands.

Schmitt took manacles from his coat pocket and clamped one around Baugh's outstretched wrist, turning the key in the lock. He fastened the other end around his own wrist, locked it, and jerked Baugh toward him.

"Let's go!"

"What the hell did I do?"

"Your name is on the list. I'm sick of seeing your ugly face every time I turn around. You asked for it; you're going to get it."

Schmitt pulled him down the stairs. Baugh tried to keep up, resisting the urge to slug the policeman behind the ear. Once outside, they crossed Kearny, then Washington Street and in a few strides were through the doors of City Hall, heading down the corridor. Schmitt led Baugh back to the detectives' room, where Capt. Lees sat at his desk, working late.

"I found this bummer over at the Bella Union," Schmitt said, lifting his wrist to display the cuffs. "I'll put him in an interrogation room. You want to sit in on this?"

Lees looked up from his paperwork. "You mind working it alone? It's been a long day."

"Suit yourself," Schmitt answered, yanking on the manacles. "Come on, you Secesh piece of shit."

* * *

Seated on a chair in a closet-sized gas-lit interrogation room, Baugh pulled against the manacle, which the policeman had shifted to an iron ring bolted to the wall. Schmitt stood over him, slapping a short truncheon lightly into his left palm.

"What are you going to do with that?" Baugh asked.

"That depends on you."

"I came to you looking for developments on the O'Gara case. I'm just interested in the story, for God's sake."

"You're from the South. You worked for the *Democratic Press*, the rag that supported Jeff Davis. You ever heard of the Knights of the Golden Circle?"

"It's some kind of secret society. Why?"

Schmitt put the tip of the club under Baugh's chin and lifted it. "I'll ask the questions."

Baugh stared back, wondering if he was going to get a beating. Schmitt leaned his shoulder against the locked door.

"Are you a member of the Knights?"

"I'm not even a Free Mason."

The detective studied him. He slammed the truncheon down on Baugh's left hand. Baugh screamed. He tucked the injured hand into his right armpit, eyes clenching from the intense pain.

Mouthing curses, he looked up at the cop. Schmitt gestured with the club.

"That's to let you know I mean business."

"You sumbitch! You broke my hand!"

"Be glad it wasn't your right, the one you hold a pen with."

Baugh glared, wishing he had not left his Starr .44 revolver back in his boardinghouse room.

"So tell me again. Are you with the Knights of the Golden Circle?"

"No."

"You're lying. I can tell by your eyes. Now, do I crush your other hand, or are you going to start telling the truth?" Schmitt held up the truncheon.

"Did you do the same to Dekker and Guthrie? Were they beaten?"

The detective stared at him for a moment. "We brought in a mule-headed bummer a while back, who was fingered for a burglary. He wouldn't talk either. When we were finished with him, he confessed—only, by then he was missing most of his teeth. You don't want to end up like that."

"I'm a member of the Fourth Estate, you dumb bastard. Anything you do to me will make the headlines."

The club blurred in Schmitt's hand. The side of Baugh's head seemed to explode. He nearly fell out of the chair. Gripping the desk with his injured hand, he gasped -- his skull vibrant with pain. Eyes watering, he saw blood dripping down onto his pants. He touched his eyebrow, glancing at his sore, red-smeared fingers.

"Do you know a son of a bitch named Thaddeus Daniels?" Schmitt asked. The policeman had the club tucked under one arm and was lighting a long slender cigar. Once he had the cigar going, he blew smoke into Baugh's face and repeated the question.

"Never heard of him," Baugh answered, panting slowly.

"I've got all night, Mr. Baugh. But I don't think you're going to last that long."

"I'm supposed to know … every goddamn fellow in town?"

"Daniels killed O'Gara. We want him, not you. Make it easy on yourself. Tell me where he is and you can walk out."

Baugh swallowed, staring at the detective. "Don't know him, and I don't know where he is."

* * *

Blake stood at the bar of the Fashion Saloon, where soldiers from the Department of California and the Military Division of the Pacific regularly met for drinks and card games. A group of junior officers were clustered around him, knocking back shots of whiskey and scotch and chasing them with glasses of beer. They were talking about making an outing to one of the tawdry fandango houses along Broadway Street, where Spanish ladies danced in sultry ways to the passionate strumming of guitars.

Face flushed with drink, Martin Tevis exhorted his comrades. "Come on, you horny bastards, let's go see those Mexican hussies!"

The others cheered, raising their glasses. "To the Mexican hussies!"

On his second whiskey and soda, Blake watched the antics of his comrades with wry amusement. They were warming up for a roaring night that would most likely end in fisticuffs and blackened eyes. Tevis came over to slap Blake on the back.

"Are you going with us, you swashbuckling duelist?"

Blake pushed off the other man's arm. "I'm not sure I want to be seen with you drunken galoots."

"We need you to protect us, in case any of those greasers decide to carve us up for ogling their ladies!"

"Go stick your head in a bucket of whiskey."

"A capital suggestion!" Tevis lurched away to wave at the bartender.

Blake had no desire to join them. He was struggling to figure out what had happened with Elena and why he had heard nothing more from her.

"We're off to see the fandango dancers. Are you coming along?" asked another soldier, his eyes bright with intoxication.

Blake shook his head. "I haven't finished my drink."

The drunken lieutenant grinned. "We'll kiss the ladies for you, Blake!"

The group headed for the door, talking loudly as they went. Blake raised his hand in a wave. When they were gone, he lifted his drink, then paused. In his pocket was Elena's letter. From the cancellation stamp, he knew she had posted it in the city before she left. What bothered him was that she had not put a return address on the envelope. He could only assume there must be no further communication between them. It pained him he could not tell her how he felt and how much he wished to be with her again. But perhaps hers was the greater wisdom—to avoid further trouble and yearning, they both had to accept fate.

Finishing his drink, he stared at the empty glass with its melting ice. He signaled the bartender for another.

CHAPTER 16

A uniformed policeman led Henry Baugh by the arm through the City Hall doors. Outside the morning air was cool, the sky overcast. Baugh turned to glance at his reflection in the glass panels of the doors. His left eye was swollen shut, the thickened flesh a bluish purple, the cut above scabbed. Numbly, he stood trying to move the fingers of his puffy left hand to see if they were broken. The taste of blood was in his mouth. The policeman waved to a taxi driver, who brought his vehicle to a stop at the curb.

"See that this man gets home," the policeman said, handing the driver a silver dollar and a slip of paper.

A neutral expression on his face, the policeman opened the cab door and helped Baugh climb in. As the door closed, the taxi rolled, pushing Baugh back against the seat. He had only chaotic memories of the night before—Schmitt's questions and the impact of the club. He noticed brown bloodstains on his shirt front and haltingly touched his stinging ear. It was swollen. Thankfully, Schmitt had not broken his jaw—though it ached, and two of his molars were loose.

A breeze streamed in through the half-opened door window as Baugh rested his head against the seat. At some point in the interrogation he had blacked out and awakened in a reeking cell in the building's basement. He did not think he had talked but could not be absolutely sure. He stared out the window as the taxi passed a Chinese grocery with bins of vegetables and fruits on the sidewalk, working its way up Washington Street. Once he was better, he would find a way to jam his .44 revolver into Schmitt's ear and pull the trigger.

* * *

Blake walked along the Vallejo Street Wharf, thinking he should have brought his overcoat. Cold bay wind swept the pier, and the fugitive sun was hidden behind high clouds. As it was Sunday, there were no workers on the pier, the usual stacks of cargo missing from the broad worn planks. Nor were there any dock loafers to be seen. Sails furled into small white banners along the spars, the ships rocked slowly fore and aft, the wind at times shrieking through their rigging. Blake had been hoping to find Serrano. Just before turning in the night before, he had remembered the dock loafer mentioning Hopkins had been refitting a ship. Looking for him now, Blake saw only the sailors on the day watch, who were huddled in nooks along the main decks, making sure no one unwelcome came aboard. Turning, he strode toward the street as fast as the stitches in his leg would allow. His eyes scanned the various saloons ahead tucked among the cordage shops and ship chandlers lining the waterfront.

It took him over an hour, but he found Serrano sitting on a wooden stool in the corner of the Indian Queen Saloon, just off East Street. Like other groggeries along the wharf, its floor was scattered with sawdust, the paint on the walls peeling. The taproom was lit in sepia tones by its meager oil lamps and redolent with raw whiskey, spilled beer, cheap tobacco, and stale sweat. Serrano sipped from a small tumbler of clear liquid—probably rum—as Blake approached, grateful to be out of the wind. A potbellied stove close by gave off a pleasant heat.

"Señor Serrano, I'm Lieutenant Blake," the soldier said, stopping at the bar. "I spoke with you the other day when I was with Detective Schmitt."

"I remember," Serrano replied.

"You mentioned Hopkins, the fellow found dead at Yerba Buena Cemetery," Blake said. "You said he was working on refitting a ship. Do you know where that was?"

Serrano shook his head. "I heard it was with a private concern, not one of the local yards."

"So you don't know where the work was being done."

"Can't help you."

"Where did you hear about Hopkins?"

"Here. He was buying drinks for all those who had stood him a whiskey or a beer when he was hard up. That was last Monday."

"Think he might have been working on that schooner that went missing?"

Serrano shrugged his broad shoulders. "Maybe. But Hopkins wasn't a boat thief. He was more of an oyster filcher. Besides, I heard others were involved in the missing pungy."

"Others?" Blake said. "Like who?"

Smiling, Serrano looked pointedly at his empty glass. Blake gestured to the barkeep to refill the dock loafer's drink and ordered a bonded whiskey for himself. Serrano sipped the refilled rum, nodding with satisfaction.

"You were talking about the pungy schooner," Blake said, gingerly sipping the bourbon he had ordered. The smooth taste assured him it was not basement-brewed rotgut.

"I heard a rumor it was the work of Liverpool Wilcox and his gang. I don't run in the same circles, so I can't say for sure."

"Wilcox being one of the local harbor thieves."

"He's more than that. You want someone killed, a cargo heisted, or a ship fired for insurance, he's your man. Of course, he works mostly for himself. He's crimped many a soul—sailors and lubbers alike."

"Crimped?" Blake asked.

"Shanghaied. Knocked in the head and sold like so much salt pork to any captain trying to fill out a crew."

Blake took a photograph from his pocket. "Ever seen this man?"

Serrano took the picture of Daniels and his lady. He smiled as his eyes took in the young woman, but he shook his head.

"This is the man that killed O'Gara," Blake said. "If you see him, let me or Schmitt know."

Serrano handed back the photograph. "Sure thing, Lieutenant."

* * *

"Come in," Guthrie said, rising from his desk chair. Azariah entered the Scot's study, holding his hat in his hands. It was a first-floor room in Guthrie's home, a row house on South Park, overlooking the long oval garden in the middle of the street. An accounting ledger was open on the desk.

"I don't wish to disturb you," Azariah said. "But I wanted to see how you fared with the police."

The short Scot gazed at him. "You've come to see if I talked. Ye should know me better than that, old friend. Whiskey?"

Azariah nodded, averting his eyes, embarrassed to have been seen through so quickly. Guthrie went to an elegant sideboard, poured gold-colored spirits into two cut-glass tumblers, and handed one to his guest.

"To the cause," the Scot toasted, clinking his glass against Azariah's.

They drank fine Highlands malt. Azariah took a seat on a small couch while the old Scot remained standing.

"Ye needn't worry. I told the coppers naething. And they dared not raise a hand to me, as I am no footpad from the streets."

"I'm sorry to have doubted you," Azariah said, shaking his head. "It's just that things have taken a bad turn. A detective got killed trying to arrest one of our fellows. And I've just had word that Baugh was taken into custody and severely beaten. The whole venture is at risk."

"Say no more. The less I know, the better." Guthrie returned to his desk chair.

Azariah sighed. "I wish I were out of it. I'm too old for this sort of business."

"One is never too old to fight the good fight. Play your cards close to the vest, and keep a weather eye out."

Azariah finished his whiskey and set the glass on the table beside him. "Thanks for the drink and for keeping mum."

He got up from the couch, Guthrie rising as well.

"Let me know if there's anything else I can do," the Scot said, shaking Azariah's hand.

Leaving the house, Azariah walked through the cool afternoon down to Third Street, feeling the Colt in his coat pocket bumping against his hip. Had he really believed he would shoot Guthrie if the man had talked? Azariah stopped at the corner, waiting for the Omnibus railcar moving slowly up the street. He shook his head, thinking the whole scheme mad to begin with, and only getting worse.

* * *

"It's very nice of you to take me out walking," Angeline said.

She rested her gloved hand on the crook of Sanders's arm. They walked along Francisco Street as it climbed a small hill overlooking the docks of North Beach. The sky was beginning to clear, patches of lucent blue showing through the ragged clouds. Several ships plied the gray white-capped water, their sails taut with wind, moving in graceful silence.

"Mother thinks it's good for me to leave the house."

"You aren't volunteering anymore?" Her cousin asked. They stopping along the unpaved street where one could look out over the water.

"Not since the incident."

"Well, I have what I hope is good news," Jim said. "Pettingill is dead. The detective brought me word just yesterday."

Angeline looked at him. She felt startled, unsure whether to cheer with elation or sob with relief. "You're sure of it?"

Sanders took a folded news clipping from his vest pocket and handed it to her. "Callard, the fellow I hired, assured me it was so."

Unfolding the paper, Angeline read the article. After a moment she refolded it and slowly tore it to pieces. Tossing the scraps, she watched them flutter away in the breeze. She pulled Sanders closer to her, then rested her head against his shoulder.

"I hope this news will set your heart at ease, Angie."

She nodded. "Perhaps it is un-Christian to feel joy over another's death, but I don't care. I'm glad he's gone."

"You're certainly entitled. He injured us both. And he was lucky to have been killed. I would have seen to it that he suffered cruelly for what he did."

"How so?"

He shook his head. "It doesn't matter now."

Sanders thought about Sally's suggestion to marry his cousin. The light pressure of Angie's head on his shoulder made him feel guilty. But he didn't think throwing away his happiness to secure Angeline's would be worth the sacrifice. *Certainly it was his fault that she had been introduced to Pettingill, but was his debt to her so great that he had to forsake all the freedoms he lived for?*

* * *

Azariah knocked at the door to Baugh's boardinghouse room in the gas-lit corridor. The door opened slightly then swung wide, permitting him to enter.

After locking the door, Baugh sat on his rumpled bed. The bruises on his face were hideous—red, black, and purple marks along the jaw and cheek, the swelling around his eye so heavy the orb was only partially visible. Daniels, scruffy and unshaven, sat in a chair placed by the foot of the bed. Azariah pulled a chair over from the corner table, looking at Baugh and feeling oddly guilty. Outside the windows, the bells of St. Mary's chimed in the distance, striking eleven.

"I waited until ten p.m.," Azariah said. "Then had Mary turn out the upstairs lights while I watched from the darkened parlor. The policeman across the street left after another fifteen minutes, and that's when I went out the back way."

"Good," Daniels replied. "What about Guthrie?"

"I went to see him, to look in his eyes, when I asked. He told them nothing."

Daniels nodded. "Well, gentlemen, what is our next step?"

"Kill Schmitt," Baugh said.

"Your motive is understandable, but we must be very careful. We've already drawn too much attention to ourselves," Azariah replied.

Baugh took a moment before he spoke, perhaps an effect of his beating or the small bottle of laudanum Azariah noticed on his nightstand. "If that sumbitch … had done this to either of you …"

Daniels raised his hand. "Easy, old friend. Schmitt will get what's coming to him, but our endeavor must take priority."

"Which is why we should do nothing for the moment," Azariah said. "We need to lay low, frustrate the police, and let them get weary. If we kill another policeman now, they will redouble their efforts."

Daniels was watching Baugh to see if he agreed. The Texan stared across the room, a stubborn look on his battered face. "I'll kill him … myself."

"What if I were to say that I would help you, once we are ready to set sail? We've many things to accomplish before that, but it will only be a few weeks at the most," Daniels said.

Baugh sat brooding, gazing with his good eye at Daniels, who frowned and continued.

"Now that my wound is healing and my ribs are less painful, I can see about getting those boarding weapons—the cutlasses and pikes."

"Too risky," Azariah responded. "I say we cease all activity for the time being. Anything you lack can be obtained in Mexico, once you have taken to the seas."

Daniels nodded.

"Or," Baugh said, "we could set a trap for Schmitt … then leave town … and stay with Cicero."

Azariah shook his head. "I need to remain here and take care of my wife. The maid can't do it alone."

"We can do it … without you. The police are watching you anyway. You'll have … the perfect alibi."

"We are at a critical juncture and must use logic, not emotion. We need to keep out of sight and do nothing," Azariah insisted.

Baugh lifted his hand, his finger raised in protest, seemingly unable to speak as emotions warred on his damaged face.

Daniels sighed. "Henry, I'm afraid I'm going to have to side with Azariah. Schmitt will keep for a few weeks. Besides, you're in no kind of shape to take him on, even if I did set him up for you."

Baugh let his hand drop but continued to glare at his cohorts.

* * *

"Go on, Captain," Chief Burke said.

Lees sat facing the chief, who was at his desk. It was Monday morning. He had come in to make his progress report on the O'Gara murder. He folded his arms across his vest and frowned.

"Unfortunately, there has been little progress. As you know, we brought in numerous Copperheads, but none of them seem to know Daniels or what he is up to. This fellow, Dekker, who used to edit the pro-Confederate newspaper—I thought he was lying when we questioned him, but I couldn't break him down. I had to release him because his lawyer threatened to file a writ. Schmitt put the screws to another one by the name of Baugh but came up with nothing. We've circulated the photos of Daniels among the department, yet it's like he has vanished."

Burke looked at him, his eyes serious. "Isaiah, you know better than I the police are all that stand between decent society and the dangerous underclasses who live in the shadows. The respect the police need to command must be absolute. Retribution for killing an officer must be swift and implacable."

"Yes sir."

"Use everything in your power. Bring this man Dekker back in for questioning. Let Schmitt do the interview."

"Yes sir."

"Talk to stable owners to see if they've rented Daniels a horse. Check at the train station and most importantly with saloonkeepers, on the chance they might have seen him. I want him found, and if he's fled the city, I want to know where he went. Is that clear?"

Lees stood up. Nodding to him, the chief went back to the paperwork on his blotter. Lees strode through the outer office and into the hallway, his face grim.

* * *

Blake was waiting at the captain's desk when Lees walked in. Schmitt sat with the other detectives, doing paperwork and ignoring him. Blake scratched his pant leg, to ease the itching stitches.

"Lieutenant," Lees said as he entered. "Any news?"

"I spoke with Juan Serrano yesterday," Blake answered but hesitated when the police captain motioned for him to stop.

"Hold on a minute. Schmitt, I need talk to you," Lees said.

The detective got up from his desk and walked over. "Captain?"

"Bring in Dekker. The chief wants him questioned again, thoroughly, and he wants you to do the interview. We need answers."

Schmitt nodded, a smile starting on his face.

"But," Lees warned, "be discreet. The man still has friends in this town."

"I'll get him to talk."

Taking his hat and coat from the rack, Schmitt left.

"You were saying, Lieutenant?"

"I spoke with Serrano yesterday about this man, Hopkins—the one found dead. Serrano told me Hopkins had been working on refitting a ship. Only, it wasn't being done at any of the local boatyards. If Hopkins was working on the stolen schooner, perhaps he was killed in order to be silenced."

"An intriguing idea, Mr. Blake," Lees replied, his eyes thoughtful. "If Daniels is mixed up with the theft of this schooner."

"His record shows he had ties to the Confederate Navy."

Lees nodded slowly, then lowered his voice to a whisper. "The chief is not happy with our progress. He wants results. I'm not certain I want to expend time on a hunch. The chief wants all the saloons and stables canvassed."

"But if Daniels is planning an operation like the *Chapman*, outfitting a ship, shouldn't we check with local arms and gun powder suppliers?"

Lees chewed his lip. "It might be worth a try. But if you come up empty-handed, report back here immediately. We're going to need every man available to cover the bars and stables. Let me take a look at the City Directory and see who you should talk to."

Blake remained standing while the captain sat at his desk and pulled a fat book from one of the drawers. He riffled through the pages until he found what he was searching for. He took a sheet paper and a pencil and started writing down names and addresses.

"There's five listed. Two are close by on California Street and another over on Commercial. Report back here as soon as you can. " Lees handed the paper to Blake from where he sat. Then he went out into the detectives' room to address the men sitting there.

"All right, gents, I want your attention. We need to make a sweep of the city's saloons …"

Putting on his new hat, Blake headed for the brightly lit lobby doors, hoping this gambit would pay off—he needed something to atone for letting Daniels get away.

* * *

Blake opened the door to the Eureka Blasting Powder Company, a squat brick building on Commercial Street. The office was small and paneled in light-brown oak. Sunlight streamed through the tall bay windows facing the street. The clerk wore a winged collar with a brown cravat, his chestnut-colored suit worn at the cuffs. Topped by gray thinning hair, the man's face was fissured with lines.

"May I help you, sir?" The clerk stood at the counter that divided the room in half.

"I'm an investigator with the police department." Blake took out the badge, engraved with the words *Special Police*, which Lees had given him. "I'd like to look at your recent sales records."

The clerk regarded the badge skeptically. "What is this about?"

"It relates to a murder investigation."

"Someone was blown up with an infernal device?"

"No," Blake answered. "The man we're looking for killed a police officer. We believe he may have done business here."

The clerk nodded but didn't move.

"Your sales book, if you please."

"You say this culprit murdered a policeman?"

"I can come back with a warrant and a squad of detectives, if you prefer," said Blake, his patience thin.

The clerk lifted a large leather-bound book onto the counter and opened it. Blake studied the clerk for a moment, then looked down at the handwritten entries. He scanned the orders, seeing nothing of interest. Neither of the two powder companies on California Street had any useful information. Frustrated, he turned the page over, thinking he had wasted an hour and Lees would be irked by his insistence on a useless line of inquiry. He moved his finger down the page until he saw a name he recognized. Glancing up at the clerk, who was watching, Blake kept his finger moving down the page. He wondered if the clerk might not also be one of the city's Copperheads. He closed the book and pushed it across the countertop.

"Nothing," Blake said. "Sorry to have wasted your time."

Outside the office, he paused in the corridor to press the sheet of paper listing the powder companies against the building's wall. He wrote down the information he had seen: Azariah Dekker, 30 kegs of powder delivered to the farm of Cicero Madison, San Mateo County.

Outside he scanned the unpaved side street for a taxi.

* * *

Responding to Mary's call, Azariah came down the stairs, seeing two policemen waiting in the entryway. One wore a uniform, the other civilian clothes.

"What now?" Azariah asked as he reached the ground floor.

"There's more questions," the plainclothes man replied, whom Azariah recognized as Detective Schmitt.

Azariah glanced from one policeman to the other as Mary took his coat off the rack, holding it for him, her eyes frightened. He slipped his arms into it. Turning to her, he pulled a small sealed envelope from his vest pocket.

"Please see that Mr. Drake, Esquire, gets this immediately."

"I'll take care of that," the detective said, plucking away the note.

"That's private correspondence. You have no right—"

The detective pocketed the paper, shoving Azariah toward the uniformed officer. "Put the manacles on him."

Schmitt stared challengingly at Mary while the officer locked the iron handcuffs around Dekker's wrists.

"This is out of line, Detective. You have no right to treat me—"

Schmitt grabbed Azariah's arm and marched him out the door.

"Save your breath, old man. You're going to need it."

CHAPTER 17

Blake hurried down the hallway toward the Detectives Room but slowed when he saw Capt. Lees conferring with Chief Burke outside the chamber. He came to a halt before them and waited for a break in the conversation.

"So far we've covered a ten-block radius around the American Exchange Hotel," Lees said. "Only one barkeep recognized Daniels's picture, at the German Saloon. But he said he hadn't seen Daniels in over a week."

"And the stable operators?"

"Nothing."

"Keep looking, Captain," Burke said. "There has to be more information out there."

"I have something," Blake said.

Both turned their heads to look at him. He told them about Dekker's purchase of the thirty kegs of powder.

"The man is in custody now," the captain said. "Schmitt's interviewing him in one of the cubbyholes."

"Confront him about the powder." Burke buttoned his coat. He held his hat in one hand. "I have a meeting with the mayor."

"Right," Lees said.

The chief headed for the front doors, putting on his top hat. Blake followed Lees back toward the cubbyholes.

"You're timing was perfect, Lieutenant. I just came back to check in, while the rest of the squad is carrying on with inquiries."

"Sir, if we alert Dekker about the powder, won't we tip our hand?" Blake asked. "Wouldn't it be better to put some men on watch at the Madison farm and see what's going on out there?"

Lees pursed his lips as he considered the suggestion. "You have the makings of a first-rate copper, young man. Let's see how Schmitt is progressing."

Down the hall, only one of the three cubbyholes had its door closed. A uniformed officer stood in front of it. The officer spoke as they approached.

"Detective Schmitt asked not to be disturbed."

Lees nodded. "Stand aside, Constable. I need to speak with him."

Dutifully, the policeman stepped away from the door. Lees knocked on it.

"Not now!" Schmitt's voice was muffled.

Lees and Blake paused as they listened to Schmitt demanding an answer again and again. A scream followed, stifled by the wooden portal. Lees opened the door. Schmitt was leaning over the small table. Dekker was seated, one hand manacled to the iron wall ring, his agonized face wet with tears. The index finger of his left hand was bent backward at an unnatural angle.

Lees looked from Dekker to Schmitt. "Any progress?"

"None yet, Captain. But there's nine fingers to go."

"I suggest you cooperate, Mr. Dekker," Lees said. "Detective Schmitt has an appetite for this line of questioning."

Dekker sagged in the chair, his face pallid, but he made no reply.

Shaking his head, Lees swung the door. As it closed, Blake saw the desperation in the old man's eyes and hoped he would have the sense to talk.

* * *

Mary O'Donovan climbed the third set of marble stairs, pausing to catch her breath before she hurried down the corridor to a glass-paneled door displaying the name E. B. Drake, Attorney-at-Law. She opened it and went inside. The office was large and well lit from the windows, the walls lined with thick books. Behind the long desk facing the door, a man in stood up, wearing a blue frock coat and dark striped trousers. He was clean-shaven and had quiet, intelligent eyes.

"What can I do for you, miss?"

"Are you Mr. Drake?" Mary asked, conscious of her brogue.

"The same," the gentleman answered.

"I work for Mr. Dekker," she said urgently. "The police have arrested him just an hour ago. Oh, sir, he needs your help!"

"What happened?" the lawyer asked, his face concerned.

"They led him away in irons, and the detective who arrested Mr. Dekker stared at me in a most horrid manner. Sure he looked like Satan himself! I know he means to harm Mr. Dekker, who tried to give me a letter to deliver to you, sir. Only, the detective snatched it away."

"Did he now?" Drake said, anger in his voice.

"Yes," Mary said. "I would have come sooner, but I had to see to Mrs. Dekker before I could leave. I'm very afraid for my master."

"Go home, miss. I'll see to Mr. Dekker, and I'll make sure he knows who alerted me."

Thanking him, she left, closing the door, and hurried back down the corridor. She whispered a prayer her employer would be all right.

* * *

Azariah sat on the edge of a wooden bunk in a dark, empty cell, trembling as he tore a strip from the tail of his shirt, using his teeth. Slowly, he wrapped the three aching broken fingers of his left hand, his breath rasping in the gloom. Clumsily, he tied the two ends into a knot, again using his teeth. He fell back against the wall, wiping the spent tears from his cheeks with his sleeve. Mercifully, he had fainted as Schmitt broke the third finger. When he woke he was being walked, his arms around the shoulders of two uniformed policemen, into the cells. They dumped him on the bunk and left. The lock of the door had clicked with a hopeless finality.

Slumped against the hard wall, he took an exhausted breath. He knew he would not be able to hold out if Schmitt continued his ministrations. The man was a mad dog. He might easily kill Azariah, while the rest of the force looked the other way, and dump his corpse in the bay. By the time it washed up, the fish and crabs would have made his face unrecognizable. *What could he do? How could he possibly escape?* He looked around the desolate, grimy cell—the ammoniac smell of the unemptied slops bucket assailing his nostrils. With withering clarity, he realized his whole life had been leading blindly up to this moment, to this wretched Gethsemane. Only, he had nothing to fall back on—no faith and no hope.

He closed his eyes as his fingers pulsated with pain. Swallowing slowly, he knew he was out of options. When they came to get him again, he would have to make a break for the building's front doors. With luck, they would shoot him.

* * *

"He's tougher than he looks," Schmitt said, pausing to sip from a mug of coffee.

Lees and Blake stood in front of Schmitt's desk. Lees kicked gently at the wooden foot of the bureau, frustration plain on his face.

"Three fingers and not a single word?"

Schmitt shrugged. "I'll work on him some more in a little while. Did we get any news on Daniels?"

"Nothing useful," Lees answered. "Dekker's lawyer showed up a few minutes ago. He intends to file another writ."

"Dekker might be awake by now. I could have another go at him."

"It might be better to let him walk out for now. Three busted fingers, and he didn't squeal. How are you going to cover it?"

Schmitt held up his pen. "I'm writing up the report now. He broke his fingers when the jailer accidentally closed the cell door on the poor fellow's hand."

"What about Madison's farm?" Blake asked.

Lees hesitated, then nodded. "Take Robson, the fellow who has O'Gara's desk now. One of you report back in twenty-four hours. Sooner, if you see Daniels."

"Where would I find Detective Robson about now?" Blake said.

"I'll send him over to your hotel once he gets back. You might as well go and get a meal and a nap as you'll be out all night. Better change out of that suit too. If things break here, I'll send word."

Blake nodded, hat in hand, and walked out, feeling sorry for Dekker, even if he had aided Daniels. It was hard to see the old man treated so brutally. However, in the deadly game they were caught up in, mercy was perhaps not only foolish but dangerous as well.

* * *

Sunset filled the western sky with streamers of red and yellow light above the shadows along Taylor Street as the carriage pulled up to the curb. The door opened and Azariah stepped down, turning to face Mr. Drake seated inside. The lawyer had miraculously appeared at the door of his cell and had gotten him released. Immediately, Drake had taken him to a doctor. His fingers splinted and wrapped, Azariah looked up at his benefactor. He still couldn't believe that he was free.

"Words cannot express my gratitude, sir."

"I think your best course, Mr. Dekker, might be to leave town for a while," Drake said, his face troubled. "The police are fully roused and bent on vengeance. Whatever connection you might have, real or imagined, with the murder of Detective O'Gara, they are not going to forgive or forget."

"Worthy advice, my friend. I will give it serious consideration."

Azariah shut the door. Walking slowly to the porch, he worked the knocker, not having the energy to use his key. He leaned against the door frame until it opened and Mary looked out.

"Praise God, it's you, sir."

She pulled the door wide for him to step into the hallway. "I believe you saved my life, young lady."

She inhaled audibly as she noticed his hand. "Are you bad hurt, Mr. Dekker?"

"It's been tended to by a physician," he said, heading for a seat in the parlor.

He sank gratefully into a stuffed chair, wishing he had asked the doctor for some laudanum. His swollen fingers were still painful. "Some brandy, if you please, Mary."

"Right away, sir. This letter came by the post this afternoon." She took a sealed envelope from the pocket of her apron, handing it to him.

While she poured brandy into a snifter, he opened it to read the handwritten message.

The hour of retribution approaches. Have dinner at a restaurant with Guthrie tonight and tomorrow night if necessary.

T. Jackson

He slipped the letter into his coat pocket as Mary handed him the brandy. Raising it, he nodded his thanks to her and took a large sip.

"I'll see to supper now," Mary said, turning toward the door.

"Just make it for yourself and the missus. I will be going out to dine tonight despite my injury. And thank you again. I will not forget what you did for me."

She smiled, gave him a little curtsy, and left. He let his head fall back against the anti-macassar draped along the top of the chair. He took another fortifying mouthful. Once he had finished the drink, he would pack a bag so that he could leave on short notice. Of the three hundred dollars Daniels had given him to live on, he still had roughly one hundred and eighty. He would leave half for Mary in a desk drawer. Whatever Daniels was planning, the police would not be idle in their revenge.

* * *

Blake shifted in the stout branches of a sycamore tree, peering out from his leafy cover with a pair of field glasses. Two hundred yards away, he could see the glinting blue of the bay and the dock at the edge of Madison's farm extending well out over the water. A two-masted schooner was tied to the end of the T-shaped pier.

Blake yawned in the morning sunlight. At the foot of the tree, Robson lay on his back, his arm crooked over his eyes as he slept. Blake swept the landscape again with his binoculars. A road led from the dock past the edge of a tilled field up half a mile to a massive stone barn and several outbuildings. Beyond these was a large white house with a pillared veranda, the ridged roof tiled with gray slate. Workers were visible, moving about the place. The distance was too great to know if Daniels was among them.

Blake let the field glasses hang from the strap about his neck and began to climb down. He dropped to the dirt on the other side of the tree from Robson and walked around to him. The policeman lifted his arm to peer up.

"I think one of us should go over to our host's kitchen and see if there's any breakfast to be had," Blake said.

"Right," Robson answered, standing up from his blankets. Several years older than Blake, he was tall and lean. He ran a large hand through his tousled brown hair, smiling sleepily.

Their host, a farmer named Samuel Walters, had been most welcoming when the pair knocked on his door early yesterday evening, introduced themselves as policemen, and asked to camp out in his fields and observe the activities on the adjacent property. Walters had pronounced his neighbor Madison to be a "first class son of a bitch" and had told them to stay as long as they liked.

"You go ahead," Robson said, holding out his hand for the binoculars. "I'll stand watch a while."

"I can't make out if the boat at Madison's dock is the stolen schooner. We're going to need to take a closer look." Blake handed him the field glasses. "Perhaps Walters has a rowboat we can borrow. "

Robson nodded. "If he does, we can row out tonight for a gander."

"I'll ask if one's available," Blake said. "And I'll bring back whatever I can—biscuits, ham, hard-boiled eggs."

"Some coffee too," Robson suggested.

Blake nodded. Putting on his hat, he headed up the path skirting Walters's fields.

* * *

Azariah woke to sunshine outside the windows illuminating the houses on the opposite side of the street. Last night he had dined with Guthrie at Delmonico's. He had been too distracted to make a decent attempt at conversation and had told the old Scot nothing of the plans that were afoot. Arriving home at a quarter past ten, Azariah had been unable to sleep and so had taken refuge in the parlor, fully dressed, with the sawed-off shotgun propped against an adjacent table, half expecting another invasion by the police. As the sky paled with the advent of dawn, he had drifted off in his armchair. He sat up, his splinted fingers aching. He stood to stretch, then headed for the kitchen.

He found Mary cooking breakfast—oatmeal, eggs, and sausage. Coffee simmered in a metal pot on the wood-burning stove. The room was filled with familiar smells, but they did little to reassure him. He poured himself a cup of coffee and flavored it with some milk from the icebox.

"Were you up all night, Mr. Dekker?" Mary asked, concerned.

"I couldn't sleep," he admitted. "I may need to go away for a few days. But I will leave some money for you to keep the house running and look after Mrs. Dekker. Is that all right with you?"

She nodded. "You needn't worry, sir. I'll see to everything."

He smiled gratefully. "When I get back, you shall have some time off. Fully paid."

"Sure, Mr. Dekker, you're going to spoil me with talk like that."

Taking his coffee, he left the kitchen and returned to the parlor to pen a note. Not wanting to know where Daniels was holding up, Azariah had agreed with the Georgian to leave messages with a newsagent on Battery Street, a one-eyed former corporal from the Army of Tennessee. Azariah wrote that he would be at Madison's farm to avoid further police harassment after tonight but did not sign it, trusting that Daniels would recognize his handwriting.

He put down the pen, folded the note, then tucked it into an envelope that he sealed with gum spirits. Waiting for the news of retaliation and the imminent countermeasures of the police was more than he could bear.

* * *

A quarter-moon gleamed like a bleached bone in the night sky, casting a wavering line of light across the dark blue bay waters. Blake and Robson lifted the dinghy by the gunwales and shoved it backward into the water, beach pebbles crunching under their boots. Blake hopped in to take the tiller, followed by Robson, sat between the oars.

"Let's stay close to the shore," Blake said quietly. "It's a flood tide, so once we get within fifty yards stop rowing. We should be able to drift close to her."

Robson nodded, moving the oars in an easy manner. They had wrapped the middles of the oars with scraps of old blanket, tied tightly with twine, to muffle them in the metal oarlocks.

Blake tucked his arm around the wooden tiller and pulled the Colt .44 from the left-side holster at his back. Peering in the faint light, he spun the cylinder slowly, checking to make sure the percussion caps were still properly seated. Satisfied, he holstered the weapon and repeated the process with the right-side revolver. He hoped they would be able to approach the schooner unnoticed—and perhaps even climb aboard to look around if there were no guards posted. A silent approach was essential, given how much light was visible from the moon, especially if there were men stationed on deck.

Blake could see the silhouettes of the dock and boat a hundred yards ahead. The dinghy seemed to move at a snail's pace. The sound of the small waves lapping at the distant shoreline sounded like the tired breathing of a sleeping man.

* * *

Baugh sat on a horse and held the reins of the second. Washington Street was silent in the early morning blackness. Gas lamps along the lane gave off oblong haloes of pale-red light. In the cool air, the two horses stood morosely, breath jetting in faint plumes from their wide nostrils. One lifted its head, pointed ears twitching. Voices came from the entrance of the Bella Union on the street corner in front of Baugh. A man in a hat appeared, arm in arm with a young woman wearing a red shawl over her head and shoulders. They walked to the corner and looked up at him.

"Hello, Schmitt," Baugh said, cocking the revolver in his free hand.

The detective halted, his face alarmed. Behind them, Daniels stepped from the shadows by the building, a derringer aimed at the back of Schmitt's head. The pistol's concussion split the silence, reverberating off the buildings. Schmitt staggered forward, fell to his knees, and onto his side. The young woman shrieked, raising her gloved hands to her temples. She continued to scream, filling the air with her cries. Daniels swung into the saddle while Baugh dropped the reins, aimed his .44 at the fallen man, and fired. Sparks and smoke spewed from the muzzle. He cocked the hammer and fired again. Schmitt's body jerked with the hits.

"Come on, damn it!" Daniels said, kicking his mount.

Haloed with gun smoke, Baugh pulled the trigger a third time. Thundering, the Starr lifted in his hand. He turned his frightened horse, then spurred it to a gallop. The saddle rocked beneath him as he followed Daniels out Kearny Street. The screams continued but grew fainter as they passed California Street and then Pine.

Daniels slowed his horse to a fast trot. Baugh did the same, catching up to him as they rode toward Market Street. The boardwalks were empty, the buildings dark and quiet.

"We got that sumbitch," Baugh said, a tight smile on his sore face. "Got him good."

They crossed Market, heading down Third Street. From there, the plan was to ride to the Bayshore Road and on to Madison's. All hell was going to break loose now. Only, he and Daniels would be well out of the way.

CHAPTER 18

Blake sat in the stern of the dinghy, steering the little craft toward the moored schooner. Robson leaned on his oars, peering now and then over his shoulder at their target. Though they were visible on the moonlit bay waters, Blake saw no movement as they approached the bow of the low-hulled ship. Scaling up the stays of the bowsprit looked to be the best way to board her.

"Ship your oars, and get in the bow to catch us," Blake whispered.

They were roughly thirty yards from the schooner as Robson swung the muffled oars in and eased the dripping blades onto the gunwales. Blake felt tension in his shoulders but ignored it. The dinghy slid forward, water lapping at its sides. Robson stood and stepped toward the bow.

"Goddamn oyster pirates!"

A figure loomed above on the schooner, moonlight shining on a long rifle barrel. The gun roared, flame spearing from the muzzle. The starboard oar rattled as the shot nicked it.

Blake pulled his left revolver, cocking the piece as he raised it to fire. He heard the shot scream off into the night, a clean miss. But the guard ducked. Robson scrambled to the oars.

Pausing until the policeman was clear, Blake fired again. Chips burst upward from the wood rail. Voices shouted on board. Shoving the tiller, Blake turned the boat in a half circle. Robson, heaving at the oars, used his back and legs to build a powerful rhythm and stayed with it. With the dinghy headed away from the ship, Blake hooked the tiller with his right arm and turned to extend his gun hand over the stern. On the schooner, heads appeared above the gunwales, rifles sliding out over the rail.

"Get us out of here!" Blake exclaimed.

Gunfire erupted from the ship, fiery smoke flashing along the rail. Minie balls struck the water around them, pocked the interior of the boat, and whined past, making a sound like spinning metallic crickets. Blake fired back at the smoke along the bow, aiming at the muzzle flashes, the slam of the .44 carrying briefly across the water. After emptying his first revolver, he drew the second and continued shooting, still aiming his shots. He had little chance of hitting anything but hoped to make the riflemen duck for cover.

Robson continued heaving at the oars. The gunfire from the ship tapered off.

"They must be reloading," Blake said, glancing at his cohort while the skin along his spine twitched. The policeman made no comment as he rowed unceasingly, eyes locked on the receding ship. A minute passed—the dinghy's progress seemed lethally slow, but no further shots came from the schooner. Robson was tiring, sweat running down the sides of his face, his breathing coarse.

"You'll to have to spell me soon," he said.

His pace was slipping, but the dinghy was a hundred and fifty yards or more from the docked schooner. Robson stopped, shipping the oars as the boat drifted to a crawl. He glanced down at his arm, shoving the sleeve of his coat up. His shirtsleeve beneath was black with blood.

"Bastards grazed me," he said. "I barely felt a thing."

Holstering his revolvers, Blake switched places with his companion. He dipped the blades into the water and sent the dinghy scudding forward, feeling a light pull on his leg stitches. As Robson steered the dinghy, he rolled back his sleeve, exposing a shallow gash on his forearm.

"That was too damn close for my taste," Robson said, wrapping a handkerchief around the wound.

Blake nodded. "Luck was with us. Had they been better marksmen, it would have been a hog shoot."

He continued rowing at a pace that was steady and less urgent than Robson's. They were beyond easy rifle range of the ship. Along the shore, Blake saw tidal grounds clotted with vegetation and shadows where they could beach the boat and walk back to Walters's farmhouse.

* * *

Angeline sat with her mother at the dining room table, having a breakfast of scrambled eggs and ham. She halfheartedly buttered a piece of toasted bread and took a tentative bite. Her stomach spasmed. Dropping the toast, she pushed herself away from the table and, rising, ran through the open door to the kitchen. The maid, holding the coffee tray, stepped quickly aside. As she reached the sink, Angeline vomited. Panting, she slumped at the sink's edge, grimacing at the bile in her mouth. She worked the handle of the pump, rinsing her mouth and washing away the mess.

"Are you all right?" Her mother stood in the doorway, her eyes worried.

"I don't know." Angeline kept hold of the pump handle as her knees shook.

"Have you had your monthly yet?"

"I'm a week late." She felt her face convulse as tears seized her.

Her mother raised a hand to her mouth for a moment, then strode forward to take her daughter in her arms.

"Calm yourself, my dear."

Unable to help herself, Angeline sobbed against her mother's firm shoulder. "What am I … going … to do?"

"You must be strong."

"Is everything all right, Mrs. Whitfield?" the maid asked, putting down the tray.

"Please tell Mrs. Harrington to send for the doctor."

"Right away, ma'am."

Angeline wiped the wetness from her face with the back of her hand. She looked into her mother's eyes, seeing determination in them. She let her head fall against her mother's shoulder, feeling desolate and very grateful for the arms that held her close. She knew she was not free of Pettingill, nor it seemed would she ever be.

* * *

Blake tapped the wedge into the Colt .44 he had just cleaned, using a small brass hammer he kept in his cleaning kit. At the other end of the kitchen table, Robson was finishing his biscuits and coffee. Walter Samuels walked into the kitchen with another San Francisco detective following him.

"You two need to report back to headquarters," the detective said. "All hell has busted loose."

"What do you mean?" Robson asked.

"Two skellums assassinated Schmitt outside the Bella Union. The girl with him gave us a description of one, who we think is this fellow Henry Baugh. The other might be that Confederate spy Daniels. She saw the photograph but wasn't sure."

Robson and Blake exchanged glances and stood, Blake holstering his guns and picking up the old cigar box where he kept his gun-cleaning tools.

"You're to ride back to town and report to Capt. Lees as soon as possible. Meanwhile, I'm to stay here and observe," the detective said.

"You'll find Mr. Walters to be an excellent host," Robson said.

"Yes, thank you, sir," Blake addressed the short farmer standing in the doorway.

"Glad to help you boys out. You best get your coats and mount up. I'll see to this gent."

Blake and Robson went to the parlor, where they had slept, having decided to stay out of the fields after the shooting affray, in case

Madison sent out search parties. Leaving their rolled blankets on the couch, they took their coats and hats and left to saddle their horses in the barn. Within minutes, they were riding at a vigorous trot out to the Bayshore Road under the bright summer sky.

* * *

"Daniels and Baugh arrived late last night?" Azariah asked.

"About four a.m.," Madison answered.

Azariah and the wealthy planter sat on the veranda, the farm surrounding them bathed in morning light. The fields were green and redolent with the growing crops. The bay glimmered blue in the distance, the masts of the pungy schooner visible above the faraway dock. Azariah sipped from his coffee cup while his host fired up a post-breakfast cigar.

"I was warned of their plan to eliminate this rabid policeman, the one who broke my fingers," Azariah said, gesturing with his bandaged hand.

The planter regarded him with steady eyes, nodding. "You're a true soldier for the cause. I've had the farm on alert the past few weeks. I have men posted at the entrance gates day and night to signal if any Yankee authorities show up. And there was trouble last night out by the *Massauga*."

"I recall hearing some noise. But I fell back to sleep," Azariah admitted.

Madison paused from his smoke. "Probably just oyster pirates. But whoever it was, the guards aboard the boat chased them off, though one was injured in the fray. A splinter from the ship's rail went through his eye. He will lose the eye, I'm told, but will live."

"That's most unfortunate. But it makes me think perhaps we should move the schooner. Dock her across the bay."

"Nonsense," Madison said, blowing a plume from this mouth. "Our plans are set. We'll sail within the week."

"That soon?"

The planter smiled. "Once Baugh and Daniels are up, we will hold a war council. If you will indulge me, I have an announcement to make but would rather wait until then."

"Of course."

While Madison enjoyed his cigar, Azariah ruminated. If the ship sailed this week, he would be left behind, with only limited resources to elude the police.

"You know," he said, "initially I intended to stay here to look after my wife. But undoubtedly the police will be looking for me after Schmitt's killing. I'm beginning to think I should ship out on the maiden voyage and have you all put me ashore in Southern California or even Mexico. It would take me some weeks to work my way home, which would give the police time to lose interest in me. Once back in the city, I can make arrangements to move my wife and sell my home through an agent."

"Where will you go then?"

"New Orleans," Azariah answered. "I'm sure I could find work on a newspaper there."

Madison nodded. "We Knights were never able to strike a blow for the Confederacy during the war, either in San Francisco or Los Angeles. But this time we will. When we fire a broadside into the Customs House, everyone is going to know that the war is on again. Jeff Davis may be stuck in a Yankee prison, but a provisional government can be set up in Cuba or the Bahamas. Southern soldiers can wear out the North with hit-and-run tactics like the Comanches use. And there are already hundreds of Confederate soldiers in Mexico. We can use it as a base for operations—California, the New Mexico and Arizona Territories, and Texas are all within striking distance."

Azariah finished his coffee, returning the china cup to its saucer. "And it is well-known the Yankees have reduced the ranks of their standing armies drastically. This may well be the best time to resume the struggle."

Madison glanced from the burning end of his cigar to his guest, a sly smile on his face.

"The South shall rise again, sir."

* * *

Blake stood next to Col. Wagner against the wall of the detectives' office, which was crowded with policemen, many in uniform. Chief Burke stared moodily at them from where he stood in the open area by Lees's office while Lees had his back against the frame of the closed door.

"Gentlemen, I am deeply disappointed ... and enraged," Burke said emphatically. "We have—all of us—failed in this matter: to bring

O'Gara's killer to justice. To add coal oil to the fire, we now have the murder of Detective Schmitt thrown in our faces. This man, Daniels, has made a mockery of this entire force. We cannot seem to find him, let alone stop him! And God damn it, I won't have it!"

He paused to stare at the faces of his detectives, many looking away.

"Captain Lees has informed me Daniels has simply vanished, that no one has any idea where he might be. This man, Baugh, whom we believe to be involved in Schmitt's assassination, has also fled. A recent search of his rooms indicated that they had been abandoned. Isn't that correct, Captain?"

Lees nodded from where he stood.

"And this newspaperman, Dekker, whom we suspect is part of whatever Daniels may be planning, is also gone."

One of the seated detectives spoke. "We searched his house this morning, confirming what the maid told us. That he had left town."

"Are we supposed to take comfort in the fact these murderers have left town?" Burke asked. "I want them found."

Lees cleared his throat. "Chief, we do have one lead: the farm that Lt. Blake and Robson have had under observation. It could be that these perpetrators are hiding out there. The farm's owner, Madison, is a former Southerner."

The chief looked at Blake. "Have you seen any of these men on the premises, Lieutenant?"

"No sir, but there is a schooner docked at the pier on Madison's property, which may be the one recently stolen. And we've seen cannons being loaded onto the ship."

"Cannons?" Burke shifted his gaze to Lees. "Raid the farm. Bring in every man on the property, and work on them until we get something."

"With all due respect, sir," Blake said. "I believe some sort of naval operation to be Daniels's ultimate objective. He has known ties to the Confederate Navy. Wouldn't it be better to wait until we can confirm Daniels's presence before raiding the farm? Better still, wait until they set sail on the schooner."

"You mean Daniels might be planning some caper like those crackpots Harpending and Greathouse tried back in 1863—privateering along the coast?"

"Quite possibly, sir," Blake answered. "If we hold back now, we could catch them as they are sailing for the Gate. Then we can hang them all for treason, not just three of them for murder."

"I'm not sure I'm willing to wait," Burke said.

"It would be quite the feather in your cap, sir, especially with the election coming up."

The chief stared at Blake. "You are bordering on insolence, young man."

"Chief Burke," Wagner said. "If I may ... I believe Mr. Blake's plan may be the better approach. If the farm is fortified and Madison's men armed, the raid may prove to be a very bloody encounter. If we wait until these secessionists take to the water, we can bring in the Navy with their guns and capture all the plotters in a nice little wooden package, at a minimum of bloodshed."

"What assurance do we have that this naval operation is their true intent?" Burke asked.

"Why else would they mount guns on a ship, sir?" Blake pointed out. "And have kegs of powder delivered to the farm?"

"The cannons looked to be six-pounders" Robson added.

The chief pondered with knitted brows. "We'll wait a week."

Blake glanced at Lees, who nodded his head gently.

"Meanwhile I want the farm under observation around the clock. And from both sides of the property. Capt. Lees, I will leave you to make up the teams and schedule them. Use Special Police officers so that the regular constables stay on their beats. I want to see notes on the number of men on the property and whatever arms they have. Col. Wagner, can you contact the Navy and see what vessels they can make available for us?"

"It will be my pleasure, sir."

"One more thing," Burke said. "No one says anything to the press for the time being. Not a word, nothing. I have, out of embarrassment, kept the reporters in the dark concerning Schmitt's death, and I have spoken to the coroner. Nothing hits the papers until these matters have been resolved. Am I understood?"

A murmur of assent rippled across the room.

"Now, let's find these bastards and stop them."

* * *

After the chief left, Blake and the colonel walked out into the hallway as the detectives conversed among themselves. Wagner turned to him.

"Well done, Lieutenant."

Surprised by the compliment, Blake straightened. "Thank you, sir."

"You are proving to be a continuous source of amazement. How did you know about the election?"

"Robson mentioned it to me, sir."

Wagner nodded, putting on his kepi. "Hang them all for treason—I suppose I should have realized this before, but you are a very dangerous young man."

Blake suppressed a smile. "I hope so, sir."

He saluted Wagner, who returned it. The colonel clapped him lightly on the shoulder and walked away.

* * *

Azariah sat at Madison's gleaming dining room table with a second cup of coffee. Daniels and Baugh were just finishing their breakfast. His face still bruised and discolored, Baugh pushed his crumb-spattered plate away with a soft belch.

"Pardon," he muttered, reaching for his coffee.

Madison stood by the head of the table, his arms folded across the front of his cream-colored morning suit. "Good thing my wife is off visiting her relatives in Arkansas. She'd give you the evil eye for such an offense, sir."

Baugh glanced at the planter. "I've done worse."

"Like finishing off a gravely wounded policeman?" Daniels asked, a smile creasing his bearded face.

"That sumbitch deserved it. You're lucky he never got to work on you."

Raising his eyebrows, Daniels made no answer.

"Shall we proceed with business?" Madison suggested. "I have good news. Right after you all brought the schooner to the farm, I wired a trusted associate in Los Angeles that we needed a ship's captain, one with the appropriate credentials, and had him make inquiries along the waterfront there. He found a man by the name of D. W. Keller, a former Confederate Navy lieutenant. I received word that he has taken a packet steamer north and should be arriving in three days."

Daniels grinned as Azariah exclaimed, "That is wonderful news!"

"And the second set of sails?" Baugh asked.

"They should be ready by the end of the week," Madison said. "Now all we need are the pikes and cutlasses."

"We'll get them in Mexico," Daniels said. "We should all stay out of the city. The police are going to be tearing the town apart to find us, or anyone even vaguely connected to us."

Madison frowned. "I could send one of my men."

"Better not to risk it." Daniels folded his arms across his chest, sitting back in his chair. "We've stirred up the hornet's nest. We can stop in Manzanillo. What about the crew? How many men do we have?"

"There's ten men among the hands working here at the farm who have agreed to ship out. The four of us. We'll need at least another six," Madison said.

"Guthrie may know a few others who might be willing to sign on. I'll send him a note, telling him we need experienced sailors who share our views or are willing to accept hazardous duty." Azariah put his empty cup on the table.

"What about cannoneers? We need a seasoned artillerist to train the gun crews," Daniels said.

Madison smiled. "Mr. Johnson, who handles the farm, was a sergeant with Scott's army during the siege at Vera Cruz. He ran a mortar crew."

Daniels nodded, looking at the others around him. "Gentlemen, our plan is fast coming to fruition. The victory the Yankees savored last year will soon be ashes in their mouths. And for the heroic men and women of the South, the fight for the cause will not have been lost at Appomattox … merely postponed."

CHAPTER *19*

Blake stood at the edge of a grassy field, saber and revolver in hand. A skirmish line was forming to rush the Confederates eighty yards away, the brown and gray of their jackets and hats visible against the tree line behind them. They clustered along a low wall of field stones. The sunlight glinted on their weapons and baked Blake's blue wool uniform, making him sweat. A voice rose, ordering the Federals to charge, and the men moved forward at a jog. Blake kept pace with them.

A ragged shout rose from the charging Federal line as they ran faster through the knee-high grass. The Confederates began to fire, muskets popping and rattling, smoke jetting from the muzzles. Blake heard the bullets zipping past beneath the sustained shouting, his guts clenched with fear. Men running alongside sprawled with each unnerving slap of lead hitting its mark. His own hoarse yell lost amid the noise, he kept sprinting as the Federal line withered. The rebel muskets roared endlessly, the wall lost in billows of white smoke.

In a momentary clearing, he saw Arzaga look at him from behind a leveled rifle, then lean down to sight the piece. Blake fired as he ran, knowing he had little chance of hitting him. Yards from the wall, he saw the rifle go off, hot sparks spraying his face, the bullet like a hammer striking his chest.

Blake jerked into a sitting position, feeling Robson's hand clamp his arm. Sweat ran down his ribs and along his spine beneath his undershirt. Gasping, he glanced at the policeman. The windows of the farmhouse parlor were luminous with gray morning light.

"You were crying out," Robson said.

"Sorry."

"Nightmare?"

Blake nodded. "I've had them for the several years now. Less so recently."

"Try to go back to sleep. We've another two hours yet before we need to relieve the other watch."

Blake lay back down, throwing off his blankets. His heart was still thumping. He focused on breathing in slow, full exhalations. For the last five days they had been watching the farm with little results. Blake had even slipped back to the city to visit the doctor, have the stitches removed from his leg, and take a good long soak in a hot bathtub. He wondered when the plotters intended to make their move. After fifteen minutes, unable to sleep, he got up and quietly rolled his blankets.

The sun had crested the brown hills of the East Bay as Blake walked the path along Walters' fields to the sycamore where the two Special Police officers were camped. He carried his jacket over one arm and a covered tin pail full of coffee in his other hand. Clary was sitting against the trunk, rubbing his face, blankets still wrapped around his legs.

"I brought you a wake-me-up," Blake said, passing the pail over to the seated man.

Clary put the metal bucket on the ground. "Bring any cups?"

Blake pulled a tin cup from the pocket of his coat and tossed it to him. Burnett scrambled down from the branches and dropped to the earth with a grunt.

"Something's up. The schooner is crowded with men. They're shipping stores—powder kegs, hogsheads of water, crates of food. Got a cup for me?"

"They're getting ready to set sail?" Blake took a second cup from another pocket and handed it to him. "I'd like to take a look."

With field glasses around his neck, he pulled himself up into the branches until he could see the dock. Peering through the lenses, Blake saw the long main deck busy with men hauling cargo nets aboard using a jerry-rigged boom with a tackle block mounted at the end. The dock was piled with barrels and crates. He saw a white-haired man in a cream-colored suit gesticulating from the dockside. Three other men stood behind him. One of them, gray-haired with a full mustache, might be the newspaperman, Dekker, but they were too far away to be certain. Blake climbed down.

On the ground, he handed the binoculars to Burnett. "I have to ride back to the city and alert my superior officer. I'll also let Lees and Burke know."

"What about our breakfast?" Clary asked.

"I'll send Robson out to spell you," Blake said.

Hat in one hand and jacket in the other, he jogged up the path back toward Walters's farmhouse.

* * *

Angeline sat in her canopied bed, looking down at her flat bare stomach, her nightgown unbuttoned at the waist. Rubbing her palm over her belly, she frowned. The floorboards out in the hallway creaked as someone approached. She re-buttoned the gown. A knock came from the door.

"Enter," she said.

The door opened, and her mother peeked in. "Aren't you coming down? Food is on the table."

Angeline stared at the frilly coverlet. "I'm not very hungry."

"You have to eat."

Lifting her head, Angie met her mother's eyes. "I don't want to have this baby."

Martha entered the room, closing the door behind her. "There is no choice in the matter. What happened to you should not happen to any woman. But we have to live with the consequences, whether we want to or not."

"A doctor can end the pregnancy. As sheltered as I've been, I still know these things can be done. And I don't want this baby."

"It's an uncommonly risky procedure—women die, as well their fetus. I forbid it."

"It's my burden," Angeline insisted. "You must let me do as I please."

Crossing the room, her mother sat on the edge of the bed. "No."

"Don't you understand?" Angie asked, hearing anxiety in her own voice. "Don't you know how ashamed I am?"

"Darling," Martha said, "you are all I have left. Your father is gone. Your two brothers died in infancy. I cannot let you risk yourself. It is dangerous enough to have a baby but doubly so to end the pregnancy before its term. I beg you—be reasonable."

Angie felt her face tense up as tears crept into her eyes. "I do not want ... that man's ... bastard child!"

Martha nodded, waiting a moment before speaking. "I understand completely. There are homes for unwed mothers, where girls go to have their babies and give them over to adoption or to an orphanage. I know of such a place in Portland. We can send you there where no one knows you. There is a physician in attendance. You can leave the baby after it's born and return home. In the meantime, we will let people know that you have been visiting relatives in Boston. No one will be the wiser. Please, Angie, it's the only way."

She looked at her mother, who took her hand in hers. "Say you will do it."

Angie stared at her mother's hand as silent tears blurred her vision. She hated what her life had become but felt too drained to argue. Defeated, she nodded her head.

* * *

Blake and Col. Wagner strode along the hallway to Chief Burke's office. Inside the antechamber they found Burke talking to his secretary.

The chief looked over at them as they entered. Wagner tucked his kepi under his arm while Blake held his civilian hat in his hands.

"I pray you have good news for me," Burke said, an undertone of weariness in his voice.

"I believe so," Col. Wagner answered. "Mr. Blake has just arrived with word that the conspirators are loading the schooner. They are getting ready to make their move."

"Do we know when they will sail? Have they filed any papers with the Customs House?"

"They have not," Blake answered. "Capt. Lees checked on that earlier. They're keeping everything under wraps, it seems."

"And the Navy?' the chief asked. "We will have ships ready to intercept these blackguards?"

Wagner spoke. "My contact at the Mare Island Naval Yard has two ships at our disposal. A steam sloop of war and the *USS Camanche*."

For the first time ever, Blake saw a smile light the chief's bearded face. "The *Camanche*? Gentleman, that is good news indeed. Whatever these villains have up their sleeves, it won't matter with such a ship at our command. Excellent work!"

As they were leaving City Hall, Blake spoke with the colonel. "Sir, am I correct in assuming you will be aboard the *Camanche*?"

Wagner looked over at him, a wry expression on his face. "I'll leave that pleasure to you, Mr. Blake. I hate the water, and so I plan to watch the festivities from the gun batteries on Fort Alcatraz, which will only be a short ride as opposed to spending the entire evening afloat and seasick."

"Where will I pick up the ship, sir?"

They passed through the front doors and out into the sunlight, donning their hats.

"I'll go over to the Wire Service and send a telegram to Mare Island to have both vessels standing by at Fort Alcatraz. Once we know the conspirators have set sail, we can take a boat out to the fort and you can board the *Camanche* there."

Blake smiled. He would be in the forefront of the action. "Yes sir!"

* * *

Azariah stood in the late afternoon sunlight with Daniels and Cicero on the broad steps of Madison's house, watching as one of the farm wagons rolled to a stopped in front of them. Seated next to the driver was a man with a fine auburn beard and wearing a dove-colored suit and a gray naval cap. He climbed down from the wagon while the driver went around to fetch the sea chest from the wagon bed.

Madison moved down the stairway. "Lieutenant Keller?"

"You must be Mr. Madison," the newcomer said, shaking Cicero's extended hand.

Azariah noticed the CSN insignia letters on the man's cap. Smiling, he descended the steps to greet the new arrival while Daniels did the same.

"These are my brothers-in-arms," Madison said. "Mr. Dekker and Mr. Daniels."

Keller had a strong grip and looked at Dekker with piercing light-colored eyes.

"A pleasure," the naval man said. He greeted Daniels the same way, then turned to Madison.

"May I see the ship, sir?"

Cicero grinned. "Straight to business, eh? I like that. Are you sure you wouldn't rather refresh yourself with a drink perhaps?"

Keller shook his head. "I am a temperance man, sir, and do not allow alcohol on board my ship except for medicinal purposes and only when prescribed by a certified physician."

Madison's eyebrows rose as he glanced at his compatriots.

"Lieutenant," Daniels asked, "have you heard of the Knights of the Golden Circle?"

"My brother belonged to a castle in Baton Rouge. I was so busy at the Naval Academy before the war, I never had time to join."

"But you know the sacred mission that the Knights are dedicated to?"

"Yes."

"Are you willing to make it your mission as well?"

"That, sir," Keller said, "is why I am here."

* * *

Fully dressed, Blake was drowsing on his bed at the What Cheer Hotel when someone knocked loudly on the door. It was late in the evening, and he taken a glass of whiskey after his supper. Rousing, he got up and crossed the room to open the door. A uniformed policeman faced him.

"Capt. Lees sent me. He's just now received word from Robson that the ship has sailed. You are to come immediately."

"Has Col. Wagner been alerted?"

"Yes, another police officer was sent to his club."

"We've been waiting two days for this," Blake said.

He took his uniform jacket from the back of the chair at his writing table and shrugged into it. He put on his kepi and took his pistol belt from the table. After locking the door, he followed the policeman down the carpeted hallway.

CHAPTER 20

The night winds on the bay were strong, the black water swirling into small whitecaps that dispersed in a hissing rush. The *Massauga* seemed to skim over the tide, the triangular main and fore sails bellied and taut, the jib and flying jib straining, masts creaking stalwartly. The ship was dark except for the port and starboard running lights, the sails giving off a spectral glint from the pale light of the cloud-wrapped moon. With the squat lethal cannons along the deck, it seemed to Azariah the ship was an angel of death—swift and silent.

Standing by the windward stern quarter, Azariah looked at his cohorts clustered around the ship's wheel, handled by Lt. Keller, who had told them he was familiar enough with San Francisco Bay to get the schooner safely out the Gate. Despite the dimness along the deck, Azariah could see Daniels's teeth as he smiled at Madison, and Baugh standing to the side, the Texan's eyes vengeful and distant. After so much planning, work, and suffering, Azariah could scarcely believe they were finally at sea, irrevocably committed to their plan. He wondered what the morning headlines for the *San Francisco Call* and the *Dramatic Chronicle* would say.

Yesterday afternoon Daniels had penned a declaration of renewed war, which Cicero and Azariah had copied and mailed to newspapers in New Orleans and San Antonio. He looked at the shoreline while the wind tousled his hair. As the schooner grew slowly closer to San Francisco, more and more lights gleamed in the dark landscape, like scattered gold dust on black cloth. They sleep, he mused, not knowing of the sword over their heads.

* * *

On board the *USS Camanche*, Blake felt the ship's metal hull shuddering beneath his boot soles. It was the vibration of her powerful engines, even though they idled. A Passaic-class monitor, the *USS Camanche* was an ironclad and the first Blake had ever set foot on. He stood in the small, round armored pilot house on the top of the ship's single turret, shoulder to shoulder with the senior officer, Captain Anthon, who was looking out the observation slits with a pair of field glasses. Behind them a sailor stood at the helm set in the middle of the turret top, his big hands resting on the brass ship's wheel. Cold salt-laden wind surged through the slits that circled the turret top at eye level. The *Camanche* hovered near the western tip of Yerba Buena Island, her bow facing the city wharves.

"It's rough tonight. Lots of whitecaps," observed Anthon—loudly, in order to be heard above the thrumming engines. "It may be risky if we have to chase them. We've only three feet of freeboard between the *Camanche*'s main deck and the waterline."

Blake buttoned his jacket against the cold air. He had left his pistol belt in the captain's narrow cabin. "And if we can't chase them?"

Anthon looked at him with steady eyes. "Then we fire."

Nodding, Blake returned to scanning the city with a pair of bin-oculars. In the distance, the gas lamps along the Embarcadero looked like a string of red luminous gems draping the waterfront. Interspersed among the lamps, the masts of the vessels occupying the dark wharves were silhouetted against the dispersed glow of the city lights. The water scudding past the city front roiled in flat white-tipped waves, moving in an ebb tide toward the fog-shrouded Golden Gate.

"Even if we can't risk a chase, the *Lancaster* over by Fort Alcatraz will run her down," Anthon said.

Blake nodded, continuing to watch through the glasses.

"I see them. They're just clearing the edge of the city front," Blake said.

At the waterline near the lower end of East Street, a schooner with faintly luminescent sails moved quickly, leaving a thin white wake atop the ebony waters. Anthon spoke to the helmsman.

"Full ahead."

Then he spoke into a brass tube, ordering the cannoneers in the turret below to ready a warning shot.

The engines increased, vibrating the ship even more as she headed out into open water. Blake glanced at the captain, unable to keep the excitement from his face. Anthon nodded, smiling. The wind gusted through the observation slits with the movement of the ship. Blake glanced at the fog bank coming in from the west. It had already swallowed Angel Island and was moving toward Alcatraz. He thought he heard fog bells clanging in the distance.

Raising his field glasses, Anthon spoke to the helmsman. "Three points to starboard." Then he addressed Blake. "By changing our bearing, we'll intercept the schooner as our vessels converge. The wind is easing a bit. That's in our favor."

"Right," Blake answered, keeping his eyes on the enemy ship.

The captain looked through his binoculars. "We'll order them to heave to and stand by to be boarded. The *Lancaster* will handle that while we keep our guns on the schooner."

The *Camanche* cut through the water, an occasional wave bursting into spray against her port side. The lines of the schooner took on detail as they closed in on the ship.

Letting his glasses hang from their neck strap, Anthon spoke into the brass tube.

"Open the porthole for the starboard gun, and stand by to fire."

* * *

"There!" Azariah shouted, pointing toward the vague outline of Yerba Buena Island, where no lights glowed. "At the waterline!"

Daniels ran to the rails, followed by Madison and Baugh, leaving Lt. Keller to crane his head from where he held the wheel beneath the taut sails. They saw the black outline of the ironclad's low-lying hull and squat malevolent turret just above the churning waves moving toward them. Shaking his head in disbelief, Azariah stared at the advancing ship.

"It's a goddamn monitor!" Daniels exclaimed.

"The *USS Camanche*," Baugh said, his face alarmed, finally stirred from his brooding.

"We're lost," Madison said. "We can't fight that monster."

Daniels ran back to the ship's wheel. "There's a fog bank up head. Make for it."

"I'll do my best," Lt. Keller answered. "But there's another ship heading toward us. I can just make out her bow, east of Fort Alcatraz."

"Hell's fire!" Daniels said, looking toward the dark amorphous lump of the fortified island marked by the lighthouse on its southern end. Close by the beacon and small in the distance, the bowsprit and square-rigged sails of a man-of-war moved just above the bay water.

He ran forward to the middle of the deck where Johnson, the gunnery officer, stood watching uneasily as the vessels emerged from the windy gloom ahead and on their starboard side.

"Ready your cannons, sir, both port and starboard sides," Daniels ordered. "Hurry! We'll give our enemies a full broadside from starboard, then fire at the city as we pass the Customs House."

"You heard him, men," Johnson shouted. "Open up the gun ports and load the cannons."

Daniels rushed back to Keller as the crew began to ready the guns. Madison stood uncertainly, looking back and forth between the two vessels. Daniels grasped the lapel of Madison's suit.

"We'll fire a broadside and run for it."

"It's suicide," Madison said.

"We've come too far to give up now!"

"We've broken no laws. If we surrender— "

"Both of us have killed for this operation. We'll hang either way!"

Keller spun the wheel a few spokes, keeping the ship headed close to the wind. Daniels pulled the LeMat from beneath his frock coat and strode forward through the shadowed main deck. Men were laboring over the guns and running them out their ports.

"Stand by, Mr. Johnson, for the order to fire."

* * *

"They're going to run for it," Anthon said. "They're not luffing their sails." He grasped the voice tube for the gun turret. "Fire the warning shot!"

An immense explosion shook the *Camanche*. For a second, Blake thought one of the boilers had burst. But the vessel continued cutting through the waters at speed toward the schooner. Water geysered yards ahead of the sailboat. Three guns on the schooner's starboard side answered, thundering fire and plumes of smokes into the brisk night. Only one missile found its mark, banging against the *Camanche's* deck. The ironclad steamed implacably forward.

"Load canister," the captain ordered into the tube. "And rake their hull!"

Blake trained his glasses on the schooner, now only a hundred yards away. Half a minute later there was another cataclysmic roar, rocking the vessel as Blake watched through the lenses. Wood fragments sprayed suddenly from the schooner's side. Tiny holes peppered in the curved main and fore sails.

"Slow ahead half," Anthon said to the helmsman. Speaking into the tube, he ordered the men to reload the starboard gun and for the gunnery officer to open the second gun port and use a megaphone to call for the schooner's surrender. Through the glasses, Blake kept his eyes on the sailboat, which seemed to be foundering. The sails were luffing now, waving and snapping in the wind like flags.

"Stop engines," the captain ordered, watching through his glasses.

A mere seventy-five yards separated the vessels. Blake felt the ironclad slow and kept his eyes on the schooner. Below him, the iron port-stopper in the turret rasped as it was swung aside.

"Heave to!" the gunnery officer bellowed. "Stand by to be boarded!"

* * *

Crouched by the mainmast, Daniels saw the lolling sails above, knowing he was being betrayed. Chaos reigned aboard the *Massauga*. In the darkness of the main deck, men screamed in agony. Others shouted in confusion—some trying to operate the cannons while their comrades stood back with hands raised helplessly. He jogged back to the helm. His face ashen, Keller kept the ship headed into the wind so that her sails wavered uselessly.

"It's the only way," Madison said as Daniels approached.

"What are you doing?" Daniels yelled, gesturing with his revolver.

"We can't fight warships—not with these light armaments," Keller said.

Yards ahead, the *Lancaster* was coming in line for a broadside, her lower sails reefed and smoke boiling from her stack. The shouts of her gun crews carried across the dark water above the clanking of the nearby ironclad.

"We have lost," Keller said. "Continued resistance would be suicide."

"We go down fighting!" Daniels shouted.

"No sir! I am master here," Keller insisted. "My orders stand!"

"Fools! Cowards! Bastards!"

Daniels raised the revolver, cocking the hammer as he pointed it at Keller. But the lieutenant remained at the wheel, firmly returning Daniels's gaze.

They heard the repeated command from the ironclad to stand by for boarding. Daniels uncocked the LeMat to holster it. Turning, he strode over to the portside rail. He swung one leg then another over the rail, glancing back at Madison, who looked on in surprise, and Keller, who watched with narrowed eyes. Daniels leaped out over the black waves.

The water was searingly cold as it engulfed him. Surfacing, he shouted with surprise, then struck out in a vigorous crawl toward the lights of the shoreline.

* * *

Azariah lay against the bulkhead of the rear companionway. A wooden splinter the size of a man's forearm was sticking out of his lower right side. His shirt and pants were wet with blood. He could breathe only in shallow gasps. If he tried to move, he felt the wood tugging at his guts. A few yards away Baugh lay flat on the deck in a thin pool of black blood, half his head gone. The wind was cold on Azariah's face and clothes. He felt profoundly exhausted.

"Forgive me, Larissa," he muttered. "Forgive me."

His vision was blurring, and it was hard to keep his eyes open.

* * *

Blake stood in a lamp-lit office of the guardhouse on Ft. Alcatraz. Capt. Lees and Col. Wagner occupied chairs adjacent to the fort's commanding officer, Major Ross. Facing the major's desk, Cicero Madison and Lt. Keller sat with their manacled hands in their laps. Madison's elegant cream-colored suit was specked with spent gunpowder and water-stained. Keller stared straight ahead at nothing.

Lees questioned the two conspirators as the soldiers looked on.

"Where is Daniels?" Lees asked patiently for the tenth time.

Keller said nothing, continuing his intent stare. Madison muttered, looking down at his soiled clothes.

"Do you men want to spend the rest of your lives here in the stockade?" Ross asked sharply.

Madison mouthed an obscenity. "This is most undignified. I demand that you free my hands!"

"You're dangerous felons. We are under no obligation—" Lees said.

"Damn it all! I am a gentleman and refuse to be treated like trash," Madison insisted.

Lees glanced at Col. Wagner, who shook his head. Returning his attention to Madison, the policeman folded his thick arms across his chest.

"I will have you unshackled, once you start providing answers."

"Oh, all right. Just get these damned things off me."

Lees looked at Keller. "And you, sir?"

The former Confederate glanced at the detective, then resumed staring at the wall beyond Major Ross.

Lees took a key from his vest pocket and unlocked Madison's cuffs as he raised his hands. Cupping the irons in his palm, Lees stepped back.

"These go back on the minute you stop talking."

Madison rubbed his wrists, glaring at the men around him.

* * *

Daniels crawled out of the frigid waters, collapsing onto the sand and small stones of a beach along the waterfront. He shivered uncontrollably. Forcing himself to move, he got up onto his hands and knees, the rocks jabbing his legs. He rose unsteadily to his stockinged feet, having lost his ankle boots during the long ordeal of swimming to shore. Breathing in exhausted gasps, he checked his wet clothes. The Le Mat was still in its holster, and his wallet was miraculously still in his coat pocket.

Squeezing water from the sleeves of his coat, he staggered along the beach toward the lights and silhouetted buildings of what he took to be North Point Dock. He hoped to find a taxi along the wharf. He would need a hotel, a hot bath and a chance to completely disassemble the Le Mat to dry, oil, and reload it. Then he had to decide to stay and fight or flee and try again.

* * *

"Now, where is Daniels?"

"The coward jumped over the side after the *Camanche* fired on us."

"Was he wounded?"

"I don't believe so," Madison said.

"Does he know how to swim?" Lees asked.

"I have no idea."

"Even if he does," Major Ross said. "The ebb tide could well have carried him out the Gate. The water is cold, even in summer. So cold it is common for swimmers to cramp up and sink."

Madison folded his arms. "To hell with Daniels."

The door to the room was opened from the outside by a uniformed soldier who ushered in Chief Burke. Blake stood aside to let the man pass. The chief's eyes were weary. They all were, as the mantle clock atop the major's bookcase read 4:38.

"Forgive my tardiness. I've been supervising the search of the *Massauga*. There was no sign of Daniels. The newspaperman, Dekker, and his friend Baugh are dead. There were crates full of arms and plenty of powder and shot, but outside of an inventory of the supplies, the only papers were these, containing some Secessionist tripe about a renewed war." The chief held up a sheaf of handwritten papers.

Lees gazed at his superior. "Daniels went over the side before the schooner was boarded."

"So we don't know if he's alive or dead."

Lees nodded. "Could be he swam ashore or was swept out by the tide."

"Damn!" Burke turned to the white-suited planter. "You're Madison, correct?"

"Yes."

"Well, what were your intentions? What was all this bullshit you wrote about renewing the war?"

Madison stared at the chief for a moment. "General Lee may have surrendered, but the rest of the South has not."

"Don't try my patience, you imbecile. Two good policemen are dead because of you bastards. Now, I want some answers!"

Madison raised his chin, staring defiantly at the police chief. Burke held out his hand to Lees.

"Your sidearm, Captain. Give it to me."

Lees reached into his coat pocket and brought out a short, slender Colt revolver, then handed it to Burke. Gripping the gun by the barrel and cylinder, he struck Madison across the face. Blake nodded, surprised by the chief's vehemence.

The planter cried out, clutching his cheek, as Keller looked over.

"We are prisoners of war," the former Confederate said. "You have no right to beat us—"

"You're common criminals," Burke replied. "You'll take what you deserve."

The chief leaned forward to grab Madison's long white hair. "Well? How did you intend to renew the war?"

"Enough!"

He let go as Madison spoke, pausing to wipe away the blood from his cheek with shaking fingers. "We were going to shell the town, fire a salvo into the Customs House."

"The Customs House?"

"To show our defiance of Federal authority. Then sail out the Gate and raid Yankee shipping. Sell the cargoes and use the proceeds for arms and ammunition."

"You were going to shell the city?" Burke repeated.

His face a mask of astonishment, the chief took a step back until he bumped into the desk. "Shell the … None of this can reach the papers! Shell the city … There would be no end to the uproar!"

Burke looked at Major Ross. "Can you keep these men sequestered on the island?"

"Absolutely," the major responded.

"Can they be tried here in a court-martial? Quietly, without a fuss?"

"We can see to that," Wagner said.

"And then hanged in a private execution?"

Wagner nodded while Madison's face went pale. Blake saw Keller's impassive expression slip.

"The civil order of the city demands it," Burke said.

"What about the cannon fire?" Keller asked, anger in his voice. "How will you explain that?"

"A nighttime naval exercise," Ross answered. "If anyone bothers to ask."

* * *

The city church bells were striking noon when Blake, in his civilian clothes, entered City Hall, leaving behind the overcast sky and cold summer breeze. He moved in a lethargic manner, weary from having had only a few hours of sleep. He had been too agitated to sleep once he got back to his hotel. A double shot of whiskey had finally lulled him to unconsciousness. He had awakened at eleven to take a quick bath, shave, and eat before the noon meeting at the detectives' bureau.

He walked along the first-floor corridor, seeing familiar faces on the passersby. Little more than four weeks had elapsed since Wagner assigned him to Ellis's murder, but so much had happened that it felt as if he had been working on the case for at least a year. The night he danced with Elena at the Donahue's ball seemed long behind him. At the end of the hall, the room was crowded with men. Blake nodded to Lees as he entered and took off his hat.

Blake worked his way to the back of the room, to lean against the wall next to Robson's desk. Conversation among the men dropped off as Lees, standing outside his inner office, raised his hands for quiet.

"We have all put in a lot of time on this investigation, and the chief and I appreciate it. But there's still more to do. Daniels, who we know murdered O'Gara, may still be loose. Hopefully, he drowned before he made it to the city. I want some of you to check with the fishing boats as they get back this afternoon. See if any of them hauled a corpse out of the bay or saw one on the rocks."

Blake looked over as a bearded man in rumpled clothes walked through the doorway, raising the Le Mat revolver in his hand.

"You're Lees, aren't you?" asked the man with a Southern accent.

Blake jerked the Colt from beneath his coat. Daniels swiveled his gun toward him. The two revolvers fired as one, ear-splittingly loud, both gushing smoke.

Blake slammed against the wall, his left arm numb. Daniels fell against the door frame but kept his feet. Lees grabbed at him as the room erupted into chaos. Daniels threw him off.

Cocking his .44, Blake fired again through the wafting brimstone. Robson's gun went off beside him. Daniels collapsed by the door, his weapon clattering on the floorboards. Blood spread from the holes in his vest and shirt. Lees picked himself off the floor, staring in shock.

"Jesus Christ!" Clary blurted, rising from a crouch. He approached the bearded assassin lying against the wall, chin on his chest, as the gun smoke slowly faded. Picking up the LeMat, he knelt to check the wounded man, fingering his neck for a pulse, then stood.

"Three fucking hits. He's dead now."

Blake slid down the wall, unaware of the bloody smear he was leaving. Robson looked down at him.

"Can you get a doctor?" Blake asked. "I'm not sure I can stand up."

CHAPTER *21*

Blake sat on the sparse grass at the rectangle of Washington Square. It was a fine summer afternoon—the sun warm in the blue sky, white cumulus clouds sailing slowly overhead. His left arm was in a sling. He held a folded newspaper in his good hand, staring down at the small bulletin for the fourth or fifth time. The paper was the *Los Angeles Star*, and the bulletin announced the wedding of Señorita Elena Caltera and Don Carlos Bejarano was to take place at the don's rancho at the end of the week. The paper was several days old when Blake had spotted it in the library at his hotel.

"Today is Friday," he said aloud to no one. "She marries tomorrow."

He looked across the square at a man and woman ambling arm in arm along the dirt paths crisscrossing the plaza and had to wonder at the vagaries of fate. Slowly, he stood from the grass, picking up his suit jacket and slipping his right arm through the sleeve. He bent over to pull the left side up onto his injured shoulder. Crossing the street, he walked slowly along Union toward Powell.

Just as Blake reached the corner, Martin Tevis came around it and stopped in surprise, staring from beneath the visor of his kepi.

"Where have you been?" Tevis asked. "I'd heard you'd been shot."

"I was in the hospital for a week. The doctor wanted to make sure my wound didn't get infected. And Wagner gave me two weeks of sick leave once I was released."

"So are you going to tell me about it? How you took a bullet?"

"I can't," Blake said. "I was sworn to secrecy."

"You're joshing."

Blake shook his head. He slapped the folded newspaper against Tevis's chest.

"Elena marries tomorrow," Blake said, resignation in his voice. "You were right. She was never mine to begin with."

Tevis took the paper, staring at his friend. Blake nodded and walked away.

* * *

Elena stood on the tiled veranda of the Casa Bejarano, looking out at the evening stars. She blinked her eyes, which were on the verge of tears. She was now Dona Bejarano. Wedding guests were singing drunkenly at the other end of the sprawling house. She took the combs from her hair, letting it cascade down the back of her decorated white gown. She was waiting for her husband and yet hoped he would not come. She wondered what he would say if she told him she loved another man.

"There you are."

Don Carlos, resplendent in his embroidered jacket and pants, emerged from the darkness of the unlit room. He was not much taller than she but broadly built. A full mustache nearly covered his thick upper lip. He walked over and stood next to her, looking up at the beautiful impassive night sky.

"I have not asked you about Santiago Arzaga. Why my most trusted friend did not come home," the don said, still gazing upward.

"It was … a misunderstanding," Elena said, surprised by his words. "He mistook my dancing with a soldier to be an insult to your honor. He insisted on dueling with the gringo, who proved … unfortunately … to be better with a knife than Señor Arzaga."

Don Carlos nodded. "I heard there was more to it. But I am willing to let it go."

He raised his hand and caressed her hair, smiling. She smiled back, a trifle uncertainly. He put his fingers deep into the thick hair at the back of her head. She moved toward him a step. His fingers closed in a fist, locking her scalp to his hand. Elena inhaled sharply, feeling her neck tense, staring at his calm face.

"I will let it go, providing you serve me well. Do you understand?"

"Yes … I understand."

* * *

Sunday morning bells rang at Grace Cathedral as the parishioners left the church to stream down the California Street hill to Dupont Avenue. Carriages and buggies crowded the sandy street, the horses straining against their harnesses as folks climbed in. Angeline and her mother walked down the wooden sidewalk with the crowd. As they reached the corner, Angeline lingered.

"Aren't you coming?" Martha asked, who stepped into the street.

"Go ahead. I feel like walking by myself for a bit. I'll see you back at home."

Her mother looked at Angeline with anxious eyes. "I'll tell Mrs. Harrington to wait on serving dinner." She turned and crossed the street with the rest of the pedestrians.

Angeline watched until she lost sight of her mother's small berib-boned hat, then strolled further down the hill and turned at Kearny Street. She walked along the boulevard, looking without much interest at the displays in the shop windows.

"Angeline, wait up."

She turned to see a soldier striding toward her, a sling about his arm, his cap tilted at a slight angle.

"Lt. Blake," she said, surprised to see him after so many weeks. "How are you?"

"I was sitting in the rear pews at church and saw you walk by. As for me, I'm …" He glanced down at the sling. "Recovering. Thank you."

"How did you come to hurt yourself? Were you thrown from a horse?"

"No." He smiled. "It's rather a long, complicated story. How are you?"

She looked in his gray eyes, thinking how friendly they seemed. She swallowed, glancing at the ground. "I'm afraid I haven't been very well."

"I'm sorry to hear that. I hope—"

Angeline looked up at him. "I'm … Things have been very bad." She heard the tears in her voice, felt her pain welling uncontrollably inside. "I'm … I'm going to have a baby."

She could scarcely believe that she was telling him but could not stop herself. "I don't know what I'm … well, yes, my mother intends to send me away … before I am ruined."

"My God," he said softly. He touched her caped shoulder with his good hand.

Angeline swallowed hard, forcing herself to remain composed. She waited to see his expression turn to disgust but saw only concern in his eyes. He stood uncertainly, nodding.

"Difficulties, indeed. Well, I … I don't know about you, but after that long sermon, I could use a good strong cup of coffee. Care to join me?" he asked, offering her his arm.

She stared at him for a moment, unable to believe his reaction, then placed her gloved hand in the crook of his right sleeve.

"I think the Cosmopolitan Hotel is the closest. Shall we go there?"

She smiled. "That would be lovely."

* * *

"Well, good night," Lt. Schaeffer said, limping toward the office door.

Blake waved from his desk, putting down his pen.

"Nice to have you back, Liam."

"Good night, old man."

Blake's left arm felt stiff, and he grimaced as he rotated it. He watched the door close behind Schaeffer, then opened his desk drawer and took out the letter he had drafted earlier in the day. Standing, he walked to the open doorway of the colonel's office, where Wagner sat looking at some papers. Blake knocked on the door frame.

"Come in, Lieutenant," Wagner said, putting the pages aside.

Entering, he stood at attention in front of the colonel's desk.

"What is it, Mr. Blake?"

He placed his letter on Wagner's blotter, returning to attention. "It's a request for transfer, sir."

Wagner picked up the letter. "Is it now?"

"I have enjoyed serving under you, sir. But I find myself better suited to chasing fugitives than counting inventories of rifled muskets."

The colonel skimmed the brief letter, then regarded Blake. "You want to go work for the provost marshal?"

"Yes sir."

Wagner put the request down on his desk blotter. "You may do very well there. Provided you can stay in one piece."

Blake nodded, waiting for the colonel's decision.

"You know," he said, opening a drawer and taking a folded sheet from an envelope, "I received this note about you from Capt. Lees, expressing his gratitude for …"

Unfolding the paper, he read, "The courage, fortitude, and perspicacity of Lt. Blake under dire circumstances."

After returning the letter to its envelope, Wagner put it back in his drawer. "That's one I'll have to remember for the fitness reports—perspicacity. I'll be sorry to see you go, Lieutenant. Your work has been quite thorough."

Blake smiled. "Thank you, sir."

"Is that all, Lieutenant?"

"No sir. I have one more request."

* * *

Standing at the bar of the Fashion Saloon, Blake looked at the evening sky through the tall saloon windows. It was pale yellow and streaked with crimson from the sun, now below the city hills to the west. Scattered cirrus clouds above the horizon glowed luminous red like dying embers. He sipped his whiskey and soda, having stopped in the saloon on his way to Angeline's house for supper. Her mother served no alcohol, so he often had a single cocktail before going over.

He and Angeline had been seeing each other three to four times a week over the last month, finding comfort in each other's presence, and there was a growing tenderness between them, which pleased him. He still thought of Elena in moments when he was alone, and rereading her last letter always left him anxious and yearning. But he had no choice. He could only look to the future; the past was gone.

* * *

When the maid ushered Blake into the Whitfields' parlor, he saw Angeline rise from where she sat by the windows. Her mother remained seated on the couch but put aside her needlepoint work. Blake kissed Angeline's smooth cheek as she smiled up at him.

"Hello, my dear," he said.

He turned to Mrs. Whitfield, bowing. "Good evening, ma'am."

"Good evening, Lt. Blake."

He gave Angeline a teasing smile, then addressed her mother. "Mrs. Whitfield, if Angeline's father were alive, I would request an audience with him. However, as he is no longer with us, I must ask you. I would like your permission to marry your daughter."

Angeline gasped, her hand going to her mouth, while Mrs. Whitfield stared at him.

"You're serious, aren't you?" Martha studied his face.

"Yes ma'am," he answered. "I've even spoken with my commanding officer, who has given his approval."

"Well, I find this rather sudden," Mrs. Whitfield said.

"Mother, please!"

Martha regarded her daughter. "Dear girl, would you leave us for a moment?"

"Now?"

"Yes, now. If you will."

Angeline walked hesitantly to the parlor doors, glancing from Blake to her mother and back. She opened the portal, then went out and closed it behind her.

Martha Whitfield advanced toward Blake until she was close enough to touch him. Her eyes never left his face.

"You are aware of Angeline's condition? That she was taken against her will?"

"Yes ma'am," he replied, matching her gaze.

"And that makes no difference to you?"

"No ma'am. Things happen that aren't always what we wish for, and life goes on in spite of it. I've come to realize how unique Angeline is—how strong, how smart, how sweet she is."

He gazed down at the thick Oriental carpeting for a moment. "We seem to make each other happy, and there's little enough of that in the world. So I'm hoping you will give us your blessing."

Mrs. Whitfield continued to gaze as he lifted his eyes to hers.

"And you can love the child she carries as well?"

"It's part of her, is it not?"

The older woman nodded slowly. "I have seen the change your presence has made with Angie, and I'm grateful for that. Her happiness is my utmost concern. I have reservations about her marrying a soldier, but I suppose if she is willing to accept you, than I can offer no objection."

"Thank you." Blake smiled. "Shall we bring her back in?"

Mrs. Whitfield resumed her seat on the couch. "Yes."

The door opened even before Blake could reach it, and Angeline entered. Her blue eyes were full emotion as she rushed to him. They hugged tightly, as though to keep the world from pulling them apart.

Author's Note: In the early morning hours of March 15th, 1863, Confederate sympathizers (and members of the Knights of the Golden Circle) Asbury Harpending, Ridgely Greathouse, and Alfred Rubery along with their crew were arrested aboard the vessel *J. W. Chapman*, as the ship attempted to sail from San Francisco harbor to begin privateering operations against Yankee merchant vessels along the West Coast. The arresting officers were a composite of San Francisco Police, U.S. Navy and U.S. Revenue personnel aboard a hired tugboat and boats from the *U.S.S. Cyane*. For a full account of the event, please see *Embarcadero* by Richard H. Dillon (Coward-McCann) 1959 and Asbury Harpending's *The Great Diamond Hoax and Other Stirring Events* in the Life of Asbury Harpending, which was initially published in 1916.